Char  the Mystery of the Blue Train

The Further Exploits of Chantecoq, Volume 1

Arthur Bernède

Translated by Andrew K. Lawston

Copyright © 2022 Andrew K. Lawston

All rights reserved.

ISBN: 9798840818725

DEDICATION

For Melanie, and for Buscemi, the Kitten of Detectives.

CONTENTS

	Acknowledgments	i
	A few words to readers	9
1	The king of detectives	15
2	The siren	30
3	Where Chantecoq's search has rather unexpected results	58
4	From mystery to mystery	78
5	Where Météor proves he's a pupil worthy of his master	108
6	Where Météor triumphs, and where Chantecoq makes an important discovery	135
7	The panther, the tiger, and the fox	162
8	Revelation upon revelation	185
9	Where Chantecoq realises the enigma that he has to untangle is more complex and tragic than he ever imagined	217
10	The final battle	236
	Epilogue	258

ACKNOWLEDGMENTS

This book was translated from *Le Mystère du Train Bleu* by Arthur Bernède, first published by Editions Jules Tallandier in 1928. The original French text can be found in full at
https://gallica.bnf.fr/ark:/12148/bpt6k936304n/

The cover design was by Rachel Lawston of www.lawstondesign.com.

A FEW WORDS TO READERS

Some time ago, I received a visit from my old friend Chantecoq, the king of detectives. I hadn't seen him in two years.

He appeared to be in better health than ever. Still thin, elegant, nervous, with a gaze that was clear, sharp, and penetrating, his face astonishingly young, he seemed, from his mocking and spiritual smile, to defy that which suits us all to call the "ravages of time".

He began by attacking me with one of his most affectionate reproaches.

"You dumped me," he said, with that familiar cordiality which is his calling card.

And, without permitting me a moment to defend myself, he continued.

"You shouldn't forget that you owe the subjects of a few of your novels all to me: *The Aubry Affair*, *Wilhelm's Spy*, *Cocorico*, and most recently, *Belphégor*."

"I remember all too well!" I protested, with all the energy I could muster. And I felt emboldened to add, "I was even going to write to you..."

"Liar!" the illustrious bloodhound declared.

I did not shrink at all from this epithet, launched as it was with the most obvious good humour, and I continued, imperturbable.

"... I *was* going to write to you, to invite you to dine with me, on whichever evening best suits you."

"Do you still have the same cook?"

"Louise… what about her?"

"Then I must accept, because she's a true cordon bleu marvel."

I must tell you, my dear ladies and gentlemen, that Chantecoq is one of the most refined gourmands that I've ever encountered. No one appreciates better than he the flavour of a dish or the excellence of a wine, but, for example, he is horrified by so-called 'modern' cuisine, that is to say eccentric and over-complicated food. And, not wishing to disrespect my charming and talented colleague Paul Reboux, the creator and distributor of special and unedited recipes, he obstinately refuses to allow his most delicate palette to make the acquaintance of one of those dishes where are found mixed, among the most diabolical seasonings, the foods least destined to share a plate.

Chantecoq replied. "Dear friend, now that I've granted you the saving of a fifty centime stamp, I suppose that you won't hesitate a single moment longer to reveal the goal behind your friendly invitation?"

"Having not heard anything of you recently, I was eager to know what had become of you."

"Didn't you once write: 'it's often when people are spoken of the least that they are doing the most?'"

"Quite so," I responded.

"Ah well," said the king of detectives, "that's true in my case, absolutely. Since our last encounter, I have been the hero of a series of adventures which number among the most extraordinary of my life, and, while you were preparing to write to me, I set out to bring you the exclusive news."

I applauded him, delighted by this windfall. "You couldn't have come at a better time. My editor and friend, Jules Tallandier, recently asked me for a detective novel, which I had promised him after *Belphégor*. I'm in that difficult period where the author, brought face to face with the blank pages piled up before him, must jostle from his brain the germ of the tale that he proposes to compose.

"A thousand projects, more or less confused, are rattling around my mind, and I swear to you that none of them inspires in me that enthusiasm which is crucial for any author who's truly anxious to 'hook his public'... And now you bring me a story."

"One story?" Chantecoq interrupted. "Oh no… several!"

I thanked him. "You're spoiling me! Because I'm already sure I'll be spoiled for choice!"

"I do hope so," declared the great bloodhound.

In his eyes a mysterious flame was dancing, which appeared to illuminate the most magnificent promises. He continued. "The fact is that I've just lived through some prodigious times, the like of which I never knew when I was an Inspector with the Sûreté, or even in the course of my career as a private detective."

"Not possible!"

"I am not exaggerating! You'll see and you'll judge! To begin with, I can reveal to you that, during the last two years, I had to disguise myself as more than twenty characters as new as they were different, from a lighthouse keeper to a perfume saleswoman. I have been murdered three times and I was even buried alive. That's not all. That's not even worth mentioning. I was King for forty-eight hours."

"A king?"

"Yes, my dear, King, with a capital K, with a real people, who were charming, and with real ministers, who were far less agreeable. I will add that I've fought with phantoms, which is much harder than fighting with living beings. I have even had for an adversary, one of the most world's most illustrious scholars, a genius who, to avenge himself for a woman's betrayal, decided to unleash on humanity the most fearsome scourge which would have desolated it and could perhaps have led to its total destruction."

"Chantecoq, Chantecoq," I cried, overjoyed, "you're making my mouth water."

"And I've not yet unpacked all my wares."

"I'm impatient to listen to you. Would you like to come tomorrow evening?"

"With pleasure! Will we be alone?"

"Naturally! Haven't you reserved for me the monopoly on your stories?"

Chantecoq was quick to reply: "Indeed. Because I know that tended by you, they won't be deformed or jollified, and that they'll reach your readers just as I narrated them to you myself."

The next evening, at eight o'clock precisely, we came to the table. Throughout the dinner, we exchanged only general pleasantries. It has long been understood between us that the king of detectives would set off his firework anecdotes only as a dessert.

When the last rocket had been launched, I thought it was barely midnight. In fact, it was five o'clock in the morning.

Never have I had a less exact idea of the time.

The fault lay with Chantecoq, so much had he captivated me with his lively, passionate stories, turn by turn tragic and gay, as varied as they were spectacular, and which he recounted with an emotion which belonged only to him, and a verve that I should so like to borrow from him.

And here is one of them: *The Mystery of the Blue Train*. At the narrator's request I have taken on, in order to reproduce it, the form that's sometimes called 'impersonal', first because it is more rapid and more direct, and then further because Chantecoq said to me:

"Just so no one thinks I was intending to write my Memoirs. I'm still too young for that."

Respectful of the will of the true author of these tales, we bow to him.

Above all, so that certain people don't believe that these lines are a preamble to fantasy; Chantecoq exists, in flesh and blood. He is not called Chantecoq, that's all. Chantecoq is the name of his country, a delicious little village in the Loire, situated between Sens and Montargis, and the nickname attributed to him by his old colleagues in the Sûreté générale because, always the first to get up early in the morning, he would use his clarion voice whenever necessary, to awake dormant energies and restore some guts to those who lacked them at the decisive moment.

That is why we're confident that those who already knew Chantecoq will be happy to rediscover him and those who are hearing of him for the first time will not complain of having made his acquaintance.

ARTHUR BERNEDE

1 THE KING OF DETECTIVES

When, abandoning Avenue des Ternes, a little before crossing the bridge which overlooks the railway tracks, you enter Avenue de Verzy, you are surprised to find yourself all of a sudden, just off one of modern Paris's most animated arteries, in a district which is calm, peaceable, intimate, and charming.

While to the right vast buildings of recent construction have been erected, buildings which one would guess are blessed with all that is fit to call modern comforts, you notice, on your left, several small houses buried, in the summer, under greenery.

Then, still half-deafened by the hurly-burly of the street, by the roaring horns of tram cars and automobiles, by the metallic fracas of lorries and all the prolonged murmurs which serve as a kind of bass to this symphony which is as discordant as it is uninterrupted, you find yourself suddenly, and with your decided approval, softly bathed in an atmosphere of silence, which in the beautiful season is troubled only by the sparrows' spiritual chirping.

You no longer breathe in those bitter aromas of petrol and oil, nor that impalpable dust that penetrates your larynx, gets in your lungs, and dulls your blood just as it wilts the leaves and dries up the sap of the trees which have had the misfortune to be transplanted into the great city.

Instead, you feel a sense of liberation, of relaxation, of well-being, and, in your joy at having finally evaded a dangerous zone, you say to yourself,

"How good it must be to live here!"

You're not wrong.

Avenue de Verzy is one of those rare and last corners of Paris where, T.S.F. aside, an intellectual worker can still set himself to his daily labour without being obsessed by the urban noise, and can still sleep at night, without being forced to put cotton in his ears or to bury his head under his pillow.

It was in one of these agreeable buildings, whose exterior architecture recalls a little that of one of those pretty Norman cottages that can be seen on the beaches of the Calvados River and the English Channel, that Chantecoq, the king of detectives had elected to reside.

That day, in a clean, attractive dining room, with its light drapes and its furnishings all Louis XV Provencal, he had finished lunching with his family, that is to say with his daughter, the splendid Colette, on whom, since the death of his wife, he had lavished all his affection, and his son-in-law, Jacques Bellegarde, the famous reporter for the *Petit Parisien*.

A fourth person was also present at this feast...

This was a thin little fellow, dry, scrawny, with the features of a clown and the gait of a jockey, a curious gaze, ceaselessly alert, with a face that was leathery, wrinkled, and to which it was so much more difficult to give an age because every time – though it was quite rare, however - that he happened to smile, his physiognomy suddenly took on an expression of youth and gaiety which immediately rendered him sympathetic to all gentlemen and… even to ladies.

For a year, he had been fulfilling for Chantecoq all the difficult and delicate functions of a secretary.

He was known only by the name, or rather, nickname, of Météor, which he owed to his skill of appearing and disappearing with a speed which bordered on prodigious.

Where had he come from? What was his past? His ancestry? How had the great man come to know him? As a result of what circumstances had he granted him better than his trust, that is to say his friendship?

Beyond Chantecoq himself, no one knew anything of it, not even Monsieur and Madame Bellegarde, who would have been reluctant to interrogate the detective on this subject because, better than anyone, they knew that this man, when he was not speaking, had serious reasons to remain silent, and they so respected his secrets that they guarded themselves from posing the least question about this Météor who, anyway, demonstrated towards his boss feelings of the deepest devotion and most sincere attachment.

Once dessert was finished, Colette asked, "Father, are we taking coffee in your study?"

"Not today, my darling," replied the detective, enveloping his daughter in a long tender look. And he added: "I'm awaiting a visit that I believe will be important enough not to be deferred. That's why I am asking you and your husband to wait in here, to savour the excellent mocha that our dear cordon bleu Marie-Jeanne will not have neglected to prepare for us."

"We'll be very comfortable in here," Jacques Bellegarde hurried to declare, in a cordial tone.

Hardly had he spoken these words, when a knock sounded in the hallway outside.

"Would this be the visitor in question already?" Colette cried.

"I think not," said Chantecoq, "the appointment is for two o'clock, and it's now only one-thirty."

The door opened, making way for a valet with a frank, open face, square shoulders, and who seemed much more suited to wear an NCO's tunic than the white apron of domestic staff.

He brought on a platter a letter which he presented to Chantecoq, who took it.

The envelope, whose address had been inscribed by a typewriter, bore this note underlined by a stroke of red ink: *strictly urgent and personal.*

The detective took a knife with which he slit one end of the envelope. He pulled out a double sheet of paper folded in four, which he immediately unfolded.

His face, from his classical profile, to his chin and his gaze of astonishing acuity, held itself immediately as if his attention was concentrated on a single object, one single thought.

His reading complete, he muttered between his teeth, "That's not something you read every day."

Then he pushed an electric buzzer.

Some seconds passed, at the end of which the valet reappeared, carrying on a much larger dish, not a letter, but four cups, a sugar bowl and a cafetière, from which drifted the suavest of aromas which is that of a marvellously successful coffee.

When the servant, slowly and with every care, had deposited his precious burden on the table, Chantecoq addressed him.

"Tell me, Gautrais."

"Monsieur?"

"Who, just now, brought this letter?"

"A constable," replied the servant with the precision, the clipped tones, of an old soldier.

"Did he have his badge?"

"Yes, monsieur."

"You wouldn't happen to recall his number?"

"No, monsieur. I could have memorised it, but I think it best to admit that I didn't think to do so."

"His description?"

"Short stature; greying hair, as well as his beard, which was well-rounded; enormous bushy eyebrows…"

"In other words, camouflaged," the detective said to his secretary, who was already scribbling notes in a notebook that, nimbly, he had taken from his pocket.

Gautrais continued. "One distinguishing feature: he limped slightly with his left leg, which did not prevent him from mounting a bicycle, seeing as…"

"That's good, thank you," the detective stopped him.

The valet sketched a gesture which was like the primer for a military salute… and, making a half-turn, he returned to the hallway.

Chantecoq was silent for a moment, his forehead tilted forward, his gaze fixed on his plate… Colette took the cafetière, filled the cups, and after having given her husband a brief glance which was not without worry, she deposited a cup before her father.

"Two lumps of sugar, father?"

The bloodhound gave a simple affirmative nod.

More and more anxious, Madame Bellegarde plunged a

pair of silver tongs into the sugar bowl when, brusquely, Chantecoq raised his head.

Instantly his face recovered its good-humoured expression, and in a voice full of high spirits and even joy, he said, "Forgive me this slight absence, and above all don't believe that I have been struck by a tile… far from it! For some time, sensational cases have been rather scarce, isn't that right, Météor?"

"Oh! Yes, boss!" the secretary said with the most pointed grimace he could manage, with the stretchy rubber from which his cheeks seemed to have been cut.

The king of detectives continued with animation. "Chantecoq without adventures, Chantecoq reduced to chasing after thieves of pearl necklaces, on behalf of American billionaires, or insurance companies! That could not last.

"Indeed, it has fallen into my lap today from the sky or… from hell… I don't know yet, a case such as I've not had since that of the Phantom of the Louvre, and at once I wonder whether it might not one day have with the public as much resonance as that which was provoked by my trouble with damn Belphégor."

"Is this possible?" Bellegarde exclaimed, all the more intrigued because he knew that his father-in-law was never bluffing.

"In any case," the detective affirmed, "it is beginning in a rather piquant fashion. After all, I don't see why I shouldn't tell you all about it. For a long time, my dear Colette, I have known that I can count entirely on your discretion. As to you, my dear son-in-law, I believe it goes without saying to ask you to forget for a moment that you're the most brilliant of our reporters, in order to remember that you are my only son-in-law.

"Anyway, we have worked together before, and it could well be that one day or another I will have further need of your services."

"They are already at your disposal," Bellegarde engaged himself with the warmest spontaneity.

"In a few words, here it is!" said the king of detectives. "I told you that I had here, in my office, at two o'clock, an appointment that I consider may be very important. Well, here's the letter that I just received."

Chantecoq took the missive that he had tucked inside his jacket pocket. And aloud he read:

Monsieur,

I have learned that you ought to receive at your home, this very day, a visit from Madame the Countess Marie-Thérèse de Roscanvel.

Doubtless you are unaware of the purpose of this visit? I am going to reveal it to you.

Madame de Roscanvel comes to ask you to help her save the head of her lover, Julien Guèret who, last March 6th, murdered her husband, on the tracks of the Paris to Monte-Carlo fast train, known as the Blue Train, between Cannes and Saint-Raphaël.

Monsieur Chantecoq, I have great admiration for you. I have followed you closer than you could know throughout the course of your remarkable career. I know that before the war, in your capacity as an agent of Sûreté générale, you had already acquired, thanks to your resounding exploits, real celebrity.

Mobilised in 1914, as a reserve officer, after having fought valiantly and having earned the Legion of Honour and the War Cross, you were put on hold and, under the control of the second office, to which I am attached myself, you gave yourself over to a hunt for spies which managed to confirm you as a true popular hero.

After the Armistice, you were given your demobilisation orders, and you opened a private detective's office. Your reputation, firmly established, and based both on your professional value and on your noble character, has won you an elite clientele, that you serve with as much intelligence as you do zeal.

I believe therefore that it's my duty to put you on your guard against the lies of the most formidable schemer, who, beneath her gentle, hypocritical features, hides an abominable soul, gangrenous with every vice and capable of any crime.

All those who have observed her closely are astonished that she was not arrested at the same time as her lover… None among them doubt that it was she who had advised, inspired, and dictated his crime.

Although, thanks to your admirable perspicacity, you're more than capable of exposing swiftly this miserable woman's character and intentions, I thought that it wouldn't be disagreeable to you to be in possession of these pieces of information, before your meeting with the Countess de Roscanvel.

I further hope to be of service to you by directing you to her past, to her origins. Countess Marie-Thérèse comes from a very humble background. Her father, Yves Tregarec, captained a fishing boat at Camaret, and her mother ran a little bookshop in the same port.

Marie-Thérèse, while still a child, demonstrated a lively intelligence and a pronounced taste for studying. She was also remarkably pretty.

Her parents, who placed on her the most legitimate hopes, worked their fingers to the bone in order to give her a first rate education. They sent her to the best boarding school in Brest, where she was raised along with all the young girls of the high Breton aristocracy.

At first they considered her to be an intruder, and pretended to keep her in quarantine.

But soon their hereditary coldness dissipated under the charm which emanated from Marie-Thérèse, and, in spite of themselves, all were forced to bow before the physical and intellectual superiority of their young companion.

Marie-Thérèse did not tarry in becoming the true queen of the convent. Not only was she always top in her class, but the gaiety which animated her during recreation times and walks, also made her the life and soul of the house.

A skilled musician, gifted with a delicious voice, she sang by turns the sacred hymns or those old Armorican songs full of mysterious and picturesque poetry.

The nuns, her teachers, cited her as an example to all, and everyone accepted that this was the case, without the slightest jealousy, without the least reticence.

Marie-Thérèse Tregarac was linked in friendship with a young girl of her age, Mademoiselle Jeanne de Roscanvel, daughter of the Marquess and Marchioness, who owned, on the outskirts of Loctudy, a very beautiful chateau where, each year, they spent the summer. In the autumn, they would return to Paris, where their fortune, very considerable, permitted them to lead a great life, but they left their daughter in Brest, preferring not to initiate her too soon in the capital's worldly life.

They also had a son, Robert, who, his studies concluded, had given himself entirely over to sports at which he excelled in any case.

One year, Jeanne asked Monsieur and Madame de Roscanvel permission to invite her friend Marie-Thérèse to spend one week of August at the chateau.

The Marquess and Marchioness had no reason to refuse hospitality to a young person as accomplished as Mademoiselle Tregarec. They were not going to be long in repenting this invitation.

Their son, Robert, who was holidaying at the family home, fell hopelessly in love with Marie-Thérèse.

Realising from his first attempts that he would not manage to make her into his mistress, he spoke of nothing less than marrying her. To the fury of his parents, but it was a futile fury.

Three months later, against the wishes of his family, Robert, who was twenty-three years old, married Marie-Thérèse, who was only seventeen. The Marquess and Marchioness cursed their son and withdrew all support for him.

Robert worried about this so much less as, shortly before his wedding, his uncle and godfather, the old Duc de Hauteroche, had left him four million clean of all rights and charges…

And the young household can, in joy and opulence, spin a little perfect love.

For five years this was, at least in appearance, absolute happiness.

But someone crashed the party.

This someone was none other than a young novelist, Julien Guèret, author of a successful book: The Secret of Loving, which had placed him at the very top rank of young contemporary literature.

How did he manage to sneak his way into Robert and Marie-Thérèse's intimate circle? No matter! So it was that he became inseparable from them, and it was soon impossible to see the one without the others.

Julien, naturally, passed as the pretty Countess's lover, and Robert as a husband who was blind rather than complacent.

Some of their friends affirmed, however, that this was only a caluminous noise. But an event which was as tragic as it was unexpected was going to inflict on them a denial that one might be right to call bloody.

The fact is certainly still present in your memory: last March 6th, the body of Count Robert de Roscanvel was found, frightfully mutilated, on the railway tracks, between Cannes and Saint-Raphaël.

At first it was believed to be an accident, then a suicide. A preliminary inquest established the unlikeliness of that hypothesis, that is to say its absolute impossibility.

The criminal version therefore imposed itself. A new inquest was ordered. It was entrusted to one of the Sûreté générale's greatest bloodhounds, Inspector Vénarède, of Marseille's mobile brigade.

With his customary skill, he managed to establish, with the aid of medical experts, that Robert de Roscanvel had been struck first by a revolver shot to the heart and that the killer had dragged his body on to the railway tracks, in order to make it appear that he had been the victim of an accident.

It only remained to discover the culprit. For the crafty inspector, this was child's play. Immediately his suspicions were brought to bear on the one who was believed, mistakenly or correctly, but much more likely to be correctly, to be the Countess's lover.

Had he not come to stay with the Roscanvels in the villa that they had rented on the Mediterranean coast, around five hundred metres from the place where the victim's body had been discovered?

Another presumption: a month beforehand, Count Robert had made a will by which he bequeathed his entire fortune to his wife.

That constituted troubling evidence, to be sure, but it was insufficient to justify an arrest.

It was then that came to pass the piece of theatre of which you have certainly read the account printed in the papers, that is to say the discovery, by Vénarède, among the undergrowth in the talus of the railway track, one hundred metres from the crime scene, of a revolver which had belonged to the victim and on which the anthropometric service discovered Julien Guèret's fingerprints.

The young novelist was arrested that same evening. It was believed that Countess Marie-Thérèse would also be… but the investigators not having uncovered against her any trace of collusion with her husband's murderer, she was left at liberty.

Since this time, Madame de Roscanvel, all the time affecting to weep for the departed, has not ceased to try everything in order to liberate her husband's murderer who, against all evidence to the contrary, has not ceased for one moment to swear that he is innocent.

Until now, she has not succeeded in convincing and disarming justice! That's why she has set her sights on you, counting on the resources of your fertile mind and on your professional skill in order to thwart those who have the mission of defending society against malefactors, and also to obtain the liberation of he whom she would then hasten to marry.

Monsieur Chantecoq, you will not make yourself the accomplice to such infamy. You will not allow yourself to be seduced by the appeals of this dangerous and nefarious siren.

You will let justice run its course and punish, as he deserves, the abominable murderer of the unfortunate Count de Roscanvel.

Confident in your honour, your probity and your good faith I offer you, Monsieur Chantecoq, my most sincere regards.

A FRIEND OF THE VICTIM

"Ah well, my children, what do you say to this missive?" Chantecoq asked, his reading finished.

"My opinion," said Jacques Bellegarde, "is that it is a bit naive and quite redundant, but that, although anonymous, it was inspired by a very good sentiment."

"And you, Colette?"

"Me, father? I am in complete agreement with Jacques. Besides, I followed this case closely. For me, Guèret's guilt carries not a shadow of a doubt."

"And you, Météor?"

The detective's secretary puffed out his cheeks, as he did each time that he had an important sentence to utter. Then he declared, "This letter is clearly troubling."

The king of detectives smiled. "Then, my children, if you were in my place, would you not receive the Countess?"

All three gave an affirmative sign.

With a faint smile, Chantecoq continued. "Allow me then to tell you that you would be making the biggest mistake."

"Why?" Bellegarde asked.

"Why, simply because Julien Guèret is innocent."

Colette, Bellegarde and Météor himself could not repress an exclamation of surprise.

With that marvellous self-mastery that, even in the course of the most perilous situations, he always kept intact, the great bloodhound continued.

"I too have followed this case with a great deal of interest. I had a presentiment that sooner or later I would become mixed up in it. And as usual, this sort of prescience of events that nature has granted me, has not let me down. Well, let me tell you that straight away I had the impression that Vénarède, although a valuable sort, had engaged himself on the wrong path. That story of the revolver served to reinforce that opinion in me.

"Let's see! Reflect a little. If truly, as it would be right to suppose, and as Vénarède pretends, this Julien Guèret made use of Roscanvel's revolver in order to murder this unfortunate, do you believe that, so little trained as he was at this kind of task, he would have thrown it in a thicket which could not, according to all plausibility and even all logic, escape the police investigations?"

Bellegarde intervened. "So you conclude from this, therefore, that it was placed there by someone?"

"You might say," Chantecoq was precise, "by the same someone who wrote me this letter. That is to say, the Count's true murderer."

Colette and her husband cried at the same time. "That would be astonishing!"

As to Météor, without even taking the time to give his

windbag cheeks the aspect of two bouncing balloons, he sang, "Astonishing, indeed! Ast-on-ish-ing!"

"On the contrary, it's really very simple," Chantecoq rectified. "First, why would the author of this letter, instead of entrusting to paper the duty of putting me on my guard against the appeals of this so-called siren, why wouldn't he come to find me himself?

"He pretends to know me well… that's right, then he believes he had to address a summary of my life to me. He must therefore believe that I have never betrayed the trust of anybody and that it is not in vain that I am often called 'the tomb of secrets'.

"If he was sincere, as he affirms he is, if he was animated only by honest intentions, if he was hoping only that Monsieur de Roscanvel's murder should be avenged, why would he hide himself like this?

"He is unaware, the imbecile, that he has just committed an imprudence which, in a time more or less approaching, could cost him very dearly."

And stirring himself little by little, the king of detectives intoned, "Come on, the era of great hunts is going to recommence for me. I can already sense my quarry. From tomorrow, I'm sure of it, I'll be on his trail. Météor, my boy, prepare yourself, we are going to have some work, but I believe we're also going to have a lot of fun."

The knock from the hallway sounded again.

"This time, it's her!" the detective murmured.

And consulting a clock hanging from the wall, opposite him, Chantecoq observed: "Two o'clock precisely. She has regal exactitude."

The door opened, and Gautrais announced with a mysterious tone, "The lady is here."

"Take her into the study."

Gautrais vanished.

Chantecoq, tranquil, took the last puffs from his cigarette, then standing, he said, "And now, let us go and listen to the siren's song."

After having given his daughter and son-in-law a respectful wave of his hand, he returned to his work office.

As to Météor, he had already disappeared like a shadow.

2 THE SIREN

In the middle of a huge room furnished with taste, decorated with pretty trinkets, and at the end of which stood a great library packed with books in rich bindings, a young woman in mourning clothes was standing, her long black veil turned down over her eyes.

Immobile, frozen in an attitude of infinite sadness, she could have been mistaken for a statue personifying grief itself.

She hardly reacted to Chantecoq's entrance.

The detective advanced towards her, addressing her with a greeting full of deference.

"Madame Countess de Roscanvel?" He said with the tone and manners of a perfect gentleman.

"Monsieur Chantecoq?" the Countess spoke in a harmonious voice.

"The very same."

Indicating to his guest an armchair placed to the right of a beautiful Louis XVI table which served him as a desk, the detective invited her: "Please be seated, madame."

While Madame de Roscanvel took her place on the seat, the great bloodhound installed himself behind his table; and, all while trying to discern his interviewee's features with his probing gaze through the thick layer of gauze, with an expression of respectful gentleness, he said: "Madame, it is pointless to reveal to me the purpose of your coming, I know it."

"How is that possible?" Marie-Thérèse said with a slight start.

"You want me to help you in saving Monsieur Guèret?" Chantecoq declared, with serene firmness.

The Countess's voice grew anxious and shrill. "Monsieur, who could have told you this?"

She did not finish, because the detective cut in. "What does it matter, madame, as I have decided to take on your case."

"Before having heard me?"

"Yes, madame."

"Why?"

"Because I am convinced that Monsieur Guèret is innocent."

A cry of joy gushed from the Countess's lips. "Monsieur Chantecoq!"

And in one brusque movement, throwing back her veil, she revealed to Chantecoq the most adorable face that it was possible to imagine.

With a forehead fringed by a curly halo of russet gold hair, her blue eyes like the waters of an Italian lake and surmounted by the marvellously painted arc of two light eyebrows like a brush stroke, a slightly aquiline nose such as that which Minerva revealed to us on antique medallions, her mouth with its coral lips that seemed to have been created only to smile, her chin of the purest oval shape, and all the natural elegance of her person, she gave an impression that one would have been able to qualify as, without the slightest exaggeration 'raphaelesque'.

Impassive, Chantecoq reflected. "I understand that this woman has inspired violent passions and even a great love, because I have rarely met one who has realised so perfectly in one person the qualities of beauty, charm, and grace. If, in her widow's weeds, she produces such an effect, what must that be when she is dressed again in bright colours or when she reflects, in suggestive night attire, the light of a thousand stars?"

Madame de Roscanvel, who had regained control of herself, continued. "Monsieur Chantecoq, do you already have proof that Monsieur Guèret is innocent?"

"Not yet, madame," declared the king of detectives, with the frankness which characterised him, "but I have faith, and that is enough for me."

"I see that this tragic business interests you."

"Enormously."

"Doubtless you have studied it in depth?"

"My God no, madame, and I know nothing more of it than the papers have told me."

"Then, what has determined for you the conviction that Julien Guèret was not guilty?"

"My flair…" replied the great bloodhound, without hesitation.

And, desiring not to reveal his entire arsenal at once, he immediately added, "And then some imponderable elements which could appear to be insignificant to the general public of mere mortals, but which are sufficient to attract and to retain the attention of those of us in the trade."

The Countess nodded with emotion. "You can not guess, monsieur, how grateful I am to you for the comforting welcome which you have granted me. Now you see me delivered from a terrible anguish, as I can henceforth count on the most powerful force, that of the most famous of our detectives, of a man for whom there are no insoluble mysteries, indecipherable enigmas, and thanks to whom, instead of a happiness destroyed forever, I will, I'm sure of it, soon find peace of mind!"

Without taking his eyes off those of his client for one single moment, Chantecoq replied. "Madame, the esteem in which you hold me flatters me infinitely, and I hope to show myself worthy of it. However, it imposes upon me an imperious duty: that of warning you that we are going to find ourselves facing considerable difficulties and dangerous obstacles to overcome."

"I am certain, monsieur, that you will succeed."

"Me too, but on one condition."

"What is it?"

"That you swear to me that you are going to respond and that you will always respond with complete sincerity to all the questions, even the most delicate, that I will be obliged to pose you."

"I agree absolutely!" Marie-Thérèse said with such spontaneity that Chantecoq, a master psychologist above all, felt, to his keen satisfaction, entirely reassured with regards to she whom his mysterious correspondent had depicted as a formidable siren.

And so, without wasting one second, he continued. "Might you permit me to begin straight away?"

"I was going to beg you to do so," Marie-Thérèse accepted. "Before that, however, I should like to speak with you on the subject of your fees, and on the total sum that I'll have to pay you."

"Madame," Chantecoq said with a smile, "I have a principle never to take a penny in advance from people who have placed such precious trust in me, such as yourself. Why, in my turn, should I not put my trust in them? However, in order to lay those matters to rest, here are my conditions: if I fail, you will owe me nothing. If I succeed, you will decide yourself upon the sum that you judge my services to be worth."

"Monsieur Chantecoq, I can only accept."

The king of detectives interrupted her. "Would you prefer, madame, that we get down to work straight away… because each minute that we waste puts us further from our common goal: the liberation of an innocent man."

"You are right, monsieur; interrogate me, I shall answer you."

"Once again, I warn you that I'm going to be indiscreet. Perhaps brutal."

"Speak, I'll tell you everything."

"As you would to a confessor?"

"Yes, as if you were a confessor."

"I see, madame, that we're going to get along very well."

"I was already convinced of that."

Chantecoq took a moment. Then, while fixing Madame de Roscanvel with his penetrating gaze, that she bore with a calm stripped of all boastfulness, he spoke slowly.

"First and principal question: were you, yes or no, Julien Guèret's mistress?"

"No, monsieur!" the Countess replied with energy. "I loved my husband as much as he loved me himself, and even when my heart did not always respond to the feeling that I inspired in his, I was bound to him by a respect too infinite to ever have even the intention of betraying him."

"Good!" said the detective, who was preparing to pose a second question.

But Madame de Roscanvel continued. "I am from a very humble background."

"I know," said the bloodhound.

And all while giving the world's brightest and most amiable smile to his beautiful client, he elaborated. "There is nothing I do not know of your past, nor of the circumstances which preceded and accompanied your union with the young Count de Roscanvel."

Marie-Thérèse replied, "I can only congratulate myself, monsieur, on observing that you are so well informed with regards to me. That will avoid a long and punishing story. However, let me tell you that, if I married Count Robert, it is not, much as his family pretended, and still pretends, that he was rich, but above everything, and I will say only, because I loved him."

"Therefore," Chantecoq concluded, "It was a love match?"

"Love match!" the young woman confirmed.

"And since then?" the detective asked.

"We have not ceased to be an excellent household and I believe it right to affirm to you, without any presumption, that my husband has been as faithful to me as I have been towards him. He adored me."

"Was he jealous?"

"Not at all! I even often heard him repeating that he did not understand jealousy It is, he said, a torture for those who feel it, and an injury for those who are the object of it."

"Consequently," the bloodhound observed, "Julien

Guèret's presence in your intimate circle never offended him?"

"Never!"

"Was he aware of the rumours that Guèret's presence whipped up around him?"

"Yes. But he was disdainful of them. He contented himself with declaring: 'the dogs bark, the caravan passes'."

"How did you come to know Julien Guèret?"

"During a trip to Norway, where that young writer had gone in order to undertake research for a book that he was planning, whose action unfolded in that country. He was a brilliant speaker. He quickly won both my husband's friendship and my own. He deserved it, because I must tell you that he has one of the noblest spirits, and the most generous and sensitive hearts that I have ever encountered."

Chantecoq again took a moment, as though he was gathering his thoughts. Then he said, "If Julien Guèret inspired in you only a very pure affection, can you then affirm that he was not in love with you?"

"Julien Guèret," Marie-Thérèse intoned, "loved me and loves me still with every fibre of his being."

"Did he declare this to you?"

"Never! But I guessed everything… then I considered it my duty to warn my husband."

"And how did Count Robert respond?"

"He took me gently in his arms and declared to me: 'I knew it! This morning, loyally, Julien told me the truth! I didn't want to speak to you about it, because I thought you hadn't noticed anything and I didn't want to trouble you. But as you *are* aware, I must tell you that our friend, with magnificent courage, has decided to leave us tomorrow evening for a long time, and perhaps forever."

Then, while two large tears welled in her eyes, Madame de Roscanvel blurted: "The next evening, Robert was murdered."

Chantecoq replied. "Forgive me, madame, to reawaken such cruel memories in you... but, alas! I have not finished my interrogation, and it is vital that I be informed exactly on every detail, on all the circumstances of the drama which unfolded there."

"That dreadful night," whispered Marie-Thérèse, who was visibly making every effort to remain brave... "that atrocious, abominable night, I have already lived it so many times that I can certainly evoke it once more."

And she continued. "Robert, Monsieur Guèret and myself were staying for around a fortnight in our property 'les Mimosas' which is situated on the coast, on the outskirts of Cassis, thirty kilometres from Marseille when, at around three in the afternoon, our friend, who was making a bad job of hiding the sadness which was prompting his departure the next day, invited us to take tea in a small rural establishment about two kilometres away in the countryside.

"As the weather was fine, we resolved to make our way there on foot. It was on the way that Julien Guèret told us that he had been summoned to Paris by his publisher, on urgent business. He added that he would return soon, and, in order to distract me, throughout the journey and the whole time that we spent sitting facing a stunning panoramic view to contemplate the sun setting over the sea, over the surroundings and enveloping them with its shadows, he affected a gaiety which, to me who knew everything, inspired a boundless compassion, that I also read in my dear Robert's eyes.

"When we were back on the road to 'les Mimosas', night

had fallen."

"What time was it?" Chantecoq asked.

"Around five in the evening."

"Thank you."

The Countess continued. "Robert suggested we take a short cut, which cut our journey in half. I refused, because it involved having to cross the railway tracks, and I hardly wanted to worry about risking an accident and even a prosecution.

"My husband teased me kindly, as he always did, and he said to me: 'You and Julien get home however you like, I'm going this way. I bet that when you arrive at 'les Mimosas' I'll have had time to prepare some splendid cocktails for you both.'

"I wanted to stop him. I didn't have time. In a few seconds he had vanished into the shadows."

"Hold on! Hold on!" said Chantecoq, whose face, which up until this point had remained an impenetrable mask, was animated by a furtive twitch.

This facial quirk had not escaped Madame de Roscanvel. "You're surprised, aren't you, that my husband, though aware of the love that Julien Guèret had for me, left me alone with him?"

"Indeed," declared Chantecoq, "I can't help but find it strange, however great and so legitimate his confidence in you, that Monsieur de Roscanvel placed you, Monsieur Guèret and yourself, in a situation which could be, for one of you, nothing but deeply painful and, for the other, extremely delicate.

Without the slightest hesitation, Marie-Thérèse replied. "In order to explain an act which, at first glance, seems justly of a regrettable inconsequence, you would need to have known Robert well. He was an impulsive sort, in every sense of the word. His main flaw, I ought to say his only flaw, was an almost total absence of all forethought.

"Life had spoilt him so much! The only chagrin that he had experienced was that caused by his parents' hostility to our marriage, and the fuss which followed it between him and them. Again this pain had been of a brief duration...

"After a year, the Marquis and the Marquess de Roscanvel had agreed to pardon him and even to receive me... in short, my poor Robert, incapable of wronging anyone, having an instinctive horror at all calculated self-interest, dreamed only of being happy while making me happy, and, as though led by this *joie de vivre* which carried him, perhaps thought no more, at the moment where he left me alone with Guèret, of the chivalrous vow that he had made that same morning.

"So long as, which would have not been astonishing, in one of his generous fits which were customary to him, he wasn't trying to offer a man who had sacrificed himself so nobly, the melancholy consolation of bidding me farewell without witnesses.

"How sure Robert was of his friend, sure of me! Anyway, the motive he was obeying doesn't matter much, I am here to relate the facts to you, and not to lose myself in sentimental considerations which would not hold any kind of interest to you."

"Make no mistake, madame," the detective assured her with insistence, "all these details are, to the contrary, very important."

And with a slightly enigmatic air, he added, "More important even than you could imagine. But continue your tale, I beg of you."

The Countess replied immediately. "We went home,

Julien Guèret and me. As you're insisting I tell you everything…"

"It's vital."

"I shall therefore tell you that, during the half hour or so that we took to reach the villa, this poor man who, in a scruple of incomparable honour, was on the eve of condemning himself to a moral exile whose bitterness you can guess at, did not utter one word, not one look which were of such a nature as to reveal to me the drama which was playing out inside him.

"He walked at a lively pace, he was talking, and he was even joking. It was only when we reached the garden that, by way of a fast, spontaneous gesture, which he had no time to quell, that he lifted one corner of the mysterious veil under which he believed he had hidden his love for me so well.

"Reaching for a mimosa in bloom, he cut a small branch from it, then, bringing it near my face, he said, 'Smell this for a moment, just one moment… and then, kiss it.'

"I did what he asked. Then, brusquely, he took the scented branch away from me, stuffing it quickly in his jacket's inside pocket. He ran quickly towards the house, very fast, like a wrongdoer who had just committed a crime.

"I approached and I heard him, in the living room, call out in a clear voice, 'Robert, old chap, where are these martinis?'

"I entered the room, my husband being nowhere to be found in there I went towards a small bar in the next room… still no one!

"I even noticed that the glasses, in which Robert had the habit of mixing his cocktails, were still in their place. I returned to the living room. Worried, I rang the bell. It was Marco the butler who appeared. Such a wretch…"

"Why?" Chantecoq asked. At that word 'wretch', which Madame de Roscanvel had just uttered with marked indignation, he had pricked up his ears.

"It was he who, along with my chambermaid Suzanne, had the infamy to swear to the prosecutors that they had caught us, Julien Guèret and me, in the act of kissing on the lips, the day after my husband's murder."

"Ah! Ah!" The king of detectives exclaimed. "Here is a fact which we can't disregard... we shall certainly take time to speak of this again later. In the meantime, madame, I'm listening."

Countess Marie-Thérèse continued. "I asked Marco if the Count had returned. He replied that he hadn't, and with his servile air, and an obsequious tone, he asked me to tell him if dinner was still set for eight o'clock. I gave him an affirmative signal and I immediately dismissed him.

"He had never been particularly pleasant with me, but that evening, I don't quite know why - perhaps I had a presentiment that I was going to have an ignoble accuser in him - he got on my nerves terribly, and then I began to torment myself. Then I said out loud, 'I'm astonished that Robert did not arrive before us... just so long as he's not had an accident while crossing the railway tracks!'

"Julien Guèret, trying to reassure me, observed that Robert could very well have met one of our neighbours and had been delayed by chatting with them.

"But the minutes passed, and my husband still didn't arrive home. At seven o'clock, unable to wait any longer, I went to look for him. Guèret accompanied me. My instincts pushed me towards the railway track, we took around twenty minutes to reach it. Julien appeared very emotional, also very anguished. From time to time, we exchanged a few words which can all be summed up as: 'Where is he? What can he have done? What's become of him?'

"Suddenly, I remembered that the blue train, which leaves from Nice in the afternoon, must have passed very soon after my husband had left us. I even remember having heard a train behind me when I had reached 'les Mimosas' and, on turning, having seen its red lights which, at a vertiginous speed, were streaking away into the night…

"My heart thumped dreadfully. Now I was no longer in any doubt, Robert must have been struck, crushed by the express train.

"I staggered. Guèret offered me his arm, I clung on to it. We approached the sidings. I thought I could make out at the top of the bank, lit by the faint gleams of lanterns, some shadows which were moving, and a confused murmur, dominated by indistinct cries.

"Galvanised, I set off towards them. But, over the tumult, a thick gruff voice shouted, 'they've just found a man mushed up on the line'.

"I heard no more… I fainted. When I returned to my senses, I was lying on my bed, in my bedroom. A country doctor was near me. He was a good old man, who came to visit us sometimes, as a friend. My first cry was 'Where's Robert?'

"Doctor Lormier responded to me only with a gesture which was meant to be reassuring and which managed only to be procrastinating. Anyway, he didn't need to speak. The terrible phrase which, two hours beforehand, had crushed me, echoed anew in my ear. No hope was permitted for me, and I said in a broken voice: 'he's dead, isn't he?'

"Monsieur Lormier murmured, 'Brave heart!' I lost consciousness again. It appears that, for a month, I was suspended between life and death.

"When I came round again, I demanded details. I was told that my husband was lying in his family's tomb. Then, little by little, with a great deal of care, I was told that Robert had not been the victim of an accident, as I had believed, but of a crime. And how great was my shock upon learning that the guilty party was none other than Julien Guèret, and that he, for more than a fortnight already, had been in prison in Marseille.

"Now, I knew that was impossible, as, at the very same hour that the police attested that my poor Robert had been killed by a revolver bullet fired into his heart at almost point blank range, then dragged on to the railway tracks, in order to make it look like suicide, Julien Guèret had been with me and had not left me for a moment.

"Convinced that my testimony would be sufficient to liberate my unfortunate friend, I left immediately for Marseille… There, I learned that Guèret had chosen for his defence counsel a young lawyer, who had already obtained great successes in the assizes court. He was called Monsieur André Barelli, and I must declare to you straight away that I can only sing his praises. He is a talented and compassionate man.

"Monsieur Barelli did not hide from me the fact that my statement could only provoke a citation of which I was going to be the object, from the prosecutor charged with the business. And as I explained to him my conviction regarding Guèret's imminent liberation, he said to me:

"'Painful as it is for me, I have a duty to put you on guard against any such illusion. Terrible charges have been brought against my client. The police, notably, have found the murder weapon, a revolver which had belonged to your husband and from which the accused's fingerprints have been recovered.

"'Certain witnesses intend to demonstrate that Guèret had a powerful interest in your husband disappearing. You know the mentality of most prosecutors. When they find a suspect, they hardly like to release him, especially when they believe in good faith – and that is the case here – that he is guilty.

"'That's why I truly fear that your deposition would hardly be useful to Guèret's cause and serves only to compromise you yourself.'

"I cried out. 'Compromise me? Why?'

"Monsieur Barelli replied with a preoccupied tone. 'Madame, I have no right to hide it from you. Monsieur the prosecutor Ribécourt is convinced that you were Julien Guèret's lover and, without yet accusing you of being his accomplice, he's not far from believing that you were aware of his schemes and that you did nothing to prevent him from carrying them out.'

"In panic, I protested. 'But that's a shameful, abominable calumny. I want to tell the world the truth, I shall do it.'

"Monsieur Barelli replied, 'Madame, permit me to advise you to tread carefully.'

"'Ah!' I cried. 'So, you too think that I'm guilty then?'

"'No, madame,' said the lawyer, 'if I had thought that Monsieur Julien Guèret was capable of such an abject crime, I should not have agreed to defend him. To kill his friend in order to seize his fortune, and then his wife, isn't that one of the most dreadful crimes imaginable?

"'But when the poor man opened himself up to me with all frankness, when he revealed to me, and in such moving terms, the secret of his heart, and when he cried out: 'how could I have hoped that she would one day be mine, even as

I was sure that she would always be his!' I understood that this man could not be a murderer and that a truly infernal machination had been contrived against him, and against you, madame, with the goal of masking another's crime.'

"Those words, Monsieur Chantecoq, brought a measure of calm to my distressed soul. I felt that I had near me a conviction which could be better than a comfort, a hope. At least, I was no longer alone in facing a battle in which the head of an innocent and my own honour as a wife were at stake, and, deciding to show myself to be both energetic and prudent, as Monsieur Barelli had incited me to be, I went to see the prosecutor.

"Monsieur Chantecoq, in your long career as a detective, you must certainly have met, alongside those magistrates with high and serene consciences, who honour their profession, those other inquisitors who are instead convinced that by showing themselves to be implacable they perform the most sacred mission of all, and who unconsciously grant themselves unlimited powers conferred upon them by the law, a conception as narrow as it rigorous.

"Monsieur Ribécourt is one of those. I only had to take one look at him, sat in his armchair, staring at me through his spectacles perched on a nose like an eagle's beak, welcoming me in with a pinched smile on his thin bloodless lips, topped by a thin grey moustache with drooping tips, to feel that I had before me not just an adversary, but the enemy.

"With glacial politeness, which further accentuated his visible hostility with regards to me, he thanked me for forestalling his summons, and asked me to tell him what I knew.

"I declared to him, just as I had declared to Monsieur Barelli, that Julien Guèret could not have murdered my husband because, at the time of the crime, he was with me.

"Monsieur Ribécourt let me speak without interruption. When I had finished, he spoke in his dry, piercing little voice, which bore into my ears like a drill. 'That's exactly what the accused said.'

"I replied. 'And it's the truth.'

"'No, madame,' the magistrate intoned. 'Let's say rather that you want to save your lover.'

"I protested. 'Monsieur Guèret has never been my lover.'

"'In my file I have proof to the contrary,' the prosecuting judge affirmed.

"'I would be curious to know it.'

"'That is my business, madame, and not yours.'

"'I would observe,' I said, indignant, 'that you are refusing me the right to confound my accusers.'

"The magistrate replied. 'The passion with which you defend Julien Guèret can only reinforce my opinion based on the declarations, as spontaneous as they are impartial, of honest witnesses who, better than any others, were in a position to be aware of your intimate life.'

"I cried with disgust. 'Servants!'

"'You admit it then!' my torturer insinuated.

"I riposted, 'I'm astonished that a magistrate who assumes such serious responsibilities can listen so complacently to a butler and a chambermaid whom I had to dismiss because I caught them both listening at doors!'

"Monsieur Ribécourt gave a little shrug. Then he asked me: 'Is that all that you have to say to me, madame?'

"'Yes, monsieur,' I responded. 'Your case is made, and I sense that you will not lend any credence to my words.'

"'You are wrong to take such an arrogant attitude,' the magistrate spat at me in a menacing tone. And he added, while twirling his finger in the end of his moustache, 'Don't forget that I could keep you at my disposal.'

"I was on the point of crying out, 'Arrest me then!' but I remembered Monsieur Barelli's recommendation, and in a more moderate tone I replied: 'Monsieur, I have my own conscience, you must do as your own dictates.'

"This response appeared to produce a more favourable impression on the magistrate. In a less aggressive tone, he said to me: 'You may leave, madame. I will certainly need to question you further. So in your own interest as well as in that of justice, I strongly advise you not to travel far from Marseille.'

"Such was my intention in any case. Convinced, *certain* that Julien Guèret was innocent, I didn't want to abandon him and I resolved that he should know that he could count on all my support.

"From that moment, Monsieur Chantecoq, my existence became an intolerable torture. I soon realised that I was being followed, spied upon by police officers in plain clothes who, from the moment I left the judge's office, dogged my footsteps.

"I returned to Monsieur Barelli. He said: 'What did I tell you?' And he added, 'I believe that the best thing is to wait for the great day of the assizes court in order to try and save Guèret.'

"The very next day, I was summoned by Monsieur Ribécourt. For three hours, he put the most insidious, the most unexpected questions to me, trying to embarrass me, to make me fall into the traps that, very skilfully, he prepared in order for me to contradict myself.

"He did not manage it.

"On my reiterated insistence, he ended up acknowledging

that it was indeed the butler Marco and the chambermaid Suzanne who had sworn to him that I was Guèret's mistress. He read me their statements, full of details as titillating as they were deceitful, and he set before my eyes a draft letter whose fragments Suzanne claimed to have found in a waste paper basket and where, in terms which could leave no room for doubt as to the intimacy of our relationship, I asked Julien Guèret, then staying in Paris, to come and join me at Mimosas as soon as possible.

"Now, Monsieur Chantecoq, I never wrote such a letter. It's a very clever forgery, I admit. I swore as much to the prosecutor."

"And how did he reply?" Chantecoq asked.

"That he was going to send my letter for analysis."

"Do we know the result of that?"

"Yes… against all hope, the experts concluded that the document was authentic."

The detective grimaced. "That proves that it's as true in Marseille as it is in Paris, and everywhere else, that technicians in this line of work are subject to error. This is just a case of demanding a second opinion."

"That's just what Monsieur Barelli advised me to do. But events have developed at such a rapid and terrible speed, that now it's all become pointless."

"What's this?" barked the great bloodhound.

"Yesterday, summoned again by Monsieur Ribécourt, I arrived at his office at eleven o'clock precisely. He received me immediately. You don't need to guess my emotional state on seeing, standing before me, cuffs on his hands, Julien Guèret, who on seeing me could not repress a cry of distress.

"I was going to offer him my hand. But Monsieur Ribécourt stopped me with a peremptory tone. 'This is not the time, nor the place, to indulge in such misplaced effusion,' he said. And he continued in that disagreeable, sour voice, which made each of his words squeal like the hinge of a very old gate: 'If I have put you in each other's presence, it is because I consider this confrontation necessary to the correct functioning of justice. I therefore order you, both of you, to respond simply to the questions that I am going to put to you.

"'As to you, Guèret, I advise you, in your own interests, to abandon this system of defence which, in denying the most solidly proven facts, will not precisely have the effect of encouraging the indulgence of those who, soon, will be called upon to judge you.

"'One last time, I ask if you will confess to having murdered Count Robert de Roscanvel?'

"With much dignity, Julien replied: 'I can only affirm, and I shall continue to do so until my dying breath, that I am innocent.'

"The magistrate continued. 'You persist in pretending that at the time of the crime, you were alone with Madame de Roscanvel?'

"'Exactly!'

"'That you are not now, and that you never were, her lover?'

"'I swear it.'

"Turning towards me, Monsieur Ribécourt, with a sardonic smile, which froze the blood in my veins, grumbled. 'And you, madame?'

"Without the slightest hesitation, I responded. 'I stand by all my previous declarations.'

"'Very well!' said the judge.

"And after having taken an oblique glance at his clerk

who, sitting at a neighbouring table, was scribbling down these words, he said in a cutting tone: 'In these circumstances, madame, I am obliged to charge you in conspiracy to murder, and to place you under arrest.'

"'Me!' I said, paling.

"Monsieur Ribécourt was relentless. 'Your successive and obstinate lies have done more than given me every right to do so, they have left me with no choice.'

"White with indignation and rage, Julien Guèret cried out. 'You are committing, your honour, worse than an abuse of power, but an abominable injustice.'

"'Silence!' the magistrate sought to impose himself. But, carried away by fury, despite the efforts of the clerk and the policeman, who were trying to keep him quiet, Julien proclaimed, bewildered:

"'One victim is not enough for you! You need two of them! And your conviction is based on a scaffold of so-called proof, of gossip, of lies, the work of dismissed domestic staff, of false reports from police or experts whose conclusions are erroneous from start to finish! Come now, it's not possible that you should commit such a lamentable double error!

"'You don't believe me! Very well, lock me up, send me to the assizes, to prison, to the scaffold, but her in prison! Ah! No, anything, everything, but not that!'

"'Calm yourself,' I told him, 'our innocence can't help but be recognised.'

"'Clerk!' Monsieur Ribécourt ordered, implacable, 'prepare an arrest warrant in the name of the woman Marie-Thérèse Tregarec, Countess de Roscanvel.'

"'I won't be party to this!' raged Julien, whose guard was having trouble keeping hold of him.

"'Gendarme!' the judge pointed at the man, 'take the accused back to his cell.'

"'But this is a disgrace! A disgrace!' the poor man howled, beside himself.

"Another guard, who had come running at his cries, entered the office, and helped his colleague to drag Guèret into the corridor. Just as they were about to cross the threshold, Julien, suddenly calming down, turned back towards Monsieur Ribécourt and, in an icy tone, which gave me the shivers, he said: 'All right then, yes, it was me… it was me who killed Count Robert. But she… she is innocent… innocent…'

"He fainted in the arms of the guards, who dragged him into a room adjacent to the magistrate's office.

"Mad with emotion, incapable of moving a muscle, I watched Monsieur Ribécourt who, with a smile of triumph, said to his clerk. 'That's all I wanted to hear him say.'

"Then he turned to me, and added: 'You are free to go.'

"Instead of heading for the door, which the judge indicated to me, I advanced towards him, staggering, half-dead. Then, breaking down in sobs, I shouted at him: 'Don't you see that if he accuses himself, it's only in order to spare me the ordeal of prison, to save my honour!'

"A sneer responded to this cry which had come from the bottom of my heart. Then, I begged this man. What did I say to him? I no longer remember. Some moving things… yes… because I was surprised to see a gleam of pity in his clerk's eyes. But not in his, oh no! There was nothing human left in him!

"Broken, I left. I went straight away to tell Monsieur Barelli. Dismayed, overwhelmed, he could only say to me: 'This poor Guèret sacrificed himself for you. What am I supposed to do in order to get him out of that?'

"I said to him, 'We must! I want to! Even if I have to spend my very last penny to shed light on this dreadful mystery, to unmask my husband's true killer, I'll do it… it's my duty! I can't leave an innocent to be condemned, when, through love for me, they push their heroism to the point of risking the hangman's noose. Master Barelli, help me, advise me…'

"The young lawyer waved me into silence. His brow furrowed, he took to pacing his office in large steps. Then, returning to me, he told me: 'There is only one man in the world capable of decoding this enigma. That's the private detective Chantecoq. You will take the first express train to Paris, ask the great policeman for an appointment as soon as possible, and tell him the entire truth, just as you have related it to me. If he consents to taking on this case, there is a much better chance that the mystery of the Blue Train will be solved and that Julien Guèret's innocence will be recognised.'

"Monsieur Chantecoq, I followed Monsieur Barelli's advice. At the beginning of this interview, you told me that you would come to my aid. Now that you are aware of every detail in the terrifying drama in the middle of which I am struggling, may I still count on you?"

"More than ever, madame," the detective affirmed, forcefully.

"Oh! I thank you with all my heart. My situation is so dreadful. My husband's family has renounced me. Even my own father doesn't want to see me anymore. Only my poor old mother has any pity for my despair. Public opinion is entirely against me. I feel despised, shamed, hounded from all quarters…

"This morning, while alighting from the train at Gare du

Lyon, I met two secret policemen who had already shadowed me in Marseille and who must have taken the same train as me. I feel indeed that if the prosecuting judge has left me at liberty, it is only provisionally, and that he still hopes I will commit an imprudent act which will betray me and will permit him, despite Guèret's sublime sacrifice, to incarcerate me too and to send me with him onto the benches at the Court of Assizes.

"Monsieur Chantecoq, you will defend me, defend us, won't you? Oh! Yes, I read it in your eyes that are so frank, so humane, so filled with willpower, intelligence, and energy. You'll save both of us. Yes, you will save us!"

"I'm going to try, madame," the famous bloodhound declared. "During your account, I have already noted in passing some details which may become very useful assets under my hand.

"As soon as you have left, I'm going to put all that into some sort of order, prepare a plan of campaign, because I never embark lightly, and I rather hope that before forty-eight hours have passed, I shall be in action."

"Meanwhile, what must I do?" Madame de Roscanvel asked.

"You have somewhere to stay in Paris?"

"Yes, monsieur, a private mansion. Number 57, Rue Henri-Heine. But apart from the fact that it would be extremely painful for me to stay there, because I've not returned since my husband's death, it would be impossible for me, for the simple reason that I've not found any servants for the place."

"Not even a night watchman?"

"Not even."

The detective was quiet for a few seconds. Then he said,

"The best thing for you would be to find lodgings with a family boarding house that is modest, but comfortable, and whose address, if you like, I can give you."

"Certainly, monsieur."

"The Calme-Abri. 49, Rue Boileau, in Auteil. I'll telephone the proprietor shortly, she's a friend of mine. You can give her a false name. That is preferable, by all accounts… For my part, you'll be asked for no information, no papers. I'd ask you to wait there until I give you a sign of activity. Rest assured, the time won't be wasted. I have a habit of getting to work quickly. And I was taking such close account of your suffering that I shall hasten to abridge it. I advise you to have, not courage, because I've just observed that you possess plenty of that, but patience, and above all do not be put off if, as I shan't hide from you, we find ourselves, as is more than probable, that is to say certain, facing obstacles which will certainly be difficult to beat."

"I shall have as much patience as is required of me," affirmed Countess Marie-Thérèse.

She stood and readied herself to take leave of Chantecoq. But he gestured to her to wait.

"We will speak soon, I'll have new information to ask of you."

"It goes without saying, Monsieur Chantecoq, that at all times and under all circumstances I remain entirely at your disposal."

"One last question for today," the detective said.

"Go on, please."

"Could you tell me if a search has been carried out at your home on Rue Henri-Heine?"

"I've not heard anything about one. If that formality took place, I would certainly have been made aware of it."

"Very well," continued the great bloodhound, "that which the prosecutor neglected, I should rather like to do."

"Monsieur Chantecoq," offered Madame de Roscanvel, "be it ever so painful for me to enter that house, where I was so happy, I am ready to accompany you there."

"It is preferable, madame," emphasised the king of detectives, "that you aren't seen there. You could then be accused of having spirited away certain compromising documents or having planted, to the contrary, some papers or letters fabricated after the fact, in the interest of your defence. It is wiser that I make this trip alone, without witnesses, so long as you see no problems with this."

"None at all, Monsieur Chantecoq. Before meeting you, based purely on what I knew of you, I was ready to follow all your directives blindly. Now that I've spoken to you and listened to you, I'll go so far as to tell you that my trust in you is boundless.

And, taking hold of her small handbag, that in the course of the interview she had placed on the detective's table, she drew from it a keyring, which she held out to Chantecoq, saying: "Here are the keys to the house, make of them whatever use you see fit."

The bloodhound took hold of the keyring, and slipped it into his jacket pocket.

"Before I go," continued the young woman, "allow me to thank you once more."

"Wait until we have triumphed."

"Then, I shall see you soon."

"Very soon, madame. One last recommendation… Don't leave Calme-Abri until I have telephoned. Don't worry, this will be a matter of twenty-four hours, perhaps less, but certainly no more."

He kissed the hand that the Countess held out to him, and led her to the hallway.

On the way, he glanced inside the dining room. Colette and her husband were no longer there.

Gautrais informed his boss that Monsieur Bellegarde had left for his paper, that Madame had gone to do some shopping, and that both of them begged Monsieur Chantecoq to excuse them.

The detective returned to his office.

Already installed behind a small table, Météor reread some sheets of paper covered in stenographic characters.

This was the whole conversation which had just taken place between the king of detectives and the Countess de Roscanvel and which, from a neighbouring room, thanks to a marvellously sensitive microphone, the great bloodhound's secretary had been able to take down completely in dictation.

"You lost nothing?" Chantecoq asked.

"Not a single comma, boss. I'll type it up for you on the machine. Only, there's a good chunk of it."

"As long as I have the whole thing before dinner this evening, that will be ample."

"No worries, boss, I'll be ready."

While familiarly resting his hand on Météor's shoulder, the detective, who seemed to be in an excellent mood, asked him, "What do you make of all that, little one?"

"Boss, I'm of the same opinion at the Marseille lawyer, you're the only one in the world capable of exposing the mystery of the Blue Train. But that prosecutor, what an evil little monkey!"

"Say what you will, everyone does a job that matches their character. His is not pretty. It's not entirely his fault. When one is born an ass, there's a strong risk of dying as one… But

I hope, very soon, to give him a not inconsiderably hard time."

"I'm counting on it, boss, and if I can give you a hand…"

"I shan't refuse you!"

"Sweet!"

"And the lady? What did you think of the lady?"

"The Countess de Roscanvel?"

"Well yes, by Jove!"

"Boss, I didn't see her, or even catch a glimpse of her, but I heard her. What a harmonious, enchanting voice. Your anonymous correspondent is right. She's a siren."

"No!" Chantecoq corrected him in a tone full of profundity. "No, Météor, she's no siren… she's an unfortunate lady."

3 WHERE CHANTECOQ'S SEARCH HAS RATHER UNEXPECTED RESULTS

Midnight was just striking on the beautiful Empire pendulum clock which decorated his studio's chimney, and Chantecoq, sitting at his table, again reread with great attention the sheets on which, with faultless fidelity, Météor had reproduced the conversation he had that afternoon with the Countess de Roscanvel.

From time to time, as was his habit, he took to murmuring reflections inspired by the work in which he was engrossed.

When he was alone, he loved to think out loud. It seemed to him that his own words, on striking his ears, stimulated his thoughts and further sharpened the double gifts of observation and deduction which complemented each other in him in such a happy fashion.

"All that," he grumbled, "is as clear as spring water, and this good – well, in a manner of speaking, let's rather say this *formidable* - Monsieur Ribécourt, a man of the north, who has certainly received some vicious sunburn in the

Mediterranean, is in the process of sticking his finger in his eye, right up to his elbow.

"But to nudge him into seeing that Julien Guèret is not Count Robert's murderer, and that Madame de Roscanvel is neither his mistress or his accomplice, it's vital to discover the true culprit as soon as possible, independently of the police.

"The first point to elucidate is to ascertain who might have an interest in Monsieur de Roscanvel's disappearance. The crime's motive can't be money, as the deceased, according to the notaries, had confirmed a month previously that his spouse was his legitimate heir and that this must be put beyond any doubt.

"A crime of passion? The Countess insists her husband adored her and was unswervingly faithful to her. Which is highly believable… but… but… that's something to check…

"A man is always a man, and, without looking to do any wrong to the gender to which I belong, I must recognise that it sometimes happens that lovers are very enamoured of taking, in passing, a penknife to their contract. The opportunity… the grass is always greener…

"Certain philosophers and even psychologists even go so far as to claim that man, whether he be Eastern or Western, is born polygamous.

"But we won't get wrapped up in that. While admitting that Count Robert was left to go in a moment of forgetfulness, in the course of a passing crisis, rapid and entirely fantastical, to give this penknife blow, it must not have been very serious and it would truly be completely extraordinary for it to have had such dreadful consequences for him.

"I believe that it can rightly be said that, often, small

causes lead to great effects. But for such a banal, anodyne cause to lead to such a tragic and above all mysterious drama, it would necessarily have been surrounded by special circumstances, of an exceptional gravity.

"A jealous lover? A cheated husband? Hum! My old Chantecoq, there's a singularly adventurous diagnosis!

"An act of revenge? From what his wife declared to me, Monsieur de Roscanvel was gifted with a thoroughly agreeable character. He led a life of ease, completely wadded by their mutual egotistical happiness. He was not even jealous… Therefore he must not have had any enemies. Let's move on."

"Armed robbery… a villainous crime? I hardly see a bandit, however audacious he might be, carrying out such aggression against a man who could have had on him only a sum of little importance and who must have been of a sufficient size to defend himself. In any case, wasn't it established by the enquiry that the revolver belonged to the victim?"

"So… suicide? For what motive? Roscanvel was rich, loved by an exquisite woman that he could only adore. And then, if he shot himself through the heart, it would have been difficult, even impossible, for him to then throw his gun in a ditch and to go and lie down on the tracks before the Blue Train.

"My word! I wasn't mistaken when I foresaw that I was going to run into some serious obstacles. Right at the beginning I am hitting the most dreadful snag that a detective has to fear, that is to say an absolute dead end, leading to darkness."

He fell silent, and plunged again into reading the papers.

After a while, he continued. "And yet, this all holds

together admirably… It's obvious that the lady is absolutely sincere. The fact of having addressed herself to me would suffice to demonstrate that abundantly.

"Don't I have, and it's my finest and most glorious title, the solidly-established reputation of having always turned away any and all improper, or even doubtful, cases? If she hadn't been absolutely sure of herself about this unfortunate Guèret, warned in advance that I would quickly bring any squalid little intrigue to light, she certainly wouldn't have come to me.

"In everything that she tells me, to the contrary of the prosecutor's opinion, I see nothing that is not believable, or highly logical, in her actions as well as in her words.

"In the course of her account, there was just one moment that made me wince, the part where she recounted that her husband, although knowing that Guèret was helplessly smitten with her, left them under the most flimsy of pretexts, to return alone to the Mimosas mansion.

"I know that she gave me one or two explanations for an attitude which, at first glance, appears rather shocking. An impulsive character, or a noble soul. Both one and the other appear insufficient to me. There must certainly have been another motive. But what? Did Monsieur de Roscanvel wish to test his friend, or his wife? Or perhaps both?

"All that seems rather complicated to me, though pulled by the hair… In any case, we will have time to occupy ourselves with this purely moral detail which is only a tiny facet of the great enigma that we have to elucidate.

"Let us therefore put it to one side, without neglecting it, without forgetting it. Who knows if it has any importance? But, as Gambetta used to say, to the questions. The first, we've decided, is to establish a firm motive for the crime.

Let's see."

While reflecting, Chantecoq set to arranging his pages in a folder which he then locked in a heavy strong box that was nailed to the wall.

And while scratching the end of his nose, which was for him the external sign of a great inner perplexity, he began to walk up and down in his vast office, his hands behind his back, and his eye fixed obstinately on the thick carpet which muffled the noise of his footsteps.

Suddenly he stopped. A joyous exclamation escaped him. "Eureka! As the wise old Greek Archimedes used to say… I've found it!"

And his face lit with a real elation, while continuing to walk around his office, he began to monologue.

"By Jove! That's it! It's obvious! It's even blinding in its clarity! The Count de Roscanvel was killed precisely in order to make it appear that it was Julien Guèret who had murdered him. The anonymous letter that I received this afternoon can only confirm me in this opinion that I am indeed close to considering as the axiom which will serve as a base for my whole enquiry.

And rubbing his hands together, the king of detectives added: "I believe that, now, that's going to purr along nicely. But let's proceed by order and method, starting with that search of the mansion on Rue Henri-Heine.

"My flair tells me that there will be nothing astonishingly useful to be discovered there. Then I shall occupy myself with this butler Marco and that chambermaid Suzanne who must certainly know more about this shady business and whose addresses I shall charge my brave little Météor with finding.

"It's half past midnight… Perfect! Have I got the keys?"

He tapped his jacket pocket, and then continued. "Yes, they're there. So, off we go."

Chantecoq, in fine spirits, reached the back of his office, opened a little door, turned a switch, and entered a well-lit room that looked like a full laboratory.

He headed straight towards a large cupboard whose doors were painted light grey. He opened them by pressing an invisible spring.

On opening, the two panels revealed, suspended from coat hangers and pressed against each other, clothes and uniforms, of all sorts.

The detective chose a black velvet suit, quite worn, and a soft old hat with the same vibe.

He placed everything on a chair and headed towards a commode from which he pulled the first drawer which was filled with cardboard boxes which all bore a label.

He took one of them and pulled out a wig with short curly hair, and a somewhat impressively brushed moustache.

Then he placed his hairpieces on a make-up table such as one sees in artists' lodgings and which was furnished with all the necessary accessories.

Changing out of his clothes, he wrapped himself in a huge bathrobe and, sitting down in front of his table, his face well-lit by the reflector lamps placed at each corner of a mirror which sent his image back to him, with a remarkable dexterity and sure touch, with the help of all the ingredients placed within his hand's reach, he entirely modified the expression of his face and even the lines of his features to the point that he was promptly and completely unrecognisable.

That done, he donned his wig and glued the moustache under his nose and, discarding his bathrobe, he dressed in the full velvet suit, burying a revolver and the keyring the

Countess had given him in the trouser pocket. And, pulling his black hat down to his ears, he returned to his office and checked his weapon. Then, from the drawer of his desk, he took an flashlight and a rectangular box that he secreted inside one of his vast jacket pockets, went out, turned off the electricity, went to the hallway, stepped outside, crossed the small garden that extended before his house, opened the grilled gate that led to Allée de Verzy, shut it, and headed towards Avenue des Ternes, before he stopped in front of a 10 HP sedan with very plain bodywork, which was parked next to the pavement.

A driver was at the wheel. It was Gautrais, who we saw earlier fulfilling the functions of a valet for the bloodhound.

Chantecoq climbed inside the car. The driver must certainly have received very precise instructions from his master, because he started up the car without anyone giving him the slightest address and stopped only at the entrance of Avenue Mozart where the detective got out, still silently.

He walked away, while Gautrais, faithful at his post, both silent and vigilant, settled down for a wait for which it was impossible for him to foresee the duration.

His hands in his pockets, without haste and with a leisurely gait, Chantecoq reached Rue Henri-Heine which was completely deserted.

He stopped in front of number 57, that is to say the private mansion belonging to the Count and Countess de Roscanvel.

The house was constructed in a very modern style. From the outside, it was very tricky to guess at the interior layout, so much did the facade, irregularly pierced by windows of diverse and unusual dimensions, bristling with angular brick outcrops, present a disconcerting aspect, which was above all confusing.

Chantecoq said to himself: "A funny case for a pearl, and as such it is hardly fit for that being of light and charm that is Countess Marie-Thérèse. Ah! Snobbery! Snobbery! What crimes are committed in your name!"

But our hero was not in the habit when, to use his own expression, he was out in the field, to waste time with artistic or philosophical considerations.

He was not there to criticise this building's architecture, but to gain entry to this strange place and to carry out a search, in the course of which he hoped to glean a few pieces of information worthy of interest.

He looked around him, and waited while two passers-by in a cordial conference, which demonstrated that they must have spent a... somewhat liquid evening... decided to continue their incoherent nocturnal stroll arm in arm, and, taking out the keyring, he headed straight for the front door which he tried to open.

But it put up such great resistance that Chantecoq concluded judiciously that it had to be locked on the inside with a chain or an iron bar. Deciding against forcing it, he looked for a servants' entrance which he discovered close to the opening with the metal shutter which surely had to serve as a garage door.

After having chosen from the keyring the key which seemed to be the best fit for the use he wanted to make of it, he slid it into the keyhole and turned it... this time, the door opened without the slightest difficulty, and Chantecoq entered freely into a narrow and dark corridor.

Immediately closing the door behind him, he took out his flashlight and examined his surroundings.

To his right, the wall was entirely unbroken. To his left,

two doors… One must give access to the garage, the other to the kitchen…

The whole of the ground floor must have been dedicated exclusively to service. At the far end was the bottom of a staircase. The detective headed for it and after having climbed twenty steps, he found himself in another long corridor which had to give access to the whole first floor…

He pushed the first door that he found before him. It led to an office with multiple cupboards and did not offer him anything of interest.

From there, he passed into the dining room, or more or less in the room which must have taken its place, because its disposition, its decoration and its furnishing was of such an aggressive originality that it was impossible at first glance or even at the second, to define its exact purpose.

Chantecoq did not wait around. A large bay closed off by a dark drape attracted his attention. He drew the curtain and saw before him a sort of hallway whose very high ceiling ended in a canopy overlooking the sharp edges of metallic pillars which would have been much more at home in a metallurgical factory or in a railway station.

On either side of the hallway, encumbered with divans, low seats and more and more bizarre items of furniture, Chantecoq, while shining the light from his flashlight around him, noticed two exits from more intimate rooms in which he did not judge it useful to venture, because he was sure of discovering nothing in these so-called reception rooms.

Taking a staircase made of imitation marble and which, starting in the hallway, led to a gallery serving the first floor, the detective reached the smaller rooms where he hoped to find richer pickings.

They consisted of a beautiful bedchamber, much less

eccentric, a vast and luxurious dressing room which was connected to a bathroom, an office for the Count, and a boudoir for the Countess.

The boudoir, in the modern style, but exempt from that excess which seemed in defiance of taste as much as common sense, formed a delicious corner, very feminine which Marie-Thérèse had doubtless wanted just so.

On a fine secretary's desk decorated with inlaid wood, there was a photo: that of Count Robert.

Chantecoq picked it up and examined it carefully.

"Very pretty boy," he said appreciatively, "very racy, kind face... His eyes are a little too intense, with a tendency to exaggerate frankness. An athlete's shoulders. Muscles developed, to the detriment of his brain, no doubt. An agreeable enough smile, but not managing to entirely hide a certain natural irony. Voluptuous lips, much more of a sensualist than a lover... a rather enigmatic forehead, a wall behind which there must certainly be something going on, which contrasts singularly with his clear gaze and which would tend to demonstrate that this poor boy was much less impulsive than his widow believes. An evidently interesting observation, but one which is not exactly made to simplify the case, which is already so complicated.

"Let's continue our visit."

The detective went into the Count's office. In there, the dreadful modernism had regained the upper hand.

Chantecoq noted in passing: "Snob! Very snobbish, even... So what hidden vice: morphine, cocaine, heroin? And yet, the portrait I just saw, and which is recent, is that of a healthy and vigorous man, much more gripped by sport than avid for morbid sensations.

"Anyway, if Monsieur de Roscanvel was addicted to

toxins, his wife would have noticed it, and she would have told me… still, let's see."

He approached a kind of desk on which there was a blotter which still bore some traces of dried handwriting.

Chantecoq removed the sheet and slipped it in one of his jacket pockets. Then he shone his lamp's beam very quickly over the walls which were covered by a dark red drape from which were hanging, at irregular intervals, and as if they had been cast there by chance, tiny chimeras woven in gold thread who appeared to be pursuing each other without ever being able to catch each other.

An exclamation of surprise escaped the detective who, yet, was not given to emotional outbursts, nor was astonished easily…

His curiosity must have been suddenly excited most singularly in order for him to get carried away with such a visible display.

Chantecoq, indeed, in examining that drape, had suddenly just remembered one of his most recent adventures that we are going to summarise in a few lines.

Some weeks before, he had received a visit from an Italian lady, Princess Gemma Rascolini, who had recounted to him that the previous night, her jewels had disappeared from a hiding place known to her alone.

At her request, Chantecoq had gone to her home. The Princess had taken him into her boudoir, whose walls were covered by the same red velvet drape sprinkled with golden chimera.

Pressing on one of them, Chantecoq remembered its position perfectly, the Princess activated the secret mechanism thanks to which a section of the drape fixed on some invisible hinges revealed a secret compartment from which the jewels had been taken.

"Ah now," the detective said to himself, "could it be, perhaps, that there's also a secret compartment in this wall?"

He tried to check at once, and sought out the chimera which corresponded best to that which he had observed with Princess Rascolini.

He pushed his finger as the Italian had done… nothing happened. But Chantecoq was not the kind of man to be discouraged over so little. Gifted with an obstinacy and indefatigable perseverance, he immediately decided to repeat his experiment on the other chimera.

On his fifth attempt, a part of the wall fell back towards him, uncovering a compartment absolutely identical to the one that Princess Gemma had revealed.

He shone the beam of his lamp inside and noticed in the hiding place a somewhat voluminous wallet, which he took.

The wallet, bulging, was secured with a steel lock, which would present a certain amount of resistance. No key from the keyring seemed to match it.

"I would be curious to know what it contains," said the detective, under his breath.

With a mechanical gesture, he tried to test the lock's solidity, and found that it opened under his first pressure.

Chantecoq stuck his hand inside the leather envelope, which was divided in three compartments and he noticed that they were hiding only old sporting journals, bereft of any kind of interest for him.

"Perhaps there's a false bottom," he said to himself.

He searched, but found nothing.

"Curiouser and curiouser…" he thought. "For this wallet to be locked away in such a well-hidden compartment, it must surely contain valuables, or documents of a quite different order of importance to these collections of *Echo des Sports*, *Auto*, or *Tennis Revue*.

"But the most unusual thing here is the basic resemblance between this secret compartment and Princess Rascolini's. It may be, after all, that she had been in contact with the Roscanvels and that she had advised them to install an invisible hiding place, similar to her own, in their home."

And, replacing the wallet in the place from which he had taken it, the detective said to himself, "Oh! Oh! My little Chantecoq, there's an explanation which is unworthy of you. It's too summary, too easy! Listen instead to your flair which, at this moment, at the same time as making you sniff a perfume of mystery which is always pleasant for a bloodhound such as yourself, is not without recognising there, knowingly mixed, certain toxic miasmas which impel you to stay on your guard."

These private reflections led the king of detectives to relive his adventure with the Italian noblewoman who, the following day, had telephoned to tell him that, thanks to an anonymous restitution, she had recovered possession of the jewels…

He recalled her silhouette which was so imperiously beautiful, so superbly dominant that her admirers called her only the Belle Imperia.

Who exactly was this woman?

The brusque manner in which their brief relationship had been terminated had not allowed Chantecoq to inform himself about her. He knew only what the chronicle had recounted.

Now, the chronicle, generally not indulgent and even disparaging towards everything that represented fortune, youth and beauty, was unanimous in celebrating not only the beautiful Florentine's physical charms, but even to praise her moral qualities, whose rich beam surrounded her with the most solid virtue.

By hovering above all suspicion in this way, Princess Rascolini had the greatest merit.

She was married at a very young age to one of Milan's most opulent gentlemen, who had promptly rewarded her truly royal gift that she had made him of her character by cheating on her with all the prettiest dancers from the Scala and the Internationale. Descended from one of Florence's most illustrious families, having in her blood that traditional pride which permitted her to elevate herself above all mundane miseries, she put up only contemptuous disdain regarding the stupid abandonment of which she was the object, and Prince Rascolini, without encountering even the slightest reproach from his wife, could give himself over entirely to the most imbecilic orgies.

But one night in Venice, the half-lunatic that he already was, losing all restraint, had the poor sense, during the course of a supper where he had drunk a little too much, to seriously attack, not just Mussolini's politics, but also his personality.

In our days, as always, in that town that is nicknamed so aptly as the Pearl of the Adriatic, and which is, for sure, one of the most joyous in the world, the palaces, the gondolas and even the canals, have always had ears, which were not only those of love, still avid to surprise the proposals of enamoured lovers, but also though, no less finely attuned, of a police who are ceaseless watchful for the greatest profit of those who inspire them and subvert them.

The next day, Prince Rascolini's idiotic utterances were repeated to Il Duce himself and, far from smiling at them, Il Duce was angered beyond anything.

Without procrastinating, as a leader who meant to be respected just as much if not more by the great as by the humble, he let it be known to his more or less conscious slanderer that he had forty-eight hours to cross the border… and that, if he failed to do this, he would be arrested immediately.

Luigi Rascolini, whose bravado was as limited as his tact and intelligence, obeyed without balking. The Belle Imperia, though she adored her country, followed him into exile without raising the slightest objection. They fixed on Paris where, thanks to their considerable fortune, they were able to lead a lifestyle worthy of their status.

Naturally, the Prince continued his revels and, as he had a marked predilection for dance, or rather for dancers, he was soon a common sight in the foyer of l'Opéra, or behind the scenes of our most famous music halls, until the day when a brutal and terrible automobile accident interrupted his choreographical exploits.

Having left one night for Deauville in a sports car that he was foolish enough to drive himself, in the company of one of his conquests, both of them were picked from the car's debris at the end of the Saint-Germain coast, from which the careless driver, who was going at one hundred miles an hour, had magisterially missed the turn.

The woman was dead. He was hardly in any better shape. He had to be trepanned. He came back from it, but only to remain plunged into that state which is so lamentable for a man of thirty, that which is commonly known as dotage.

A remarkable spouse, Princess Gemma solemnly renounced the world, with all its pomp and ceremony, and transformed herself into a nurse, spending most of her time around her husband, escorting him, while a servant pushed him in his little wheelchair across the garden of the magnificent mansion that Rascolini had bought on Chaussée de la Muette, some days before his accident.

She took her revenge in this way, as a heroine, as a great Christian, for the injuries that this vanquished fool had inflicted on her during the first five years of their marriage.

That was all Chantecoq knew of the Belle Imperia.

"For the moment," he said to himself, "let's relegate that superb shop puppet of accessories and continue our search, because, I have a feeling that it will furnish me with still more surprises."

Chantecoq was not mistaken.

But the discovery that he was about to make surpassed, by a long way, anything he was expecting to find or to see.

Indeed, one can only imagine his stupefaction, upon re-entering the Countess's boudoir, of observing that an electric lamp in the ceiling was filling the room with bright light.

Yet he was sure he hadn't activated any switch. And yet those lamps could not have switched themselves on.

Alert, Chantecoq grabbed his revolver and listened. No noise disturbed the surrounding silence.

As he looked around him, the detective noticed, leaning against the photo of Count Robert, an envelope on which there was an address.

He approached on tiptoes, and read these words in a distorted handwriting which was visibly misshapen:

To Monsieur Chantecoq: URGENT AND PERSONAL

The bloodhound took the strange missive, but before learning its contents, he went, on tiptoes, over to the door which opened on to the Countess's bedroom and, brusquely, his revolver in hand, he opened it wide.

The bedroom was plunged into the most complete darkness. No noise being heard, Chantecoq returned to retrace his steps into the boudoir, closed the door as a precaution, and to avoid any unexpected attack, he pushed home the bolt.

Then, replacing his revolver in his pocket, but ready to grab it and make use of it in the case of sudden danger, he tore open the envelope and read the following:

Monsieur Chantecoq

In spite of the warning that was given to you this morning, by one of the friends of the unfortunate Count de Roscanvel, who doubles as one of your most sincere admirers, you have followed up on the attempted approach, at your home, of a miserable woman, justly suspected of having conspired in the murder of her husband and whose arrest is just a matter of time.

This time, I consent to pardoning you but, understand this, it will be the first and last occasion.

I do not hesitate to declare to you, if you persist in occupying yourself in a business that has nothing to do with you and to hamper the work of justice, I will not answer for your existence.

Do not believe for one moment that I am bluffing. The best proof is that earlier, barely a few minutes ago, I held you under the muzzle of a certain pistol, with which I do not encourage you to make better acquaintance.

You are, Monsieur Chantecoq, a very remarkable policeman, and I willingly recognise that you have in no way usurped the title of king of detectives that public opinion has granted you.

I have no wish to go to war against you. You inspire no hatred in me. Far from it! I repeat, I have only admiration and esteem for you.

But above all I intend for Count Robert's murder to be avenged and that his murderers should receive the punishment that they deserve.

Therefore, take care not to make an implacable enemy of someone who has only excellent intentions towards you.

I just gave you a sample of my skill, do not force me to continue. This time, beware, you are not dealing with one of those criminals who, however skilful, crafty, and audacious they may be, always end up presenting a critical error to your demanding eye, but with an invisible person who is following you, observing you, attentive to the slightest of your steps and who will not miss you if you give him occasion.

Farewell, is it not, dear Monsieur Chantecoq, it would be much better for you, as for me, than to force me to say to you 'au revoir'.

The message bore no signature. Calmly, Chantecoq put it in his pocket along with the photograph of Robert, and the blotter that he had already stowed away. Then, with one hand on the butt of his revolver, he went to the door, pushed the bolt, switched off the light, and armed with his flashlight, went into the Countess's bedroom.

Advancing carefully, he reached the hallway which led to the gallery, went down the stone staircase, crossed the hall, the dining room, the office, took the service stairs, walked the length of the corridor, reopened the door, locked it with the key, and found himself in the street.

A few minutes later, he was being driven in his car which took him back home.

The mysterious events that he had just experienced didn't trouble his serenity. Never had he appeared calmer, more in control, more aware of his strength.

A light smile of satisfaction wandered across his lips, whose fine contour lent a spiritual expression in marvellous harmony with his gaze which had never been livelier, or more alert.

At that moment, Chantecoq gave the exact impression of a man who is greatly amused and intends to distract himself further.

"The plot thickens," he murmured, "the plot thickens even in a completely unexpected manner. So much the better! To vanquish without peril is a triumph without glory. And if my anonymous correspondent, however redoubtable he is, and doubtless he is, thinks that he's going to intimidate me, he is mistaken!

"Now I'm sure of it, it was he who carried out the murder! As if I would relinquish such prey! The rogue pretends to know of me! What a joke! In any case, I'm going to prove to him shortly that I have more than one trick up my sleeve. And it won't be the 'farewell' that he's banking on, that I will be bidding him, but an expressive 'au revoir' accompanied by an energetic 'soon'!"

Gautrais, impassive, let his boss monologue away… the faithful servant had seen and heard many others. It was felt that he was one of those 'who don't care', not because he was gifted with that rudimentary philosophy that is commonly called egotism, but because he had a faith in his master that could be equalled only by his affection and his devotion.

On arriving at the entrance of Allée de Verzy, Gautrais stopped and asked the detective: "Boss, what are your orders for tomorrow?"

"What time is it?" Chantecoq asked.

"Three o'clock," replied the chauffeur, checking the car's clock.

"I've kept you up, poor old chap. I can't still ask you to bring me my hot chocolate at seven in the morning!"

"Why not, boss? While you were busy, I slept in the car,

and then, we're nearly there!"

"Four hours of sleep though, that's not enough," declared Chantecoq, "we're going to need all our strength."

And he concluded: "Bring me my hot chocolate at nine o'clock, instead."

"Very well, boss."

"Let's go, have a good quarter of a night, my brave man!"

"Good quarter, boss!"

While Gautrais went to return his 10 HP to a neighbouring garage, Chantecoq returned home.

After having deposited in his strongbox the paper blotter and the letter that he had uncovered on his nocturnal expedition, he went to discard his costume in his laboratory; and, having changed into comfortable pyjamas, he returned to his bedroom which was situated on the mansion's first floor, went into his bathroom where he prepared himself a good warm bath that he finished with a fine shower, and, after having rubbed in some Eau de Cologne with a loofah, he went to bed.

Five minutes later, this man, or rather this super-man, was sleeping like a baby.

Count Roscanvel's assassin needed only to wait quietly… the king of detectives was now on his trail.

4 FROM MYSTERY TO MYSTERY

When, the next morning, at precisely nine o'clock, Gautrais brought Chantecoq his hot chocolate, he found his boss set up in his studio, behind his desk and hard at work with his secretary.

The great bloodhound appeared as fresh and alert as if he had slept eight to ten hours together.

His physical fitness equalled his mental health, and just as he was immune to these moral failings, which make individuals lose as much as three quarters of their performance, he was also free from all fatigue, all depression, such was the perfect balance of his being and of his mind that sheltered him from all misfortune.

These advantages were most precious, and they were what permitted him, at a mature age, to develop levels of activity which would have been the envy of so many young people, he owed them both to a steely will, to the rigorous observation of perfect hygiene, and to the moderate and rational practice of certain exercises for flexibility thanks to which he had conserved all his strength and his suppleness.

His son in law, Jacques Bellegarde, who had for him as much admiration as he did friendship, said of him: "My father in law stopped ageing at the age of forty; barring accidents, there's no reason why he wouldn't still be in the same condition in another forty years."

This is why one must not be astonished if, after a night that had been so fertile in unforeseen incidents, Chantecoq found himself, that morning, in better shape than ever.

Gautrais, after having put down his platter in front of his master, was going to retire discreetly, but Chantecoq called to him with a cordial familiarity.

"Not too knackered, old boy?"

"Oh no, boss. In fact, one tries to follow your example. One doesn't always manage it, but in the end one does one's best."

"As soon as you smiled," declared the detective, "I was happy."

"With you, how could I not be smiling?" the excellent lad exclaimed. "Aren't you the best of bosses?"

"Gautrais, you know that I hate flannel."

"It's not flannel, it's the truth. Marie-Jeanne, my wife, said to me again this morning: 'dear monsieur, it doesn't feel like being in service, but like being in a family'. But I'm not trying to shave you, sir, you've known me a long time. I never dish out blandishments. What I say is what I think. Ah well! If all bosses were like you, certainly there would be no shortage of servants."

And, clicking his heels, he said. "At what time might you be needing the car, my captain?"

"Rest today," the bloodhound declared.

"Monsieur is not going out?"

"Oh yes, but I intend to make use of taxis or to frequent

one of those numerous public transport options which are dispensed to us by our good city of Paris."

"Then, if you don't mind, boss, I shall make the most of it by helping Marie-Jeanne to polish her brasses."

"Whatever you like."

"Thanks, boss."

Gautrais dashed off a military salute and left, his heart at ease.

"What a brave lad!" Chantecoq mused. "That one is no ingrate!"

Météor observed: "He's not forgotten that, during the Great War, you, his Captain, you went out to look for him in the barbed wire where he'd fallen, grievously wounded, and that you brought him back to the trench at great risk to your own life."

"And I," affirmed the great bloodhound, "I have not forgotten that six months later, he did me the same service. You see, lad, that creates bonds of solidarity, of fraternity, powerful in different ways to those forged by banal sympathies or common interest."

And, while dipping a piece of toast in the cup of vanilla-flavoured hot chocolate, which was giving out a delicious aroma, Chantecoq added: "Now, down to work. Citizen Météor, you have the floor."

The secretary took a notebook from his pocket and opened it.

He was about to read a passage from it, when the king of detectives, his brows slightly furrowed, raised a finger. "So, still taking notes?"

"Boss, I'm not yet sure enough of myself not to."

"I'll forgive you, because of your frankness. But remember what I told you about this. If you want to become a good detective one day, and you have the raw material to be one, you must get used to recording in your memory everything that you see and everything that you hear and to be, in a word, a thinking Kodak, not a scribbler on little bits of paper, which risk blowing away in the wind and falling into the hands of those for whom they were not exactly intended."

"Understood, boss," declared Météor, "and I'm going to apply myself again to following your advice."

"Good. Now, read me your grimoire."

Météor puffed out his cheeks, then consulting his notebook, he read out loud.

"The butler Marco is in Paris at the moment. He arrived a few days ago in the service of Princess Rascolini.

"Hum!" the bloodhound interjected.

"Chaussée de la Muette, number 77," Météor continued imperturbably. "As to the chambermaid, Suzanne Morlier, she also visited the so-called Princess on the same day. It's beyond all doubt that she's Marco's mistress. Full stop, that's the lot."

"And it's very good!" Chantecoq congratulated him. "Ah! Now, lad, tell me how you were able to procure all this information so rapidly?"

"Boss, it's very simple," replied the secretary and student of the king of detectives. "Thanks to your friend Menardier, from police headquarters, I was able to request Marco's address from the foreigners' directory. In reality he's called Marcolini.

"Then I made a little enquiry around Chaussée de la Muette, where the Princess resides. A very dandy mansion, a real palace with a large garden, where there's a man who's wheeled around in a little carriage. It appears that this is the

Prince… and a grand brunette lady, very beautiful, and who does not exactly give the appearance of being on honeymoon. It seems that this is the Princess.

"Quite a large world. But they were not what was interesting to me, what interested me was Marco and the shepherdess, wasn't it?

"I settled down to observe, and soon I saw leaving through a small servants' door, a young governess, my word, very pretty, but with a scampish air to her… Ah! Boss, the kind of attitude that would make Saint Anthony's pig's curly tail wiggle!"

"Monsieur Météor," Chantecoq interrupted, shocked, "I suggest you refrain from these preposterous similes."

"Sorry, boss, I shan't do that again."

"We shall see. To the facts."

After having puffed up his cheeks again, the secretary continued. "My instinct warned me at once that this young person who was strutting before me, tapping the high heels of her elegant boots on the asphalt, was that same Suzanne that you had charged me with locating and, instantly, I set to dogging her footsteps.

"But the gallant lady, who had to me all the airs of a thin fly, turned immediately and, taking in my appearance, to which I had voluntarily added an amorous look, she gave me a stare that was much more ironic than angry.

"'I should warn you that you're wasting your time.'

"'Mademoiselle,' I tried to protest, greeting her respectfully and treating her to my most gracious smile.

"'I don't like gigolos!' she cut in with a voice that was dry and disdainful.

"'I'm not a gigolo!'

"But I had hardly proffered this affirmation which was so

truthful and so easily testable, than I received out of nowhere a formidable kick which, though I was solid on my legs, however made me tremble on my base.

"I turned and found myself face to face with a tall brown-haired bloke, an officious fop, who grabbed me by the collar before I could even try to take evasive action.

"But Suzanne intervened. 'Leave him, Marco! With his ratty face, he's really not worth the effort of correction.'"

Météor continued. "Now, Boss! I don't know if I have a ratty face, but what I am sure of, is that at that moment I had a furious desire to deliver to this Marcolini one of those swift left jabs whose secret you passed to me. But I stuck to the principle that you've instilled in me, that wise axiom from which all good police officers should take inspiration: 'avoid all pointless conflict'.

"I contented myself with disengaging timidly and picking up my hat from the pavement, and beating a hardly dignified retreat.

"What good could that have done me? I had completed the mission that you entrusted to me. Not only had I procured the address of the butler, Marco, and the chambermaid, Suzanne, but I had discovered that they were lover and mistress. All that was well worth a toe up the arse."

"Météor," Chantecoq congratulated him. "I am very pleased with you, you did an excellent job yesterday."

"All I ask is that I can continue."

"You'll not be lacking in work."

"Even better!"

"You're going to set out again straight away to the countryside."

"Posh!"

"Oh! Not too far away!"

"Too bad!"

"I need to be kept informed very precisely on all Princess Rascolini's comings and goings. But as you've been burned by her butler and her chambermaid, you'll therefore be forced to construct a new skin, that is to say to camouflage yourself in such a way that it will be impossible for them to recognise you. Do me the service of going immediately to my 'laboratory'. I leave to you the choice of character which will best fit your temperament, as well as the circumstances.

"When you have completed your transformation, return to me and I'll explain to you then, in more detail, what you'll need to do."

"Understood, boss."

Twirling around on himself, nimble as a squirrel, as rapid as a shooting star, Météor darted into the laboratory, inside which he disappeared like one of those film characters that one sees suddenly melt from the screen.

Chantecoq picked up his telephone and asked for a number.

Without doubt he benefited from special grace, either that or he knew how to inspire kindness in the young lady from the P.T.T. on the other end of the line, in any case he placed the call with particular ease.

"Hello!" he barked into the machine. "Is that Calme-Abri? It's Monsieur Chantecoq here… could you please let the proprietor know that I need to have a word with her, with some urgency… thank you, miss."

The bloodhound waited for a few seconds, then continued. "Hello! Is that you, Madame Derigny? Sorry to bother you at such an early hour. Yes, I know that you're a morning person. That's why I allowed myself… you're well? You're still happy? Very good!

"Hello! Yes, me too, fine, everything's going great… You're completely wonderful… I would like to know how the young lady that I sent to you yesterday is getting on? Good? Thank you… Yes, she is completely charming… Would you be so kind as to let her know that I will be visiting her today, definitely before lunch? Understood… Thank you, Madame Derigny.

"Could I stay to lunch? I truly regret that I have such a busy day that I will barely have time to devour a sandwich… and yet… see you soon!"

Chantecoq hung up the receiver and headed towards his strongbox from which he pulled out the paper blotter and the letter that he had deposited there the previous night.

He returned to his table on which he piled the two documents and, armed with a huge magnifying loupe, he began to examine the letter closely.

"There's no doubt," he said, "it's certainly a woman's handwriting, quite skilfully forged, but which, nonetheless, conserves certain signs which are more than distinctive enough to unveil these lines' true author. Now let's study the other piece."

The king of detectives took from a drawer a mirror on a small stand. He placed it in front of him and held up the blotter sheet in front of it, whose traces of handwriting, quite crisp in any case, were reversed. The mirror switched them back to normal.

Chantecoq instantly read: "M728i… M459O… 5321A… BI04L… U951E… T991R… A604I… N228+…"

All the rest was completely blurred, illegible.

"That," the detective said to himself, "has every appearance of being an encrypted message and must, as a consequence, contain some important secret… the numbers certainly form some kind of code, to which one must have the key. No point in asking them for the key, as they'd refuse to tell us, with that strength of inertia which belongs only to inanimate objects.

"Rather let's see what we can get from an assembly of these letters placed to the left and right of these mysterious numbers."

"Still holding the paper blotter up to the mirror with one hand, Chantecoq took his pen in the other and began to write on a blank sheet of paper.

"MI… MO… SA… Mimosa," he murmured. "The name of the Roscanvels' property. Hold on… hold on, hold on…"

And continued to transcribe the following letters, he obtained: "BL… UE… TR… AI… N+"

"Blue train!" the detective exclaimed this time. "The Blue Train that hit Count Robert."

And, intrigued, he chanted, "Mimosa… Blue Train… Blue Train, Mimosa!"

Then he added. "That's not trivial. Now that I've discovered the meaning of those letters, I would gladly pay two thousand francs just to know what the numbers mean."

"There can be no mistake. The whole secret behind the drama is there."

Once again, his gaze went to the mirror that displayed the paper blotter's reflection, which he stared at ardently, as if he wanted to tear its secret from it.

Then, he said: "This is a female hand, too… In fact…"

His eyes fell on the letter, then returned to the blotter. Several times he switched his gaze like this, sometimes slowly, sometimes with haste.

Then after remaining entirely immobile for a moment, he spoke.

"There's no chance of any mistake here. The two documents come from the same hand. That is to say, that of…"

Then he interrupted himself, and grumbled. "Chantecoq my friend, let's not get ahead of ourselves. Remember your fundamental principle: we must never get carried away by 'clues'. Certainly, it's curious to encounter in the home of the Count de Roscanvel, a hiding place identical to that which I had already spotted with Princess Rascolini and it is still more troubling to observe, that the noble Italian has taken into her service Marco and Suzanne, who accused Julien Guèret of being the Countess's lover and furnished, from this boss, to this peculiar Marseillaise prosecutor, one of his case's most serious elements…

"But let's be wary of drawing conclusions from all this that are too formal, too decisive. A mystery such as this of the Blue Train will not be elucidated in twenty-four hours, nor even in forty-eight. If we cling to a tiny thread that must guide us through the labyrinth, in which we are wandering, we must be aware that if we yank on it too hard, it will break between our fingers."

After having reasoned in this way, Chantecoq replaced the mirror in its drawer and went to replace in his strongbox the two precious documents that he had just examined, thanks to which he now glimpsed a tiny light in the shadows where he was engaged so resolutely.

Just as he had completed this operation, there was a knock at the door which led to the hallway.

"Enter," he said, thinking that it was his valet who was bringing him a dispatch, a telegram, or a letter.

He was mistaken. An old man, with stooped shoulders, his hair swept back like an artist, with his beard and moustache cut close to his nose, which was imposing and serving as a support for a pair of tortoiseshell glasses, dressed in a black redingote topcoat of an unsightly cut whose tails were beating against the legs of a pair of trousers who had lost their creases months ago, stepped forward, holding in his hand a black hat in the shape of a cake, and with a very large brim.

In a nasal voice, he announced: "Monsieur Joseph Martigné Ferchaud, from the Institute."

Chantecoq gave an amused smile. "Brave Météor," he said, "this is one of your most successful compositions! One note, all the same…"

"Go on, boss, please."

"You've left a bit too much of your ear showing. Alas! When one wants to personify a man of sixty-five to seventy years old, one does not want to see an ear that's as pink as a kitten's nose."

Patting his secretary's shoulder affably, the king of detectives continued. "You see that I too can get carried away with your little game of comparisons."

Météor looked at his reflection in a mirror that was fixed to the wall. "Boss," he acknowledged, "as always, you're right."

And modestly he added, "Before becoming a master of disguise like you, I have a rough path to travel."

"But you're on the right path, in any case."

"I'll run along and sort out the ears."

"One moment!" the great man said, taking his young collaborator by the arm, which was the only way to prevent him from vanishing.

And he continued. "I'd like to know right now, why you have given yourself this venerable scholar's likeness."

"Boss, it's really very simple. I recall having read recently in a paper that Princess Rascolini possessed a superb collection of ancient coins that she had succeeded in smuggling out of Italy under the nose of the illustrious Mussolini's customs men. You will not be unaware that Monsieur Martigné Ferchaud is one of the most distinguished numismatists around. There's therefore nothing shocking in him desiring to take a look at a collection which is reputed to be one of the most splendid in the world."

"Very well imagined."

Météor observed. "I believe that this is a very plausible way of getting close to the Princess and of familiarising myself with the interior layout of her mansion; in a word, of sounding out the terrain on which I shall be adventuring."

"Very good." Chantecoq nodded his approval. "But that's not all. As soon as possible, I will need to procure a sample of the Princess's handwriting."

Météor puffed out his cheeks under his make-up. Then he spoke with conviction. "You'll have it this evening, boss. In fact, now that I come to think about it: around the time of the theft of her jewels, didn't the Princess write to you?"

"No, she paid me a visit and I corresponded with her only by telephone."

"Boss, forgive that reflection."

"I wouldn't dream of it. It proves that you're thinking of everything. Anyway, go and age your ears. I'll need to change my skin as well."

And while entering his laboratory with his secretary, the detective said: "Our modern police officers are wrong to attach such total disdain to disguise. I know that it's an art that demands much study, much care, much patience... and that's perhaps why among my official and private colleagues, there are so few adepts. I remain one of them and I shall always remain faithful to it, because I owe my greatest successes to it. The old methods remain useful, on condition that one adapts them to the times we live in, and I have decided not to change my methods."

While speaking, Chantecoq had opened the wardrobe of outfits, and chose a cassock and priest's hat.

Less than half an hour later, he was transformed into an old missionary who seemed as though he had just arrived from China or from the depths of equatorial Africa.

His own touch-up finished, Météor had not taken his eyes from his master undergoing the transformation of his person. As he put it, he took it into the very grain of his being. He could do it. Never had any actor, except perhaps the great Guitry, attained such perfection in the method of constructing a character.

Chantecoq, indeed, did not content himself with the exterior incarnation. He also identified the character through his gestures, his way of speaking, his bearing, his attitude, his character, his temperament, his very soul. It was perfection itself.

And so, by the time Météor took leave of him in order to reach Chaussée de la Muette, he had the impression that a real missionary was shaking his hand and wishing him good luck.

For one moment, he almost asked him for his blessing.

Chantecoq transformed into a Holy Father returned to his studio, and though he was certain that under his ecclesiastical disguise, the most observant eye was incapable of recognising him, he slipped his revolver into the pocket of his cassock, as well as the little rectangular box that he had carried the night before and which he had not had, however, any opportunity to make use.

And he left, carrying a suitcase that he had picked up in his laboratory.

He already had that slightly flustered air that our capital always inspires in anyone who has not set foot there for a certain number of years.

On Avenue des Ternes he got in a taxi and ordered the driver to take him to the address for Calme-Abri.

When they arrived at the boarding house run by Madame Derigny, it was around eleven o'clock.

After having settled his fare, he rang at the door of a house with a simple but comfortable appearance. A young maid, from the welcoming home, came to the door.

"Madame Derigny," the detective asked.

"This is her place, father," replied the servant.

"I'm here for a holiday."

"Please come inside."

The chambermaid led the detective into a pleasant waiting room which, decorated with a certain taste, bore no resemblance to those sad rooms with faded wallpaper and obsolete furniture, such as are seen in many establishments of this sort.

Chantecoq was not kept waiting for long.

A young woman who also had nothing in common with those aged, respectable, but severe women, or indeed with those corpulent, bustling, and over-friendly gossips who sometimes preside over these houses, called families, appeared immediately.

With a smile which was not at all commercial, she advanced towards the fake missionary while saying to him with deference: "Father, please sit down."

"Thank you, madame," Chantecoq replied, changing his

voice, "I'm used to standing."

"You came here, so my chambermaid tells me, for a holiday."

"Yes. A holiday of about half an hour."

Madame Derigny looked at her guest with a slightly astonished air. She asked herself if the tropical sun hadn't warmed his brain a little too much or if, simply, he was making fun of her.

"What?" Chantecoq teased. "Dear Madame Derigny, don't you recognise me?"

"No!"

"However, I telephoned you not two hours ago."

"You… father."

"Why yes, Madame Derigny, in order to ask you if the young person that I sent to you yesterday…"

"Monsieur Chantecoq," the charming lady exclaimed, "Ah! Indeed, I would never have suspected for a moment…"

And in a pleasant tone, she added: "I had no idea that you had taken holy orders."

"Not for long!"

"The cassock and missionary beard suit you very well. You look as though you've worn them forever. Now, tell me how I can be of service."

The detective replied. "Allow me first to thank you for the service that you have rendered me in welcoming that young lady."

"Could I do any less for a friend such as you? When I had a bad time, didn't I find you?"

"Shh, shh! Let's not talk any more of that," Chantecoq interrupted. "Your husband was one of my comrades on the front line. He had praised you, confided in me… Didn't I have the strict duty, when he was no longer around, to lend you all my moral support?"

"And material support."

"Madame Derigny, we'll start to argue, and as we'll then have to reconcile, that will waste a considerable amount of our valuable time. Now, I need to speak for a few moments with your new lodger."

"Madame Fegreac?"

"That's the one, Madame Fegreac."

"What a delightful woman, Monsieur Chantecoq, whom you've sent me as a client. She immediately gave me such glowing praises of you that she was instantly agreeable to me. I'm going to go right away to tell her that you're here."

Madame Derigny left. The great bloodhound took the opportunity to cast an eye through one of the living room windows, which looked out on the street.

He noticed on the pavement opposite two men of around forty years in age, with good-natured attitudes and proper bourgeois clothes. They were pacing quite a narrow stretch of pavement, while never taking their eyes from the front of the boarding house.

He grumbled to himself. "I observe that the Marseille prosecutor's orders are carried out in full by the Parisian police. There we are then, I was right to bring what was necessary in my suitcase."

The door reopened to reveal the Countess de Roscanvel. At the sight of this old missionary, she remained silent.

Straightaway, Chantecoq asked: "Didn't Madame Derigny warn you?"

"She told me that Monsieur Chantecoq was asking for me," Marie-Thérèse replied.

"Ah well, Monsieur Chantecoq, that's me."

"I recognise your voice now, but I would never have

suspected…"

And seized by an instinctive anxiety, the young woman asked: "You must have a very serious motive, to disguise yourself like this."

And without giving the detective time to answer her, the Countess continued. "Yesterday evening, I noticed that I was being followed by some suspicious people."

"Let's call them policemen, shall we?"

"Doubtless they discovered my address?"

"It's highly likely, even certain. The proof is that at this moment, there are two of them in the street waiting for you to leave, in order to dog your footsteps."

"My God!"

"Don't worry, madame, and above all maintain your composure."

"Last night I dreamed that Ribécourt had given the order to have me arrested."

"It could well be that he intends to. But I guarantee you that he won't manage it… on the condition, as always, that you follow all my instructions."

"I'm ready, Monsieur Chantecoq, to obey you blindly," Madame Roscanvel replied.

"I'll tell you soon what you will have to do. In the meantime, I need you to answer several questions."

"Please go ahead."

"They were inspired by the results of the search that I carried out yesterday evening in your home on Rue Henri-Heine."

"Interrogate me," declared Madame de Roscanvel, "I'll respond without the slightest hesitation and with the most complete sincerity."

The detective articulated his question carefully. "Are you

aware, madame, of the existence, in your husband's study, of a secret compartment constructed inside the wall?"

With an expression of utter astonishment, Marie-Thérèse replied. "No, monsieur, and Robert must also have been unaware of it, otherwise he would certainly have told me about it."

Chantecoq continued. "Did Monsieur de Roscanvel order the house to be built or did he buy it already built?"

"Yes, already built," the young lady repeated.

"Had it already been inhabited?"

"Yes, by its owner."

"Could you tell me their name?"

"Prince Rascolini."

Hello, thought Chantecoq, *we're on the right track after all.* Out loud, he said, "Monsieur de Roscanvel and yourself, at the time of purchasing this building, were either of you in direct contact with Prince Rascolini?"

"No, monsieur; Prince Rascolini had just had an accident. He was in no condition to receive anyone, much less to undertake any business. It was his notary and our own who got together. My husband and I had only to add our signatures to the deeds."

The bloodhound interrupted. "And Princess Rascolini?"

The Countess replied, "I know only that she exists but I have never met her, directly or indirectly."

"And Count Robert?"

"Him neither."

"You're sure of that?"

"Absolutely. I even remember that one day, while we were talking, my husband and I, about our home's previous owners, my husband cried out: 'it seems that Princess Rascolini is a saint. She has all the more merit as she is, shall we say, a marvellous beauty.'"

"Do you remember, madame, on what date Monsieur de Roscanvel spoke those words to you?"

Without the slightest hesitation, the Countess declared: "The night before our final departure for Marseille."

"How long before the crime?"

"Three weeks exactly."

"Good!" Chantecoq said with gravitas.

As he remained silent, Madame de Roscanvel timidly spoke up. "Monsieur Chantecoq, I know that you don't like to be interrogated, but judging by the question that you asked me, I believe that you are not without suspicions…"

"No one yet!" the detective cut her off sharply. "I'm seeking to inform myself…"

And reining in that train of thought, he continued. "The most pressing matter, for the moment, is to put you beyond reach of Monsieur Ribécourt's attacks."

"You believe that I'm going to be arrested?"

"I'm sure, to the contrary, that you won't be."

"After all," the young woman cried in a tone of sudden despair, "they'll do what they want with me."

"What's all this?" Chantecoq said with a parental, scolding tone. "How is it that just yesterday I was admiring you for your courage, your resilience, your composure, and yet here you are today, and I find you helpless and even ready for all sorts of madness, just because two police inspectors are patrolling the area?"

"I'm not afraid of prison, and I've started to ask myself if it wouldn't be better to give up the struggle rather than to continue leading this existence as a hunted animal, a wretch who no longer has a single moment of respite nor a corner in order to weep in peace for her lost happiness and her honour in tatters."

The detective reproached her kindly. "So, you no longer have any faith in me?"

"Oh! Of course, Monsieur Chantecoq."

"I understand that you are anxious for this all to be over but, yesterday, I loyally warned you that you would have to be patient. The questions that I was forced to ask you, and the shadowing of which you have been made the object have been wearing on your nerves…

"I beg you to calm yourself, I can't yet tell you anything precise other than that I have already gathered together a few clues. I'm pulling on a thread. But all that is still too vague for me to be able to give you any details.

"I told you and I will repeat, we will have to overcome difficult obstacles, perhaps extremely difficult ones. And you will not improve matters by getting yourself arrested. It is vital, instead, that you remain free. I will certainly have need of you again. And furthermore, I consider that it's already quite enough having one innocent under lock and key.

"You are going to listen to me, aren't you, madame? You must! You spoke to me earlier of your honour in tatters… your honour demands that justice be done!

"And then, think of he who sacrificed himself so heroically. We have to fight as much and even more for him than for you. It's his head that's at risk. I shall say no more to you about this, I can read in your eyes that we are in agreement.

"Yes, Monsieur Chantecoq," Marie-Thérèse acquiesced, wiping away her tears.

"All in good time!"

"I beg you to forgive my moment of weakness."

"Brave heart! The only thing that I ask of you, madame, is

to hold on to the bitter end. It's faith in victory that makes the victors."

"I promise you that I shall be valiant from this moment forth."

"And that you will listen to me?"

"Like an oracle."

"Don't judge me if I put you to the test straight away."

And in a plain tone of calm decision and benevolent authority, Chantecoq continued. "It's absolutely vital that you evade this dreadful ring of surveillance that Judge Ribécourt has organised around you. Your presence having been spotted at Calme-Abri, you can't stay here any longer."

"That's a pity," declared Marie-Thérèse, "because I was so well received here that I would be happy to stay longer…"

"I'm quite sure of that," conceded the detective, "but your safety trumps everything. I'm therefore going to ask you to leave with me."

"And those agents watching me?"

Showing her the suitcase that he had placed on an armchair, Chantecoq explained. "In here I've brought you everything you need to pass under their noses and their moustaches without them recognising you."

And he clarified, "It's a nun's habit, with her wimple, naturally. I'm going to take you to a convent where I defy the most cunning of our official detectives to discover you and where you'll be able to wait under the protection of sure friends, as sure as myself, for the moment of truth and of justice."

"That's understood, Monsieur Chantecoq, and I'll ask you only one thing."

"Speak!"

"That is to let Julien Guèret know that we are working to

save him."

"I promise you that, madame."

"I thank you, Chantecoq." And with a deep sigh, Madame de Roscanvel added. "It only remains for me to don this costume. Who knows if I might not end up living out the rest of my days under a coarse habit. My life is forever broken. I have nothing more to hope for down here."

"Madame," replied the great bloodhound, "it's not my place to give you any advice on that subject. I'm a man who is too prudent, too discreet, to allow myself the slightest incursion into a domain that's not my own.

"However, though I only met you yesterday, I believe that I know you well enough to have, more than the right, that is to say a duty to affirm that you are the last person in the world who ought to abandon yourself to such discouragement and to such an excessive renouncement.

"This is a subject that we can discuss one day at greater length, if you wish… but not today."

And his nostrils twitching, as though he already scented approaching danger, the great bloodhound cried out: "Let's get moving first, at top speed!"

And he pressed the switch on an electric bell placed to the right of the chimney, as he continued. "I believe it is time to flee. Also, I ask you, madame, if you would be so kind as to go to your room and dress yourself as a nun."

Leontine appeared. Chantecoq said to her, "My girl, would you please let Madame Derigny know that I have something to say to her?"

"Yes, father."

The Countess and the maid left the salon.

Chantecoq went over to the window. On the pavement opposite, a third person, who belonged to the same order as those who were staked out in front of Calme-Abri, had met those men and spoken to them with a certain amount of animation, all while pointing at the boarding house every so often.

"One might say," continued Chantecoq, "that events are running away with themselves. Ah well, so be it!"

Madame Derigny entered. Straight away, the detective crossed to her, saying: "My dear friend, I'm taking Madame Fegreac away from here."

"Already?"

"It can't be helped! In two words, here's the thing: this lady, who bears a great name, is a victim of both a calumnious accusation and of the blind obstinacy of a prosecutor struck by that incurable disease which is a deformation of the profession.

"He wants to see her as a guilty woman, at all costs, and quite wrongly. This unfortunate - I use that word quite deliberately - has been placed under my protection. I mean to grant her that protection in full. She deserves it, and her case is truly one of the most interesting.

"The police have found her, and her arrest, judging by certain signs I detected which never let me down, is now only a matter of hours, perhaps even minutes.

"In a moment, I'm going to help her fly from here disguised as an Evangelical Sister. I chose this costume, because its wimple hides a portion of the face.

"In case of emergency, I'm Father Gardin, and this lady is Sister Saint-Magdeleine, my niece. If as I foresee, someone comes to arrest my ward, that is to say the Countess de Roscanvel…"

"It's her then!"

"Absolutely. Well, my dear friend, you may answer that

this person has never been with you, at least not under that name. And if, as is more than likely, you are shown her photo, you will cry, with every appearance of the most profound surprise: 'I recognise her, that's her, that's definitely she who came last night to ask me for a room under the name of Madame Fegreac. But she spent just one night under my roof, and she left this morning, after settling her small bill with me.

"In this way, my dear friend, you will risk no consequences, neither you nor me. And after all, you will only have made a tiny adjustment to the truth, which is sometimes necessary, especially when one is trying to save an innocent."

"Understood, Monsieur Chantecoq, your instructions will be carried out to the letter."

The noise of a car stopping outside the front door attracted the bloodhound's attention.

Quickly, he went back to the window, then grumbled, "There we are! I just hope the Countess is ready!"

In one bound, he returned to Madame Derigny and spoke to her in a low voice.

By successive nods of her head, Madame Derigny seemed to agree with all of his words.

A bell rang in the hallway. The proprietor of Calme-Abri withdrew quickly, after having given the fake missionary one final nod of understanding.

Chantecoq, under his beard, gave a smile that was not without irony.

Then, rubbing his hands, he said, "He who laughs last, laughs longest."

Voices were raised in the hallway, a noisy discussion suddenly broke out.

Leontine, dominating the tumult, chirped: "I'm telling you that madame is busy and that she is speaking to a priest in the lounge."

A gruff, brittle, masculine voice was heard next. "This isn't a priest you're dealing with. I'm a police commissioner and I want to speak to your boss straight away."

Chantecoq, who had opened the door a crack, now flung it wide open, saying, "Then come in, commissioner."

Upon seeing this priest whose venerable appearance had imposed respect on the wildest miscreants, the magistrate, suddenly appeased, raised his hat and spoke politely.

"Father, forgive me for disturbing you."

But Chantecoq, playing his role with tremendous theatrical skill, insisted, "You're not disturbing me at all, commissioner, and I would not want to present the slightest hindrance to you in carrying out your duties. Come in, I beg you!"

And addressing the two officers in plain clothes who were standing in the hallway, he added, "You too gentlemen, you're not too many, quite the reverse!"

The commissioner and his subordinates could do no less than defer to this holy man's invitation, as he appeared to dominate them all with his peerless virtue.

They entered the lounge one by one, hats in hands, better than proper, deferential to this old missionary who was welcoming them with such cordial amiability.

And yet, the commissioner was astonished. "Madame Derigny isn't in here?"

"She went to find my niece, Holy Sister Magdeleine, of the Evangelical order, who came to spend a few days in Paris and whom I'm going to take back to her convent in Brioude, of which I have just been named chaplain."

And the detective who was looking to buy some time, continued. "These are my invalids! Bear in mind that I spent almost forty years in the colonies. It's hard, it's so hard… even when one is animated by the ardent faith of the apostles. And then, France is still France… and when one has escaped disease, ferocious beasts, men or animals, and avoided the fate of martyrdom, one indeed has earned the right to beg Providence for permission to return, in order to spend the little time one has remaining, in the country of one's birth.

"But do sit down, gentlemen. I feel almost at home here… I am a very old friend of the Derigny family. We are even related… very distantly related. But we have never lost touch."

And Chantecoq talked, and talked, ready to recount to his enforced interviewers, if need be, all the stories that his fertile imagination could inspire in him.

But the commissioner was beginning to grow impatient. He had not come to listen to the rambling of a faintly senile old missionary, but to carry out a mandate that, at Ribécourt's request, the chiefs had ordered him to execute.

The detective noticed this, and with his paternal attitude he carried on. "You are doubtless pressed for time, commissioner?"

"Very pressed indeed, Father."

"Ah. Well, I'll go and look for Madame Derigny myself."

"Father, you really are too kind, I can still wait a while longer."

"No, no, I'm going," insisted the devious performer, heading towards the door.

But it opened first, making way for Madame Derigny who, while feigning a deep astonishment, advanced towards the commissioner saying: "I was told, monsieur, that you wanted to speak to me?"

"That is correct, madame."

"One moment, please?"

And turning towards Chantecoq, she said in the most natural tone in the world: "Father, Holy Sister Magdeleine is ready and awaits you."

"Thank you, I'll go and fetch her."

And the king of detectives left, greeting them all. "Commissioner. Officers."

As he was crossing the threshold, the magistrate took on a severe air and declared to Madame Derigny, "Madame, you must have here a certain Countess de Roscanvel."

"Commissioner, you are mistaken, I have no one here of that name."

"You're sure of that?"

"Absolutely sure."

"However, police reports confirm that she came here yesterday afternoon, entering your home and that she spent the night here."

"Then she came and checked in under a false name. Would you like me to show you my books?"

"There's no point."

And brusquely taking a photo from his pocket, the commissioner held it up and asked, "Do you recognise this person?"

"Oh, of course!" Madame Derigny replied with every sign of the most perfect candour. "She called herself Madame Fegreac."

"No, Madame!" the magistrate cut her off. "She is the Countess de Roscanvel, and I'm charged with arresting her on suspicion of murder."

Feigning a swoon, Madame Derigny cried out. "What are you saying, commissioner? What, I received a criminal in my home, sheltered them under my very roof?"

"Oh, yes!"

"How could I ever have suspected such a thing?"

"No one would dream of incriminating you, madame. I'm asking you only one thing: that's to bring me to this woman."

"That's impossible, commissioner."

"Why?"

"She left this morning at nine o'clock, after having paid her bill."

The magistrate's face betrayed his disappointment, then clinging to one last hope, he said, "Did she tell you where she was going?"

"No, but she asked me, if I received any letters in her name, to forward them to Marseille, by return post."

"That's a useful piece of information."

And, turning towards the inspectors who, sheepish and confused, had listened to Madame Derigny's declarations attentively, he cried out.

"Ah! You lot, how did you manage to let this woman flee, even after you'd been given her description, as exact as it was detailed?"

One of the inspectors replied: "Commissioner, I swear to you that since seven o'clock this morning, my friend and I have not ceased watching all the comings and goings, all the entrances and exits, of the lodgers and tradespeople of Calme-Abri."

His colleague weighed in. "And if the person in question had left, as madame says, we would all the same have picked her up and brought her in, as we were ordered."

Perplexed, the commissioner asked Madame Derigny,

whose face had retained all its customary serenity, "Is there another way out of your house?"

"No, monsieur."

"Well, this is extraordinary."

"Commissioner, if you don't believe me," Calme-Abri's owner declared, "you can always carry out a search."

"That's exactly what I'm going to do," the magistrate declared with a scowl.

"I shall take you around the place myself."

"Very well, let's go." And, turning to the two officers, he said, "Gilot, you come with us, and Lacoste, you stay at the door and keep watch."

At the point where they were all about to leave the lounge, Leontine appeared, holding a letter in her hand.

"It's for you, madame," she said to Madame Derigny, handing her the missive, on which no stamp or post mark could be seen.

As it bore the note: 'urgent', Calme-Abri's owner tore it open straight away and scanned through it.

Then, holding it out to the commissioner, she said, "Take it."

The representative of the law read what follows:

Madame

Please forgive me for leaving you so abruptly this morning, and if my brief stay in your house causes you any difficulty.

It would have been infinitely agreeable to me to stay longer with you but thanks to persecution by a police force who are determined to view me as guilty, I find myself forced to find another retreat, where I will be able to prepare my defence in peace.

As soon as truth triumphs, I shall make it my duty and my pleasure, Madame, to express my sympathies to you.

*Countess Marie-Thérèse de Roscanvel,
AKA Jeanne Fegreac."*

Literally thunderstruck, the commissioner turned the letter over and over between his fingers, looking between Madame Derigny and the two officers with a suspicious and furious gaze.

Meanwhile, Father Gardin and Sister Saint-Magdaleneine were travelling in a taxi with all speed towards Saint-Germain-en-Laye.

5 WHERE METEOR PROVES HE'S A PUPIL WORTHY OF HIS MASTER

Our readers will certainly not be angry that we'll now be introducing them to Princess Gemma Rascolini directly, a character whose name has cropped up quite frequently from our pen, and who is playing such an important part in the police drama that our friend Chantecoq is revealing to us.

Let's go deeper inside that superb mansion on Chausée de la Muette, which serves as a showcase for the Belle Imperia.

It's eleven o'clock in the morning. The Princess is about to leave her bathroom where, aided by her maid, Suzanne, she has just decided on the tiniest details of her ensemble.

Dressed in a day dress whose sober elegance further augments her regal beauty, she pauses for a moment to contemplate herself in front of a tall and wide standing mirror that reflects her image back to her.

A strangely voluptuous smile sketches itself over her lips. An ardent flame sparks in her eyes.

Could she whom her invariably rebuffed admirers have nicknamed The Marble Lady, suddenly become The Fiery

Lady?

No! Because she instantly resumes her attitude of coldness, sovereign insensitivity and, without even uttering a word, makes a gesture to her chambermaid Suzanne who, carefully and with no noise begins to tidy away the crystal flasks containing the most subtle and precious perfumes. She goes into a neighbouring room which, from its position, decoration, furnishing, paintings, missals, and books of hours that it contains, resembles more a noble Renaissance abbess than the boudoir of a great modern lady.

But she simply crosses it and enters a gallery, a true museum hallway, where admirable masterpieces of sculpture and Italian painting are piled up.

After having cast a rapid and proud glance over these marvels, Princess Rascolini heads towards a hallway where she finds the top of a wide staircase whose cast iron railing comes from one of the oldest chateaus in France.

She slowly descends the steps with that look of instinctive majesty that she would put on while climbing the steps to a throne.

And so she arrives in a second hallway, vaulted with columns of pink marble and mosaic tables that dominate the whole ground floor.

Three large doors leading to the apartments called reception rooms, seem to invite her. She goes through none of them and takes a small door which, hidden in an obscure corner to the left of the staircase, almost blends in with the wall.

A simple push is all it takes to open it. So she enters a small room whose appearance offers a striking contrast with those that we have just crossed in the Princess's company.

It looks like the office of a businessman, closed against all thoughts of art and exclusively monopolised by the calculation of figures and ideas.

The walls disappear completely behind filing cabinets. Behind a desk in the American style, a huge strongbox whose solid shell seems to defy the expertise of the hardiest burglars. Opposite, two leather armchairs appear ready to receive visitors.

A window which looks out on the garden is garnished with bars that are just as solid as those found in prisons and, quite a curious detail, the access door which, seen from outside, seems to form an integral part of the wall, presents, when opened, a metallic thickness of ten centimetres which, when it is locked, must render impenetrable this fort for the businessman who wishes to shelter at once either his secrets or his wealth.

After having closed the door behind her, Princess Rascolini, who appears to be unaware of the need for any keys, contents herself with resting her thumb on the desk's right hand corner.

Immediately the cylinder lifts. Quite a bundle of post is in there… a dozen letters in sealed envelopes, newspapers still tied in a bundle. She doesn't even look at the papers. She takes them as they are and throws them disdainfully into a waste paper basket.

Then, armed with a letter opener, she slits open all the envelopes in succession, pulls out the letters and unfolds them one by one, skims some, reads others with more attention, but always without her face losing for one moment that Olympian serenity which we saw crack for a few seconds just now.

That done, the Belle Imperia, who does not seem in any way pressed to respond to these various correspondents, replaces the letters in their envelopes meticulously, puts them in a file next to the desk, and presses on an electric buzzer placed within reach of her hand.

Almost immediately the secret door opens. A man of around thirty, tall, quite skinny, somewhat tanned, clean-shaven, shifty eyes, feline movements and an obsequious air, walks towards the Belle Imperia.

His black suit takes on the aspect of a livery, so much does this character reveal himself from first glance as a stooge, in every sense of that word which conveys such antipathy and unpleasantness.

With one brief, mechanical movement, that demonstrates the suppleness of his spine, Marco bows before the Princess.

"How is the Prince?" she asks him in a haughty tone.

"He was very agitated during the night. But at the moment, His Excellency is resting," the valet responds.

"The doctor has not yet come?"

"No, Princess. He telephoned to say he was delayed by one of his gravely ill patients, and that he could not be here before noon."

"When he presents himself, you will tell him from me that Princess Rascolini does not allow this sort of behaviour. I pay him… and dearly. As a result, I demand that he be at my disposal when I need him. Not according to his schedule, but to my own," the Princess declared, frowning. "As to his other invalids, I couldn't care less about them, may they all drop dead!"

The Belle Imperia had pronounced those last words with an accent of implacable cruelty, and the butler didn't seem to be surprised at it.

A small smile wandered over his thin lips. Then he replied in an insinuating tone. "Has the Princess considered this carefully?"

"What?" said the Belle Imperia with a start, visibly shocked by this demonstration of familiarity.

"The order that she just gave me," Marco explained without departing from his attitude of total respect and humility.

"Oh, that!" scolded the Italian. "Do I make a habit of speaking badly or in haste?"

"Forgive me, Princess," replied the servant, "but my devotion…"

He stopped, as though he already feared having said too much.

"Your devotion," intoned Gemma, "I know its extent."

Marco, flattered, widened his smile, but the Florentine continued. "I know that it is in direct proportion to the benefits you can extract from it and, as a consequence, it is considerable. But I did not suspect that it would reach the point of discussing my instructions and giving me advice."

"The Princess misinterprets my words…"

"I guess all too well, to the contrary, what you are trying to tell me. That I'm wrong, aren't I, to sack this charlatan? How much did he pay you, that you've grown so attached to him?"

"Princess, never has Doctor Angelotti honoured me with even the smallest gratification."

"There we are then!"

"I swear it!"

"I don't believe you!"

Marco spoke cynically. "He loves money far too much for that."

This protestation must have made a certain impression on the Princess, because she said: "So… why are you defending him?"

The butler, fluttering his eyelashes, declared, "He's so very... convenient."

"So convenient?" she repeated. "What do you mean by that?"

Marco replied, taking on a mysterious air. "I might suppose that one evening, His Excellency might not be able to sleep because he is too nervous or because he suffers from an attack of pain that is too violent, and that Your Highness might give me the order to double the dose of Veronal or to give His Excellency an extra morphine injection."

"And?" Gemma asked, nervously.

"I would obey immediately," the butler confirmed, "first because I will always do as my Princess demands, and also because it would truly be a great act of charity to appease or even to abridge the torment of the true martyr that is His Excellency. I suppose therefore that the following morning, His Excellency might not wake up; in a word, that I would find him dead in his bed."

"Ah! Marco, you're mad!"

But Marco continued, implacably. "With Doctor Angelotti, there's nothing to fear. Everything will be for the best in the best of all possible worlds. He would declare His Excellency's death to be from entirely natural causes, and he would not arouse the suspicions of his colleagues in the civil service... while with another doctor, you never know...

"That's why, just now, when the Princess commanded me to dismiss Doctor Angelotti, I could not prevent myself from displaying my astonishment and my fears to Your Highness."

"So," the Belle Imperia replied coldly, "you are suggesting I murder my husband in cold blood?"

"Not murder him," the foul rogue corrected her, "but

save him."

"You're mad!"

"Not at all. I have, to the contrary, all my wits about me."

"And you dare to offer yourself to me, as the instrument of a crime that is so abominable that I dare not even think of it."

"Your Highness is indeed wrong not to have faith in me."

And in a tone under which lurked a serious threat, the Italian added: "I did believe, however, that I had proved once and for all that she could count on my services."

The Belle Imperia considered Marco with a much less disdainful air.

"I know," she said, "that you are an excellent servant."

The cunning rascal, profiting from the advantage that he had just won over the Florentine, then outdid himself with a certain boldness. "I am even more devoted than Your Highness guesses, and I have not forgotten that Madame's father, the illustrious Count Grambaldi, one of the most noble lords of Florence, took me in when I was an orphan, and never ceased to take an interest in me.

"Should Your Highness deign to remember that when her noble father died following a terrible hunting accident, I had the honour to be his first valet, that I attended him during his final moments, and that I was there when he breathed his last, and Your Highness closed his eyes."

Faking an emotion that he was in no way feeling, the butler continued. "At that moment, I swore to rest forever faithfully attached to Your Highness. Your Highness has always been so good to me, that I owe her a debt that will end only with my own life. That's why, when I see Your Highness condemned, by her duty, to spend the best years of her life around an invalid who can't be cured, I ask myself if that duty might not have limits… and I will swear to Your Highness, on several occasions, I have been tempted, without telling anyone, to…"

"Be silent, Marco!" the Belle Imperia interrupted severely.

"Your Highness is angry with me?" the wretch asked, with an attitude of servile humility.

Gemma was silent. The valet shot her a look in which burned the flame of all vices, of all lusts…

As the silence of the Florentine dragged on, Marco continued in an insidious voice. "Forgive me, Princess, but time is getting on. It will soon strike noon. What should I say to Doctor Angelotti when he arrives?"

Princess Rascolini thought for a few seconds, then she decided. "You will take him, as usual, to the Prince, and you will inform me immediately."

Marco bowed, and left.

When he had vanished, Gemma, whose splendid face suddenly took on an expression of implacable cruelty, began to murmur to herself.

"This wretch may be right… but…"

A telephone rang nearby. The Princess grasped the receiver, brought it to her ear and after having listened to the person who was on the other end of the line, she spoke into the machine.

"Did you say Monsieur Martigne-Ferchaud, from the Institute? Ah! Yes, very well… I had forgotten. Show him to the gallery, I shall receive him straight away."

The Belle Imperia closed her American desk, then headed towards one of the large cartonnier filing cabinets placed against the wall, and simply pressed the index finger of her right hand on one of the mahogany studs that served to frame this imposing furnishing.

She must certainly have activated an invisible mechanism, because the cartonnier swung open, pivoting on an axle, revealing an opening wide enough to allow a person free passage.

Gemma went through it, turned a switch that operated an electric lamp. This illuminated a narrow staircase that she ascended right away.

After having climbed fifty steps, she found herself facing a reinforced door similar to that which led to her ground floor office. She pushed it and, just like the other, it opened easily and with no noise.

In one stride, Princess Rascolini found herself in her oratory, where she caught her breath. Next, she went to the gallery to meet her visitor, that is to say Météor, who, under the disguise of the old scholar, was preparing to complete the mission that Chantecoq had assigned him: to procure a few lines of the Princess's handwriting.

Météor felt at once both very excited and very touched.

In the year that he had been in the famous detective's service, this was the first time that he had been entrusted with such a delicate task.

If he succeeded, it would be the definitive affirmation of his professional skills in the eyes of a master who knew them better than anyone.

If he failed, he would certainly be diminished in the esteem of the man whom he tried every day to emulate and, as a result, for himself, a bitter disappointment and true heartbreak.

But young Météor, though he had not yet had the experience that can only be acquired with time, was too steeped in Chantecoquian principles to have embarked on such a difficult business without having thought it through long and hard, and without having worked out a plan that only unforeseen circumstances could make him modify.

Convinced that a reflective mind must be the foremost quality of a good policeman, he was not unaware that a good policeman sometimes sees his best studied plans turned upside-down in the blink of an eye by some sudden, unexpected incident which forces you into immediate and bold improvisations.

He therefore stood ready for all eventualities.

Princess Rascolini presented herself to him in her usual guise, that of a very noble lady, who seemed to incarnate the most melancholy pride.

On seeing her advance towards him, beautiful as Venus, proud as Juno, mysterious as Minerva, Météor who, at various times, had seen all sorts of Parisian fuss, puffed out his cheeks immediately and thought, dazzled, "Christ alive! What a chick!"

The Florentine, with a soft Italian accent that lent an additional charm to her naturally harmonious voice, began. "My dear Sir, don't judge me too harshly for not receiving you yesterday. My whole day was taken up… Today, it is with the keenest pleasure that I place myself entirely at your disposal.

"Prince Rascolini asked me to tell you how deeply he regrets being unable to show you the wonders of his collection himself. I shall attempt to replace him as best I can."

"Princess," Météor said in a comical nasal voice, "this visit will only be the more precious for me."

"Then please accompany me, my dear sir," invited the great lady.

In her wake, Météor entered a second gallery, less vast

than the one he had just left, but which, marvellously lit, concealed a double row of windows locking away one of the world's most valuable coin collections.

As soon as the Princess appeared, a man, with a silhouette that was full of youth and vigour, who was writing at a small desk near a window, stood up hurriedly.

"Sit down, Gabriele," said the Belle Imperia gently, "and continue your work, don't worry about us."

This person, three quarters of whose face was concealed under a sort of black mask which only revealed one very attractive eye and the corner of a cheek traversed by a deep scar, sat back down with his papers and, docile, returned to his task.

Gemma breathed in the fake numismatist's ear. "He's an invalid from the Great War… his face was mutilated. He is descended from one of our most ancient Italian families. He was poor, but as attractive as a god. All the ladies in the Roman aristocracy doted on him, and the young girls battled to marry him.

"Shrapnel transformed his noble face into an object of terror. What adds still more horror to his situation, is that he has completely lost the power of speech."

"The poor man!" said Météor.

"I took pity on him," replied the Princess, "and I took him on as a secretary. I can only congratulate myself. His terrible misfortune has not enfeebled his character nor atrophied his heart. He is an exquisite being, very intelligent, very vibrant, very artistic. At the moment, he's rewriting the catalogue for our collection. He knows it all backwards: painting, sculpture, poetry, music. He's a true artist in every sense of the word.

"Not only does he give me the very best service, but

furthermore he helps me to bear an existence rendered so painful by the incurable illness that afflicted my poor husband."

Météor listened to his target with an attentiveness that was more and more captivated. He felt, despite himself, enveloped by the fluidity that emanated from the Belle Imperia, a fluidity of fascination, of witchcraft, and he said to himself:

"In order that my boss requires, at all costs, a sample of her handwriting, he must suspect her of having meddled in some villainy. Ah well, that's not possible, and I'm sure that this lady is incapable of any malicious action."

But an internal voice was also murmuring to him. "Watch out Météor, don't get muddled here. You know damn well Chantecoq is never wrong. Get a grip, my lad… you're in danger of slipping on the slope. Mind you don't get it soapy with your own hands."

While he was engaged in these reflections, Princess Rascolini, showing a first display to Météor, who cared about as much for coins as he did for his first milk tooth, began to explain to the fake scholar the origin and significance of these rare coins of which several, even individually, were worth a fortune.

Météor, who was once again fully in control of himself, pretended to admire them with a fervent compunction.

Having purchased, the day before, the *Perfect Coin Collector's Manual* under the galleries of the Odéon, and having read up on it for most of the night, he chanced his arm from time to time with a technical appreciation, all while carefully avoiding making any fatal gaff that might risk compromising him.

Everything, in any case, had to follow her desires because,

from time to time, he puffed up his cheeks under his make-up, which meant not only that his soul was untroubled, but also and especially that he was preparing himself to pronounce some important words.

The tour lasted around ten minutes. The pseudo-Martigne-Ferchaud, after having been in ecstasy in front of several unique coins that the Marquess had brought out from their glass cages, in order that he could contemplate them more easily, stopped in front of a case labelled 'Caesars' and which contained an almost complete collection of coins representing the features of the Roman emperors.

"Splendid! Unheard of! Sublime!" Météor declared.

Then, pointing with his finger to a coin that was a little battered by time, but on which one could still clearly make out the profile of a warrior with a long moustache, the fake member of the Institute exclaimed:

"Isn't this the famous coin, called the 'Vercingetorix', of which there no longer exists more than one example, and which was struck to mark the occasion of Julius Caesar's triumph?"

"Alas, no!" Princess Rascolini declared. "The famous Vercingetorix is missing from our collection."

"What a shame!" replied Météor, who was playing his character joyfully. Then he insinuated, "No doubt it lies in some Italian museum?"

"No, dear sir," the Belle Imperia corrected him, "the Vercingetorix in question is in Paris."

"In Paris!" Chantecoq's secretary repeated. "In Paris?"

With a rueful look, he added, "I had no idea… Princess, I'm going to look like the last of the pedants and sots…"

"No one knows everything," the great lady said forgivingly. "Especially as very few people are aware of this."

Météor replied. "Would I be indiscreet, Princess, in asking you who might be the fortunate holder of such a treasure?"

"The Marquis de Sorrento."

"The Marquis lives in Paris?"

"He is attaché to the Italian ambassador, who resides at 57, Avenue d'Eylau."

"How happy would I be to inspect that marvel."

"I'm certain that the Marquis will be happy to show it to you."

"If he could allow me to take a photograph of it…"

"I don't see why he would refuse you. Sorrento is a lovely man…"

"You are personally acquainted with him, Princess?"

"His wife is one of my childhood friends, and we have remained close."

All while adopting a slightly confused air, Météor, skilfully, insinuated further. "Princess, the wonderful welcome that you have bestowed upon a modest scholar…"

"Let's say a great scholar, monsieur."

"No, Princess, upon a modest scholar such as myself, emboldens me to ask if it might be possible for you to give me a letter of introduction for the Marquis de Sorrento?"

"My dear master, you have no need of a letter… isn't your name alone sufficient to open all doors to you?"

"Princess, I assure you that one word from you would procure for me all the facilities that I need."

"I'm more than happy to write it."

"I would be infinitely grateful."

"Then let us return to the gallery."

She led them back, while Météor who, though joyful with his stratagem's success, managed to conceal his light spirit.

The facially mutilated man didn't appear to react to the

departure of the Princess and the fake scholar.

Plunged deep in his work, he had apparently lost any notion of that which surrounded him.

Once in the gallery, the Belle Imperia sat in front of an exquisite Louis XVI table on which she had a beautiful engraved blotter, a gilded bronze inkwell that bore Caffieri's signature and was worthy of figuring among the works of art that embellished the Louvre or the Palace of Versailles. Nearby lay a huge golden pen-holder whose remarkably finessed chiselling evoked the genial manner of a Benvenuto Cellini.

Princess Gemma took a sheet of vellum from the blotter, on which she traced the few lines for which the pseudo-Martigne-Ferchaud had asked her.

After having dried her note with gold dust that she had taken from a cherry-red bottle, she folded the sheet delicately in two and slipped it inside a large envelope on which she transcribed the ambassador's attaché's address.

Handing the missive to Météor, who showered her with thanks, she said, "I am delighted, my dear master, if I succeeded in being of assistance to you."

Now that he had won the round, Météor now had just one wish: to do a bunk.

His retreat was facilitated by the entrance of the butler, Marco, who was just coming to inform the Princess that Doctor Angelotti had arrived.

"Excuse me, my dear master," said the Florentine, "The Prince is not well, and I had to send for his doctor."

Chantecoq's secretary did not ask for any more details.

After bowing before the Belle Imperia, he reached the door before which stood Marco, who showed him out.

As to Gemma, she went to the Prince's private

apartments, which took up the mansion's second floor almost entirely.

In a huge bedroom with heavy curtains that let daylight penetrate only grudgingly, on a big bed in the middle, an emaciated man with a pale face, thinning hair that was already greying, and excessively bony hands, was lying, inert and wrecked. Only occasional twitches of his lips and nostrils, and some slight movements of his eyelids indicated that the death that was clearly lurking nearby hadn't already transformed this ruined body into a cadaver.

Doctor Angelotti, standing nearby, had seized the wrist that the Prince, plunged into a stupor, had abandoned to him.

Barely thirty-five years old, with an elegance that was subtle and not over-refined, and the appearance of a professional dancer more than a doctor, blessed with a beauty all too reminiscent of Don Juan, Angelotti well deserved the nickname bestowed upon him in the society and almost-society circles where he practised his twin professions of therapist and seducer: the babe mirror.

As soon as he noticed the Belle Imperia, he left his invalid brusquely and came running to her, and seizing the hand that she held out to him, a hand as beautiful as if it had been sculpted by the immortal Canova, he pressed his lips there a little longer than suited the Princess, because she disengaged herself from his grasp.

"Stop that, Angelotti," she said in a displeased tone, "you know very well how I hate those games."

With an accent and attitude whose obsequiousness almost equalled that of Marco the butler, the doctor cried out.

"I know that you are both the purest and most divine of women... but how, in the presence of such beauty and charm, could one not be exposed to certain temptations…"

"Be quiet!" Gemma interrupted. "You're going to talk nonsense again… Rather, tell me about my husband."

"The poor man!" Angelotti said with a sigh.

"He's lost, isn't he?" the Princess murmured.

"I'm not saying that," Angelotti protested. "I'm even confident he could yet live for many years."

"How reassuring."

"So long as no accident befalls him…" the doctor specified.

"What kind of… accident?"

"An embolism, cerebral haemorrhage, a sudden heart attack, septicemia, who knows! The Prince is what we might call a general invalid. All his organs are more or less gravely afflicted."

"His spinal cord especially."

"Yes, but he is gifted, in spite of everything, with an extraordinary vitality that permits him to fight against the assaults which have assailed him from all quarters and which still assail his being. There can be no thought of curing him, but he can be kept alive, and as you desire it, Princess, I shall try my best to do just that."

Approaching the Prince, who appeared absolutely incapable of being aware of what was happening and what was being said around him, Angelotti continued.

"And yet, just look at him! He's only thirty-two years old, and he looks like an old man. Beyond the odd lucid periods, which have become less and less frequent, he lives in the shadows, both metaphorical and actual, of permanent brutalisation.

"He can no longer act, he no longer knows how to think. He knows nothing but an existence that I would qualify as mineral. Would it not be better for him, as well as for those who surround him, to embrace the tomb's eternal peace?"

"Take care," the Princess observed.

"Of what?" the doctor asked.

"If he should hear you!"

"That's impossible! While admittedly he still perceives sounds, he is incapable of understanding the meaning of words."

"The poor man!" the Florentine sighed.

"You pity him?"

"With all my soul."

"You are heroic."

"Why?"

"He made you suffer so."

"That's my business alone."

"Was he not the architect of his own ruin?"

"Has he not been punished more gravely than he ever sinned?"

"You are mercy personified."

"As are all women who have long wept."

"You loved him, then?"

"Adored him! I owe him a year of happiness such as I did not dream was possible on this earth. Its memory is like a dry flower through the pages of a book of misery."

"Princess, I can only bow before the nobility of a sentiment worthy of Ancient Rome."

Keen to take the conversation in a different direction, Gemma replied. "In the case of an acute crisis, ought we to continue with the morphine injections?"

"I see no reason why not. Do you still administer them yourself?"

"Of course, you know, Angelotti, that I've taken on the

role of nursing my husband, and not for anything in the world would I want my unskilled hands to fail to give him the care that I am happy to provide for him. Isn't it the best consolation, the surest remedy that I might bring to my isolation and my sadness?"

The doctor declared. "Who could have predicted that the Belle Imperia would one day become a sister of Charity?"

The Florentine wore a smile of disabused melancholy.

Angelotti continued. "I trust you will still permit me to express to you so in such familiar terms the deep admiration that you inspire in me."

"No, my friend!" Gemma responded. "I have built for myself such an interior life that now I am insensible to everything."

"That's frightening!"

"Why?"

"Because a woman such as you has no right to impose such an implacable cloistering on themselves."

"She is very soon to impose another," the Princess affirmed, slowly, seriously.

"What are you saying?" the doctor exclaimed.

"The truth."

"What? You would think to…"

"Pay close attention to what I'm about to say to you, Angelotti."

And the Italian spoke, in a tone that betrayed her unwavering will. "The day that I realised that my husband no longer loved me, my life was broken, ended…

"I stayed near him because I comforted myself with the useless hope… that he would rediscover his love for me. Perhaps he would have returned to me, if illness had not brought him down. So I am riveted to his bedside, that is to say to my duty. I will be a slave to that duty, to him, until the very end.

"Now, remember this part, it's a confidence that I share only with a very small circle of friends. I trust that, like them, you will keep it to yourself."

"I swear it."

"The day my husband passes, I too shall vanish."

"Princess!"

"Don't worry! I shall not seek oblivion in suicide, no. I shall go and cloister myself in a Spanish monastery where I am expected, and none shall ever know what became of me."

Sincerely troubled, the doctor asked: "What did they say, the friends to whom you have announced this sinister project?"

"Much as you intend to do, they strove to oppose it."

"They were right."

"No, Angelotti, they were wrong. To live among the world, that would be a condemnation for the worst supplicant. To live, instead, in God's presence, will appease my soul, put an end to my tears, and nothing, you hear me, *nothing* will make me go back on my decision."

Angelotti, understanding that he would only irritate his client by trying to make her give up on her resolution, and bowing respectfully before her, contented himself with saying: "Whatever happens, Princess, know that no matter what time of day or night, I am and I will ever remain at your complete disposal."

"I thank you, Angelotti."

This time the Florentine did not offer him her hand to kiss, she contented herself with ringing for Marco and giving him the order to show the doctor out.

When she found herself alone again with the living dead

creature that was her husband, the expression of resigned sadness which had filled the Princess's face was wiped away completely. And the Belle Imperia's mask was composed of hardness and ferocious cruelty.

Her eyes which, just moments before, had brimmed with the tears that she was forcing herself to repress, lit up with the light of inexorable hatred.

Her mouth twisted in a rictus of rage which threatened only to explode. And approaching the Prince who, dazed, mummified, was staring at her with his round, vacant, eyes, she spoke to him in a hissing voice.

"Do you hear me, Luigi, do you hear me?"

The Italian, leaning over the Prince, fancied she noticed a slight movement of his lashes, a tiny tremor of his eyelids. Bitterly, she continued.

"You're listening, yes, you can hear me. Perhaps you also heard what Angelotti said just now, that you could live like this for many years… an ignoble wreck, a lamentable ruin, a hideous piece of detritus, an infamous waste."

And the Sister of Charity who had become a sister of cruelty stated atrociously:

"I could curtail your torment. One slightly stronger dose of morphine or Veronal would be enough. No one would suspect me. And even if it was discovered that I had hastened your demise, who would blame me for it, knowing what you were? What court would be brave enough to condemn me, as it would have been two tortures, my own as much as yours, to which I'd have put an end?

"But be assured as, despite everything, you still cling to life, as though you keep in your heart some imbecilic hope that you will return to health someday. No, I will not kill you! I still want to repay myself through your suffering and at the same time to buffet you with my contempt and hatred. I want to be able to scream at you for many days yet. Luigi, you never wounded my love, because I never loved you, but you injured my pride, which is worse!

"Well, the day on which your vices nailed you like an inert lump to this bed that you leave only for the little cripple's cart that takes you down your garden paths, me, your wife, me the disdained, forgotten, outraged wife, I took my revenge, and *such* revenge!

"I have a lover! And what a lover! A being of admirable beauty, who adores me as hopelessly as I adore him, a lover who is here, in this house, who lives ceaselessly by my side, who spends his nights with me… in my bedroom… below your own, so close that you can hear, in the nocturnal silence, in the solitude of your crushing prison, the cries of passion that fly from our swooning mouths rising up to meet you. Eh, Sylvio, am I not well-avenged?"

After having shot one last terrible glance at the Prince whose eyes were now burning with a strange and intermittent gleam, the Belle Imperia stepped back, as though to better savour the pitiful spectacle offered her by he of whom she had in turn made a victim.

When she had disappeared, leaving lingering traces of her perfume in her wake, Sylvio Rascolini, still immobile, loosened his discoloured, thin lips. His clenched jaws relaxed, his mouth parted, forming a gaping hole from which soon exhaled a prolonged death rattle while his chest was rising slowly with effort, and the gleam in his eyes sharpened, fixed, intensified, soon transformed into the light of hatred.

Then… one word… only one… one insult imbued with the smell of ditchwater escaped this body that might have been described as ready for the coffin.

"Bitch!"

***

The Princess roamed the first floor gallery, heading towards her rooms, when her secretary, Gabriele d'Orvieto, approached her.

Though it was impossible, under the mask which hid his face almost entirely, to make out his expression, it was easy to guess from just his gait and his body language that he was prey to a dreadful anxiety.

"Gemma," he said in a low voice, "something very serious is going on."

"What's that?" the Italian asked.

"Earlier, when you left the coins room, I was seized with a sudden suspicion."

"Suspicion about what?"

"That Martigne-Ferchaud?"

"The old scholar?"

"Yes."

"What of him?"

"I had the impression… or rather an intuition that you were doing business with an impostor."

"Surely not!"

"Exactly! And I was not mistaken… In order to ease my nerves, I immediately telephoned that member of the Institute. Unfortunately I couldn't get hold of him immediately; it was only after ten minutes that I was able to get Monsieur Martigne-Ferchaud on the end of the line."

"And then?"

"Then… that honourable person confirmed to me that he had not left his home all morning and that, as a consequence, he could not have been visiting Princess Rascolini at eleven o'clock."

Frowning, the Princess cried: "So who would have the audacity to present himself to me in his place?"

Gravely, the mutilated man replied. "He, by Jove, who undertook the task of exposing Jules Guèret's innocence."

"Chantecoq?"

"Himself."

"Then, according to you, it would have been he who, earlier, introduced himself to me under the guise of this coin expert?"

"He or one of his agents."

"To what end?"

"That, as indeed he managed, of extorting a few lines of your handwriting from you."

"Why?"

"To compare them with those he already possesses."

"But…"

Gabriele d'Orvieto replied in a sarcastic tone. "I did warn you that one does not trifle with such a man with impunity."

More vexed than worried, the Belle Imperia replied. "What proof does he have against me?"

"None yet," declared the tall man, "but the way things are going, he won't take long to procure some."

"I defy him to do so!"

"Gemma! Gemma!" Gabriele reproached her. "Why did you act so imprudently? Why did you provoke this formidable detective, who would certainly never have thought of you if, as I advised you, you had remained silent? Giving way to your impulsive, prideful nature, you have brought over your head a storm that only threatens to burst."

"All is not lost!" observed the Belle Imperia who, instead

of bristling against the reproaches her secretary was addressing to her, was beginning to lose some of her poise.

"No doubt," the mutilated man admitted, "but all is seriously compromised. You don't know Chantecoq; I can't repeat this often enough, he's an adversary before whom you must shrink rather than opposing him.

"You'd thought to intimidate him once by addressing to him, despite my advice, a typed letter. Just as I foresaw, you only succeeded in stimulating his ardour. I then begged you to stay calm… you didn't listen to me and, instead of planting, as I wanted to do, a bullet in his heart or his brain, you wrote to him in your own hand, this time, a letter of provocation at which he could only smile.

"Wasn't I right when I tried to prevent you from carrying out that act which was as dangerous as it was futile? Now, indeed, Chantecoq possesses two samples of your handwriting. He is going to compare them and, as he can't fail to do, careful as you may have been to disguise the writing in the letter that he found in Rue Henri-Heine, he will discover inevitable similarities between them, he will draw serious conclusions as a result, capable of putting him on the right path and of attracting incalculable damage to both of us."

At these words, spoken in a measured tone, but which were no less of an accusation for all that, Princess Rascolini responded almost timidly.

"I think you may be exaggerating."

"No!" said Gabriele forcefully. "I even feel that the time has come to honour the promise that you made me."

The Italian shuddered.

Without appearing to notice her unease, Orvieto continued. "Have I not kept mine?"

"Do you regret it?" Gemma said, flushing.

With perfect calm, the mutilated man continued. "That is not the question. Out of fear or sadism - both perhaps - you persist day by day in shrinking from a decision that, you have declared to me formally, ought to have been immediate.

"If, as you had undertaken to me to do, you had put, according to your piquant euphemism, 'an end to your husband's suffering', today, clear of all obstacles, freed from all servitude, we could already have realised our dream…

"We would be you know where… that's to say liberated from this infernal jail that they call the modern world, radiant sovereigns of that happy isle towards which, since many long weeks ago, we ought to have sailed.

"Instead of that, we are still here. You, playing nurse to a spouse that you despise, with good reason… me… playing the role of a soldier wounded in the War, forced to hide his face from all and playing out an absurd, odious, unbearable farce all day long."

"Are you forgetting our nights of voluptuous ecstasy, then?" The Belle Imperia said, trembling with passion.

"No!" Gabriele replied, "but I ask myself, while falling asleep, if, in the morning, we're not going to be woken by the police. Come, Gemma, just admit that you have shown yourself to be very imprudent."

Angered, Gemma cried out. "Why didn't you warn me of your suspicions? Why didn't you tell me that, beneath this Martigne-Ferchaud, you had detected an enemy? We could have sent someone to run after him, trap him, take back my letter from him."

"I told you," riposted the secretary, "I couldn't place the call straight away and, when I tried to warn you, our man had fled and was already far away."

"We must, at all costs, get that letter back from Chantecoq!" The Italian insisted, stamping her foot.

"Impossible! First, it is too late. And then, don't imagine that he who is so justly nicknamed 'the king of detectives' is the sort of man to let himself be robbed of such a precious document."

"So, what do we do?" interrupted the Princess who, now that her mask had slipped, was beginning to give the first signs of a certain fearfulness.

"Finish it!" Gabriele pronounced, with conviction.

"You mean…" the Belle Imperia began, then stopped. Her eyes had met her lover's. They needed no more, either of them, to understand.

The huge door to the gallery opened, and Marco the butler announced in a ceremonious voice:

"Your Highness, lunch is served."

"Let us take lunch, Monsieur d'Orvieto," said Gemma, recovering her goddess-like attitude.

As she passed in front of Marco, she said with a detached air, "Doctor Angelotti found the Prince in great pain. He fears a terrible attack tonight."

And slowly, emphasising every word, she continued. "So you may, this evening, double his dose of morphine."

"Very well, Princess," said the wretch.

And as the mutilated man passed the servant in his turn, he whispered in his ear.

"This time, Marco, your fortune is made."

6 WHERE METEOR TRIUMPHS, AND WHERE CHANTECOQ MAKES AN IMPORTANT DISCOVERY

Although Chantecoq had great faith in Météor who, in the year that he had been in his service, had given him great proof of his devotion, intelligence, and even initiative, the detective was no less anxious to know how his young collaborator had acquitted himself on the mission that had been entrusted to him.

Now, at about midday, when the brave Gautrais was just telling him that lunch was served, Météor, still disguised as the old scholar, presented himself before him, and after having puffed out his cheeks, declared in a tone of evident satisfaction and justified pride:

"Boss, it's done! I won the eggcup."

"Then," cried the great bloodhound, "you're bringing me…"

"A letter from the Princess's hand, that I have the honour to place in your own hands."

Météor gave the envelope to Chantecoq who, also

enchanted, cried out.

"Bravo, little one, that's wonderful! Quickly go and change your clothes and reclaim your normal physiognomy, I'm going to tell Gautrais to put your cover opposite my own."

"Boss," the young secretary blushed under his make-up. "Boss, are you inviting me to lunch?"

"I'm inviting you."

"What a feast day!"

"Isn't it already a feast day, as you've pulled off a real success?"

"Boss, I'm overcome!"

"Go on, hurry up. Because if you make her stewed apples 'sticky', Marie-Jeanne will curse you, and she would have a point."

Météor had already vanished. Ten minutes later, during which Chantecoq had munched some hors-d'oeuvres, Météor reappeared in his natural shape, and sat down to eat.

"Now," the policeman invited him, "tell me how it all went."

While doing all honour to the simple but excellent meal that his master had decided to share with him, the young secretary gave an exact and detailed account of his meeting with Princess Rascolini.

When he had finished, the king of detectives replied.

"I can only compliment you sincerely. You manoeuvred most skilfully. I gave you free rein because I wanted to test your knowhow. And your success is plain. It was swift and complete. I could not have hoped for more."

"Yet, boss," declared Météor, by no means wearied by these tributes, "thinking about it, I feel I may have made a gaffe."

"Ah! You think so!" Chantecoq underlined, with a mischievous smile. And he added, finely, "It would in no way displease me to see you make your own critique of your operations. That proves that you are not conceited. Now, I'm listening to you."

Météor puffed his cheeks, then blurted out: "Boss, my gaffe, the way I see it, was this: putting myself in the skin, or rather, having endorsed the character of a known individual such as Monsieur Martigne-Ferchaud. You understand me, don't you, boss?"

"Go on."

"I suppose one thing: that one day Princess Rascolini finds herself in the real Martigne's presence, that she talks to him about his visit, and that he swears to all the gods he never set foot in her home."

Météor stopped.

"Continue, continue," pressed the detective, who seemed to be enjoying himself.

"There's the other more serious eventuality," continued the apprentice bloodhound. "Suppose that once departed, the Princess had any doubts, that she'd telephoned old Ferchaud!"

"And what then?" Chantecoq cut in.

"Well, boss, it would be a disaster."

"Ah! You think so?"

"Yes."

"Well, lad, you made a grave error… for which I forgive you, due to your success this morning, and… due to your inexperience. Do you think then that I too hadn't thought of this objection, that you just addressed a little belatedly? Do you imagine that if I'd considered it to be dangerous, that I'd have let you leave on the mission, dressed like that? Come on!

"It may well be as you fear, that the Princess scents, or has already scented the plot. What harm can that do us, as we have her letter, and I am going to once more demonstrate the veracity of the ancient dictum that pretends that with a few lines of his writing, one can trap a man, and more to the point a woman!

"Even if she knew that it was me who made her fall into the trap, I would be very happy, first, because that would prove to this strange person that I am not afraid of her... and then, because she would feel, not yet hunted, but all the same threatened and then she could not help but commit some imprudent act from which, I don't need to tell you, I would manage to profit from.

"So you see then that your critique was in no way justified."

"Boss," said Météor admiringly, "you're a super bloke. With you, there's always something interesting to learn. Listening to you is an education in itself."

"It's your turn to talk..." the detective encouraged him.

"Me, boss..." Météor exclaimed, "but I've nothing more to tell you, I've emptied my sack completely."

"Error, lad! Grave error!" intoned the great bloodhound. "And what about everything you observed there? Because I'm certain that you will not have neglected the opportunity to examine, without making it obvious, and yet with the greatest attention, the appearance of the surroundings as well as the attitude of those who live there."

"Boss," the student detective declared with frankness, "I would prefer to confess to you that I was so preoccupied with my mission, that I had hardly any leisure for observations which, I acknowledge, would have been very interesting. I am not yet, as you are, an Argus Panoptes with a hundred eyes, for whom the entire universe is theatre…"

"Don't worry, lad. That will come."

"All I can tell you on this matter, boss, you know as well or even better than I. I will teach you nothing new in telling you that Princess Rascolini is a superb lady, who has a pair of peepers to damn a saint, that the mansion where she lives is certainly one of the most beautiful and sumptuous in Paris, that her collection of coins, though I'm hardly an expert on the subject, appeared to me to be of the highest order, and that alone the gallery where the Princess received me contains several millions in artworks: paintings, sculptures, furnishings, trinkets, such as all the antiquarians of France and Italy would be incapable of matching."

"What effect did the Belle Imperia have on you?" the king of detectives asked him brusquely.

Météor puffed out his cheeks, then replied. "The effect of a goddess that you'd really like to see come down from her Olympus to pay you a little visit between midnight and one in the morning."

"That's a very natural point of view for a lad of your age," said Chantecoq, who knew how to be a marvellous deadpan, when he wanted to be.

And he went on. "However, I was expecting better from you."

Stung, Météor, who never let himself get caught off-guard, riposted. "This was only a first impression, boss. The Princess inspired others in me, and of a completely different order, which, I hasten to assure you, immediately destroyed that which I just revealed to you."

"I like that better."

Météor continued. "My first shock, once cushioned by

the necessity of not allowing myself to be distracted for a minute from my professional duty, I began, according to your principles, sheltered by my glasses, to explore, while speaking, my target's eyes, and I noted, beneath her gentle demeanour, a flame which was not precisely that of uprightness and goodwill."

"Good."

"I also observed that the mask of melancholy renunciation and conjugal abstinence into which she was sinking was not sufficiently glued to her face to hide the projection of considerable pride and the impatience of an excessive temperament."

"Better and better. And what else?"

"That's all, boss."

"You're sure?"

"Yes, boss."

"I bet it isn't."

"I assure you…"

"Did you see Marco?"

"The butler?"

"Yes."

"Yes, boss. He wasn't the one who opened the door, but it was him who showed me around."

"And the chambermaids?"

"Other than Suzanne, no more than there are hairs on the palm of my hand."

"And Prince Rascolini?"

"Nowhere to be seen! But his noble spouse didn't hide from me that he was very ill, and she even left me to go and meet his doctor, who was just arriving."

"You didn't gather, in passing, any other details?"

"No, boss."

"Spot anyone else at all?"

"No, boss… that is to say, yes."

"You see… Come on, then. Tell me quickly what you saw."

Pausing only to puff out his cheeks, Météor replied. "The Princess's secretary."

"She has a secretary, then?"

"Yes, boss, an Italian called Gabriele d'Orvieto, the heir to a ruined family and, on top of all that, a war invalid, with a mutilated face. And he must have been seriously messed up, because his face was entirely covered in a kind of mask. You could barely make out quarter of an eye, a bit of his cheek, and the lobe of one of his ears.

Chantecoq, visibly interested, cried out. "And you were pretending that you had nothing more to tell me! But there we are, lad, better than a detail, a fact that I will qualify as capital."

"That, boss, I was not expecting…"

"You'll see. But one more question: where was he, this secretary?"

"In the room with the coin collection."

"What was he doing?"

"He was working on a catalogue."

"Did the Princess seem to treat him as an inferior?"

"Not at all. I even noticed that, whenever her eyes settled on him, their expression instantaneously became benevolent and were even imbued with a certain degree of tenderness."

"And that's perfect!" Chantecoq cried. "Straight after dinner, you're going along to the police precinct, you'll ask at the foreigners' service for the pedigree of this Gabriele d'Orvieto and you'll report it back to me with your habitual alacrity."

"Understood, boss!"

And, radiant, the king of detectives cried out. "I would gladly wager my own head that this Gabriele is no more called d'Orvieto than I'm called Fanfan la Tulipe or Ratapoil, that his face is no more mutilated than yours or mine, but that he is the lover of the Belle Imperia, of the virtuous Princess, and that he is also… but we mustn't get ahead of ourselves!

"Finish your coffee, Météor. We've both got work to do and if I am not mistaken in my deductions, which would astonish me, I believe that we may mark this day with a white rock."

In one gulp, Météor absorbed the rest of the succulent and aromatic brew and, in a voice full of youthful ardour, he said, as he rose from the table:

"Boss, goodbye, and see you soon."

"All my compliments, once again," said Chantecoq, holding out his hand.

Shaking it with deference, the young secretary cried out. "Never, boss, I will never manage to express to you how happy and proud I am to work under your orders."

Chantecoq tried to give him a friendly pat on the cheek, but Météor had already vanished into the hallway.

"I'm relaxed about his fate, he'll find his path. He will even go very far. So much the better! He's such a brave child!" the king of detectives murmured to himself with a happy smile.

His first act was to return to his strongbox, to take from it the paper blotter and the letter that he had brought from Rue Henri-Heine and to spread them out on his desk.

Taking from his pocket the missive that his secretary had given to him before lunch, he set himself to the extremely intricate task of making comparisons between that letter and the other two documents, when there was a knock at the door.

"Come in!" he said with a slightly irritated tone, because he hardly liked to be distracted, especially when he had such a delicate job to do.

Gautrais's silhouette lurked on the threshold.

"Boss," said that excellent chap, "sorry to disturb you. There's a lady who's asking to speak to you."

Chantecoq cast a rapid glance over his notebook before replying. "I have no appointments this afternoon and I am very busy. Ask this lady to write to me as to the purpose of her visit, and I shall find time to see her, but… another day."

"This person told me that she had a word for you on behalf of Monsieur Bellegarde," Gautrais replied.

"That's different, then. If Jacques is sending me someone, it's certainly not to waste my time."

And, as he shoved his papers sharply into the middle drawer of his table, he ordered, "Gautrais, show in this lady."

A few seconds later, the visitor entered Chantecoq's office.

She was a lady of about fifty years, dressed in black, and with great distinction. Her face, ravaged by a pain which must have been as recent as it was profound, bore the vestiges of a rare beauty.

Chantecoq stood, and showed her to a seat. "Madame, you are welcome."

The stranger handed him a letter which the bloodhound scanned immediately.

It was thus composed:

My dear father-in-law,

I present to you Madame Kérénot, the widow of my colleague and friend who was my colleague at the Petit Parisien for so many long years. Madame Kérénot will tell you the purpose of her mission herself. I know you well enough to be sure that your excellent heart will be deeply moved by the misfortune of this poor woman whose very noble existence and high moral qualities are respected everywhere.

I thank you in advance for anything you can do for her.

If you are not too busy, we will come this evening, Colette and myself, to spend some time with you after dinner.

With great affection,
Jacques Bellegarde.

His reading finished, Chantecoq said immediately, "Coming on behalf of my son-in-law, you could not, madame, be more welcome here. I knew your husband, in any case. He was a journalist of great talent, as well as being a noble and honest man. Rest assured that in his memory I will be delighted to oblige she who was such an admirable companion for him."

"Monsieur," replied Madame Kérénot, in a voice trembling a little with emotion, "Monsieur Bellegarde told me that I should find a very comforting welcome from you. I can see that he was not mistaken. I am, to him as well as to yourself, extremely grateful."

"What may I do for you, madame?" asked the detective.

His visitor replied. "Monsieur Chantecoq, you see before you a woman who is very unhappy, and who is paying dearly for the years of clear and simple happiness that have been interrupted by the death of the best of husbands.

"From the day that I had the tragedy of losing he who had made me so happy, I have experienced every sadness, every anguish, every bitterness.

"But I don't want to burden you with complaints. I know, Monsieur Chantecoq, that you are a man whose time is infinitely precious, and with whom one must get straight to the point. I shall do so.

"I have a son, twenty-eight years old. Last January 3rd, he disappeared. At my request, the police carried out searches. They were executed most professionally, I have absolute proof of that. Alas! They remained unfruitful, and I come to beg you, Monsieur Chantecoq, on Monsieur Bellegarde's advice, to please help me to locate my son."

"In principle, madame, I accept."

"Thank you."

"But before anything else, I require certain information."

"Monsieur Chantecoq," replied Madame Kérénot, "first, here is a photo of my poor Raymond."

She handed a small photo to the bloodhound, who examined it immediately with persistent attention.

Raymond Kérénot was a very handsome young man, whose well-cut suit highlighted his supple and elegant athletic physique.

A sportsman, for sure… but a worldly sportsman, one who must also frequent trendy dance halls no less assiduously than the tennis courts.

His eyes were provocative to the point of insolence, his sensual, ironic, and disdainful mouth… his confident chin…

Though he must have inspired more than mere passing interest among a certain category of women, for whom the muscles make the man, Chantecoq took from his picture an impression of anger… anxious even, which, at first glance, rendered him unsympathetic to the point of inspiring immediate suspicion…

Chantecoq, imperturbable, asked Madame Kérénot, "Did

you say, madame, that your son is twenty-eight years in age?"

"Yes, monsieur. Anyway, here is a note which I prepared for you and which, better than I could manage speaking out loud, will bring you up to date on my unfortunate child's life."

Chantecoq took the document held out to him by the poor woman.

It was composed thus:

Raymond-Charles-Etienne Kérénot, born in Paris, on January 2nd 1900, was a mediocre student at Lycée Carnot. He was even expelled during the War, shortly before taking his first Baccalaureate. Took up employment with a large automobile dealership on the Champs-Elysées. Only stayed there for a few months.

Passionate about sport, became a competitive cyclist, winning some prizes. Military service at Nancy. Sentenced to one year in prison, following a refusal to obey orders. Following his return to Paris, simply refused to make any effort to find serious work.

Following a violent argument with his father, broke off all contact with his family, who soon learned that he had signed up as a dancer in a Montmartre nightclub…

Spent three years without giving any sign of life to his relatives.

On the death of Monsieur Kérénot the father, three quarters worn out by two years of war and two and a half years of captivity in a prisoner of war camp in Western Prussia, Raymond then reappears, attends his father's funeral, claims his share of the inheritance, fifty thousand francs, and leaves again, setting up a nightclub in the area near Place Pigalle, in association with an Italian man who flees with the cash register after three weeks.

Bankruptcy, judicial pursuit, threats of arrest.

Madame Kérénot pays her son's debts. He swears to amend his behaviour through working and seeks, or pretends to seek, a position.

One day he announces to his mother that he has been named general administrator of an establishment which has just opened near Bois-Colombes, under the title of 'Sporting Palace'.

His situation, this time, seems serious and even brilliant. He resides in a ground floor apartment on Avenue Henri-Martin, for which the rent is ten thousand francs a year, and which he has furnished most luxuriously. He even has a lovely car. He leads the high life, frequents the top restaurants, spends money lavishly and without keeping accounts.

From time to time, he comes to pay brief visits to his mother, to whom he has returned the sums that she had paid out for him.

He declares to her that he is brewing some huge deals, that he's on the path to making his fortune, that he is happy, enchanted…

Madame Kérénot believes him, and rejoices for him.

Then, brusquely, after New Year's Day, after coming to see his mother, he disappears. After eight days, Madame Kérénot begins to worry. She phones Rue Henri-Martin. They confirm that he is not answering his door.

Madame Kérénot goes to her son's building. The concierge tells her that he left on January 3rd, in a car, for an unknown destination, and that she has not seen him since.

Madame Kérénot goes to the Sporting Palace. There, she receives a nasty shock. She is told, indeed, that Raymond Kérénot has never belonged to this establishment's administrative department, in any position.

Why did he lie to his mother? Through what means did he procure the considerable amount of money that his lifestyle required?

Madame Kérénot who, despite everything, retains a deep maternal tenderness for her son, leads a first enquiry herself, which brings her no results.

For all, friends as well as creditors, Raymond Kérénot's existence is a mystery and the origin of his financial resources is inexplicable.

Madame Kérénot, more and more anguished, manages to persuade the concierge, who was doing his housework, to hand over the keys to his apartment.

She hopes to find among her son's papers some clues that will allow her to piece together his life and perhaps to pick up his trail.

But a new surprise awaits the vanished man's mother.

On entering the Rue Henri-Martin bachelor pad, she observes that it has been burgled.

The locks on all the drawers, dressers, tables, have been forced. Everything has been searched, rummaged through... The mattresses, the bolsters, the pillows, right down to the bedsprings, everything has been disembowelled. All correspondence has vanished. It is impossible to find even an account book.

Madame Kérénot's fear redoubles. She asks herself, terrified, if her son might not have been murdered.

She reports the matter to the police, who order a search. But, for three months, all efforts have been in vain.

The opinion of Inspector Menardier, charged with finding Raymond Kérénot, is that the missing man must have been lured into an ambush, and murdered.

There ended the notes that Madame Kérénot had given to Chantecoq.

After studying in vain the detective's face for the impression made by reading these lines so moving in their sincerity, the poor woman continued with effort.

"You must think, monsieur, how much it costs me to spread before you the whole sad existence of this so unfortunately delinquent child. But as I asked you to locate my son, I was under a strict obligation, dreadful as it was, to tell you the whole truth.

"In any case, I knew that you're the tomb of secrets and that gave me the courage required to write these sentences, which are not the denunciation of a mother against her son, but the complete and faithful exposé of reality.

"Has Raymond really been killed, as Inspector Menardier believes? I can't accept such an awful eventuality. I refuse to let it end there. I love him still, Monsieur Chantecoq, he's my son, isn't he? My only child! I am alone in the world! All alone! I always had the illusion that once his wild oats had been sown, Raymond would come to understand the necessity of an ordered life.

"I had even come to believe that it was done, that this luxury acquired by him was due to his labour. Such wilful blindness!

"Monsieur Chantecoq, you are my last hope. But do I have any right to hope? Is Monsieur Menardier right? Oh! Anything rather than this abominable uncertainty.

"If he was killed, prove it to me. If he's alive, return him to me!"

Madame Kérénot had spoken these last words with a tone so desperate that Chantecoq found himself deeply moved.

Keen to prove right away to this tearful mother how much he empathised with her suffering, he replied in the most delicate tones.

"Though I am caught up at the moment by several and especially one case of the highest interest, and of an extreme urgency, I must declare to you, madame, that from this moment, I shall take on board the research that you have asked me to carry out, and that I will cease only when I have obtained a decisive conclusion.

"What will that solution be? I can't yet tell. But though I am in possession only of the facts with which you have just furnished me and which, despite their precision, are insufficient for me to form an opinion or even a hypothesis,

I believe I can confirm to you that you will be answered in relatively short order.

"I don't want to pass an unfavourable judgement on Inspector Menardier. I know him well and I hold him in great esteem for his interpersonal skills, his hardiness, his bravery, and his industry. He has on his trophy wall a very fine collection of murderers and thieves. He has rendered, and will continue to render a huge number of services, but he is a little lacking when it comes to psychology. And that's rather crucial in a case such as this.

"*A priori*, indeed, your son's disappearance can be explained in only two manners: a runaway… or murder."

And as he took Raymond Kérénot's photo and stared attentively at it, he said, "If this young man had been lured into a trap by bandits who wanted to rob him, in a word, if it consisted of a villainous crime, Menardier, I'm certain, would already have uncovered the mystery. That's his speciality, and he is unbeatable in that regard.

"In my opinion, in the present case, never has the old principle '*cherchez la femme*' been more appropriate. It's therefore on that track that I'll direct my preliminary investigations."

Chantecoq took a moment, and then continued. "Madame, I should like to pose you a question which will doubtless offend your maternal heart… but it's the first thing that comes to my mind, and despite my repugnance at saddening you further, I consider that it's my duty to put it to you.

"Speak, monsieur," Madame Kérénot invited him. "Anything rather than doubt, yes, anything!"

"Inspector Menardier must certainly have looked into your son's private life?"

"Yes, monsieur."

"And must have reconstructed, as a result, his past and present liaisons?"

"Exactly! I must say that they were multiple. But Monsieur Menardier declared to me formally that it wasn't on that side of things that he needed to search."

"Naturally, as he'd got it into his head that it involved a villainous crime."

"So, in your opinion, Monsieur Chantecoq, it was a crime of passion?"

"I am not so rigid in my opinion, madame, and I even doubt that he was murdered at all. What's most important to find out, is where your son found the resources he needed to make all his costly purchases."

"Monsieur," said the mother bitterly, "I know all too well."

And, with a gesture of distress and shame, she hid her head in her hands.

Respectful of this immense pain, Chantecoq remained silent, not daring to further question this mother who, in order to locate her son, or rather to learn in what lamentable drama, in what sinister adventure he had definitively sunk, vanished, found herself in the atrocious position of being obliged to spread before him all his flaws, all his vices, all his infamy.

But, stiffening against the momentous desperation that had afflicted her, Madame Kérénot raised her head and, bravely, continued.

"Monsieur Chantecoq, forgive me for this moment of weakness, but that which remains for me to tell you is so dreadful, that I hesitate to speak. He's my son, isn't he! Then, thinking… telling oneself that he was capable of such a vile, base act… it devastates me."

"Calm yourself, madame," advised the detective. "And tell yourself that you're speaking to a lay-confessor, but one who is just as respectful of the secrets confided in him as a true priestly confidant."

"I'm sure of that, Monsieur Chantecoq, and I'm no less convinced of the necessity for you to be up to date with everything. So, I shall hide nothing from you. Here it is! My son was the lover of a very rich lady…"

Madame Kérénot stopped, choked by tears. But valiantly, she tried to continue.

In a gesture of deferential benevolence, Chantecoq, anxious to shorten her torment, stopped her, and spoke again.

"Do you know this lady's name?"

"No, monsieur."

"Do you have any suspicions?"

"None."

"Then… pardon me for insisting…"

"Please…"

"How could you have learned that?"

"On New Year's Day, my son came to wish me a Happy New Year. He had indeed become very kind to me, and if his visits were not very frequent, he would always behave towards me in an attentive, considerate manner, and even brought me numerous presents, that today I blush to have accepted. But how could I have suspected their source?

"That day, Raymond was more affectionate towards me than he had ever been. He even stayed to dinner, and then went to the kitchen, to give a tip to the old maid Françoise, who had known him as a child.

"He left me, after having kissed me tenderly, and even

with a certain emotion, in such a way that I've often asked myself if at that moment he didn't have some intuition that he'd never see me again.

"I felt a great sadness upon his departure. Presentiments, we mustn't seek to explain them, they strike us, that's all. And it's not the first time that I have noticed that they're not always misleading.

"I retired to my room and I admired the very beautiful roses that Raymond had brought for me, when Françoise came in, an open envelope in her hand.

"'Madame', she said. 'I just found this in my kitchen, after Monsieur Raymond left. It's a letter that he doubtless dropped from his wallet, when he gave me a fifty franc note.' I seized the envelope, I looked at the address, whose handwriting was clearly feminine, and without reading its contents, I locked it in my desk, promising myself to return it to my son as soon as he came again to see me.

"Several days having passed without having the slightest news from him, I went to his rooms, as I recounted to you just now. His mysterious disappearance, complicated by false declarations that he had made to me about his situation, incited me to read the letter that Françoise had given me. It bore no signature, but it was composed in such terms that it was impossible for me to retain the least illusion concerning my son's moral degradation.

"That revelatory letter, Monsieur Chantecoq, is here. Perhaps it will provide you with some clue, put you on the path to the truth."

As he grasped the missive, the detective asked, "Has Inspector Menardier had access to this document?"

"No, monsieur," Madame Kérénot responded categorically.

"Then it's perfectly excusable that he went down the wrong route," the great bloodhound declared.

"I realise that I was wrong not to show him this letter, but wasn't I also justified?" the poor woman replied. "Is there anything more frightful for a mother than being forced to sully the reputation of her own child? And then, by law, aren't the state police duty bound to bring to light the most well-hidden secrets, the most unknown shames?

"The press gets hold of things. How could he be reproached for it? Isn't it his role to inform the public?

"As a journalist's wife, I have no right to judge him, or to blame him for it, but I shudder at the idea that all this misery would go to be spread out in broad daylight. That, in this *Petit Parisien* where the great honest man who was my husband had published such wonderful articles for so many years, my son's name might be handed over to the indignation of readers.

"I then regretted having notified the police as soon as I had discovered that my son's apartment had been burgled. Because if I had read that letter sooner, I would perhaps have kept quiet. And yet an insatiable curiosity was pushing me, still pushes me, to discover the truth.

"I cling to the hope that my son is still alive… and that, morally or materially, there is still time to save him.

"This is why, Monsieur Chantecoq, I will never forget what you have agreed to do for me! I am not rich, but…"

"Madame, please," Chantecoq interjected, "Allow me to assure you that there will be no question of money changing hands between you and I. You are the widow of a man for whom I had enormous respect. I have not forgotten that on several occasions, in his remarkable articles on both the official and the private police, he cited my name and accompanied it with praises which I found so much more touching as they were sincere.

"Furthermore, you were sent to me by my dear Jacques Bellegarde, who is for me more than a son-in-law, that is to say he is a good friend. Finally - and now it's the detective who's talking and I believe that he has a little say in the matter - the case that you're bringing to me interests me greatly, and it is still I, madame, who is obliged to you."

"I see, Monsieur Chantecoq, that your delicacy is equal to your talent," declared Madame Kérénot. "But I do not want to take up any more of your valuable time. I'll leave you with this photograph and this letter."

"I'm going to examine them with a magnifying glass, and under a microscope if needs be," declared the great bloodhound, "because, be assured, madame, this is what will provide us with the key to the mystery."

And guessing what his new client was thinking, without daring to voice it, he added: "It goes without saying, madame, that, whatever the result of the enquiries to which I am committing myself, it will forever remain your secret, and mine."

"I don't doubt it for a moment."

"I don't quite dare schedule our next appointment because, as I told you, I am on another very serious case, that is taking up much of my time… but don't worry, I can lead them both, working on two fronts! One consists of saving an innocent, for the other I have to seek out a guilty party. Therefore it's crucial to move fast and it won't take long, I swear to you."

After having thanked the detective again, Madame Kérénot left, if not reassured, then at least less anxious.

As soon as she had taken leave of him, Chantecoq took

the revelatory letter back out from its envelope.

Hardly had he glanced at it than he cried out. "Ah! This is too much!"

Quickly, he searched in the drawer where he had placed the letter he discovered on Rue Henri-Heine, and that which Météor had just brought him. He immediately set to an examination of comparisons which only confirmed his first impression.

The handwriting in all three messages, though different, revealed certain distinct signs that even an ordinary graphologist couldn't help but notice.

Now, Chantecoq was a past master in this art, and for him, there was no shadow of a doubt: it was the same hand that wrote these three messages, Gemma Rascolini's hand.

Enchanted by this sensational discovery, the king of detectives cried out in glee.

"Now, beautiful Princess, I'm going to prove to you that if speaking too much cooks, then writing too much kills."

And he added: "Certainly, more than ever I can see that the old proverbs are right, and that a good deed is its own reward. If I'd sent away that poor Madame Kérénot, I wouldn't now possess this letter, which will perhaps give me the key to this enigma that is the mystery of the Blue Train.

"My instinct tells me, indeed, that these two cases are linked, but divine bounty! What can there be written here?

"All the same, my son-in-law wasn't wasting my time in sending this brave lady to me. It's certain, where the police experience lucky breaks, there's Providence for private detectives.

"But that's not all. Time marches on. Chantecoq, you've crowed enough… get to work and be quiet. First let's see a bit of what Princess Rascolini was writing to Raymond

Kérénot."

And Chantecoq read the following:

My love.

I must scold you… gently, but firmly… You promised me you wouldn't touch any more cards, and now here you are forced to confess to me that you still made a loss of fifty thousand francs the day before yesterday in the game at Sports Réunis, and that this loss has completely absorbed your resources.

I don't want to leave you embarrassed, so I'll send you the cheque you asked me for. But make no mistake, however great my love is for you, that this is the last sacrifice of this kind that I will allow you.

I want, more than ever, for you to have a happy and easy life. That's why I demand that you make a permanent break with habits which would soon degenerate into a passion capable of leading you to worse depths.

Anything, rather than see you persevere down such a cursed path.

I hope that you will read between the lines that which I may not write to you, and that after some thought, you will understand that it's high time for you to become that which I wish you were.

Yours, despite everything.
Your very sad friend.

"Here's a letter which should enable me to knit together a fair few facts and also a fair few theories," murmured Chantecoq. "First let's see the postmark."

The bloodhound took the envelope and checked it over. The postmark, quite legible, indicated that the letter had been launched into the mail on December 26th, at the office on Place de la Bourse.

Chantecoq thought to himself.

"I begin to see clearly in this saga, which now seems

much less complex than I believed at first. Raymond Kérénot was the lover, how to put this right… the interested and barely interesting lover of the Princess.

"At the threat, which was disguised but sufficiently transparent, that the Belle Imperia made to cut off his living if he persisted in teasing the Queen of Spades, the no less pretty Raymond will have riposted with an attempt at blackmail, and the Italian, who perhaps has Lucretia Borgia's blood in her veins, or at least that of the Medicis, will have responded by radically suppressing her… how to put it… her lodger.

"What gives further weight to my reasoning is that young Kérénot's apartment has been ransacked, that all the papers that its owner held have vanished, and if he had not dropped this vital letter in his mother's kitchen, there would not have remained the slightest trace of a liaison which must have been as secret for everyone as it was costly for the Princess, and profitable for the… ah! This time let's just say it, for the gigolo.

"Therefore, now, it's clearly established that the Belle Imperia, far from being the martyred spouse, the resigned saint that she passes herself off as to the world, is worse than a wretch, she's a swine who's perfectly capable of committing one crime, and even several.

"A lady of her rank, of her situation, who tumbles so low, and manages to hide her ignominy under her misleading exterior, couldn't she be capable of anything?

"In any case, I have a formidable weapon against her, and I wouldn't be surprised if she is swift to give me occasion to make use of it.

"However what scares me a little is that, while ever more convinced that there's a link between Kérénot's disappearance and Roscanvel's murder, I don't see, at all, what it can consist of.

"Why would Rascolini have killed Count Robert? To avenge herself? To rid herself of Guèret and, as a consequence, Countess Marie-Thérèse?

"Now, the Countess affirmed to me that neither she nor her husband was acquainted with the Princess, and I have no reason to doubt that young and charming lady's sincerity.

"Finally, what role does this Gabriele d'Orvieto play here? Is he Kérénot's successor?

"Would I be wrong, rather, in assuming him to be the Princess's lover? This is where the thread becomes particularly tangled.

"But I can't beat myself up about it. In forty-eight hours, we have done a very good job and I already have several assets in hand. Now we're going to make use of them."

And Chantecoq, grabbing a sheet of paper, folded it in eight sections, which he separated with the help of a penknife.

On each of them he wrote the name of one of the principal characters of the drama in the middle of which he was struggling.

Roscanvel
Guèret
Kérénot
Marco
Prince Rascolini
Princess Gemma
Madame de Roscanvel
Suzanne

He began by placing them in this order, one after the other. Then he tried all sorts of combinations, changing, swapping the small squares like pawns on a chessboard.

He could have been mistaken for a fortune teller dealing out tarot cards.

Then he went to his strongbox, taking out the photo of Monsieur de Roscanvel, putting it on the table and comparing it with that of Kérénot.

"You couldn't say they look alike," he murmured after a moment. "Their features have nothing in common. These are two handsome lads… two beefcakes, as a vulgar person might put it, and just the type that ardent Florentine must love.

"Supposing, contrary to Madame de Roscanvel's account, that the Belle Imperia, whose letter to Kérénot demonstrates starkly that she was weary of him, had set her sights on Roscanvel and that this latter might have become her lover. Their liaison would have been brief, as Kérénot's disappearance dates from January 3rd, and Roscanvel's murder took place on the 6th.

"In fact, who's to say that Rascolini wasn't capable of harnessing two and that Roscanvel, unbeknownst to his charming wife, was not her lover for a while?

"Then why would the Princess have had him silenced? Might she have been inspired by Marguerite de Bourgogne's tradition, who when her lovers had ceased to please her, sewed them up in a sack and tossed them into the Seine?

"In any case, it's a clear fact that she signalled her crime by writing me that letter where she forbade me, on pain of worse reprisals, to involve myself in the Roscanvel case. That's already a great deal…

"It's now nothing more than a case of loosening her

tongue, as well as those of her two accomplices, Marco and Suzanne.

"Come on then, I'm happy, the skein begins to untangle. We're now going to start the active phase. The trench warfare is over! Now for the charge! Onward!"

Chantecoq tidied away all the documents in his coffer and he was about to go to his laboratory, when Météor rushed suddenly into the studio like a jack-in-a-box.

"Boss," he announced, "as you predicted, there isn't, in Paris, any Italian going by the name of Gabriele d'Orvieto."

"Ah! Ah!" Chantecoq chanted.

And immediately, he added: "It would be very important to find out, as soon as possible, the date on which this pseudo-Gabriele entered the Princess's service."

"That's done, boss."

"What, you thought of that?"

"Yes, boss. I went back to Avenue Henri-Martin and, subtly interrogating some suppliers, I ended up discovering that the Gabriele in question had moved in with the Princess on January 8th."

"In other words," Chantecoq said, "forty-eight hours after Monsieur de Roscanvel's murder."

Météor was about to speak but, with an energetic gesture, the great bloodhound waved him into silence.

Then, slowly, he said, as though talking to himself, "It's absolutely essential that I find out whose face that tall invalid is hiding beneath his mask."

7 THE PANTHER, THE TIGER, AND THE FOX

The mysterious character that we shall continue to call by the name of Gabriele d'Orvieto, as we don't yet know him by any other, continued his work peacefully in the coin collection, when the Belle Imperia appeared in an elegant dressing gown.

"Yes?" the masked man asked, with a sharply anxious expression.

"He's still alive!" the Princess declared.

The mutilated man made a sign of impatience, then spoke. "Are you sure," he said in a curt tone, "that Marco doubled the dose yesterday evening?"

"I'm all the more certain," affirmed Gemma, "given that I prepared the injection myself."

"Decidedly," sneered Monsieur d'Orvieto, "this man's soul is nailed to his body."

"I shall try again this evening," said the Florentine, coldly implacable.

"Let's hope that you have more success," Gabriele wished

cynically, "because I won't hide from you that I grow tired of this mask in which I'm forced to dress up, and of the stupid role you make me play in this household."

"I thought you loved me," cried Princess Rascolini in a somewhat disenchanted tone.

"If I didn't love you," sighed her confidant, "would I have consented to that which you have demanded of me? Would I have become a…?"

"Be quiet!" the Italian interrupted.

"Why?" hissed Monsieur d'Orvieto, "do the walls here have ears?"

"No!"

"Are you afraid?"

"Fear, I think I have proven to you, is a sentiment I do not possess."

"Then I don't understand."

"I only fear that you don't speak any words which could make me think that you regret…"

"I regret nothing," the masked man cut her off, "Aren't we henceforth riveted to each other, by bonds that nothing may break?"

"Those of love."

"And those of crime."

"There is no crime in love!" cried the ardent Italian.

"That's your opinion, it also happens to be mine," purred Gabriele, "but it's certainly not that of the institution that has come to be known as 'justice'…

"Therefore, if we must be happy, we will be so together, and, if we must succumb, so be it! We shall both succumb together."

"Why would you want us not to be happy?" the Belle Imperia cried.

Monsieur d'Orvieto held his tongue.

"What do you fear?" Gemma continued, "Remorse?"

"No."

"Complacency?"

"Even less."

"Boredom?"

"Not a jot."

"So?"

"I'll tell you. I fear Chantecoq."

"We need no longer fear Chantecoq," the Belle Imperia affirmed with a triumphant air.

"What would you know about it?"

Princess Rascolini explained.

"Becoming aware, as you said, that I'd committed two seriously imprudent acts: one in sending a written warning to this detective, and the other in giving that impostor Martigne-Ferchaud a letter of introduction for the diplomat from Sorrento, I wanted to repair this double stumble."

With a voice full of ironic scepticism, Gabriele declared, "I'd be curious to know how you managed that?"

Gemma replied. "In the most direct fashion, the only one which had any chance of success, anyway.

"Having learned that Chantecoq had a secretary; a young man named, or rather nicknamed, Météor, I sent my chambermaid Suzanne after him, giving her instructions to bamboozle this boy and to offer him a significant sum of money if he managed to liberate from his boss the two documents in question and to return them to me as soon as possible."

Shaking his head, Monsieur d'Orvieto blurted out: "You would have done better to talk to me about it before putting such a plan into operation."

"Why?"

"Because I'd have tried to dissuade you."

"Is it that bad, then?"

"In every respect. And it presents one formidable risk."

"Which?"

"If Météor refuses?"

"He accepted, and he must bring to me himself, this morning, both the letters, in exchange for one hundred thousand francs that I'm going to pay him."

"He's not here yet!" Monsieur d'Orvieto observed.

"The meeting is fixed for ten o'clock, and it's now only half past nine."

"I hope he'll come," replied Gabriele.

"He'll come. Suzanne assured me, and that girl's too shrewd an operator to let herself be played, even by Chantecoq's secretary."

"We'll soon see!" said the masked man. And in a mordant voice, he added, "In any case, if our plan failed, there is another way that I thought of since yesterday, and which has the advantage over all the others of being more radical: that's to silence Chantecoq, just as I already wanted to do."

"I thought of that too," revealed the Florentine, "and if I didn't do it, it's… oh, but what use is it to tell you, you'll only mock me again…"

"I think I can guess… you've been consulting old Eusebia again?"

"Yes, I must admit it."

"And she forbade you from killing this accursed detective?"

"No, she simply said to me: 'the day you touch a cockerel's feather, it will be the cockerel who plucks you."

Monsieur d'Orvieto let out a sarcastic peal of laughter.

"How," he said, "yes, how is it that a woman of your education, of your intelligence, and your sophistication, how can such a woman believe such twaddle?"

"Eusebia has never let me down," the Florentine said seriously.

"What a superstitious one you are!"

"Superstitions must not be mocked, neither, especially, predictions from those whom nature has granted the gift of second sight."

"It's said that you're descended from the Medicis."

"I'm proud of it!"

"And you only need do like your great-aunt, Queen Catherine: attach yourself to a new Ruggieri, who will help you protect yourself from the attacks of your enemies, and to get rid of them for you, which would be much simpler by bewitching them with the help of a needle jammed into a wax statue.

"Don't mock these practices!" the Belle Imperia cried. "They're real, they've brought undeniable results, and who knows if they might not work again?"

"Ah! So you believe in sorcery?"

"You believe well enough in radio waves!"

"That's science."

"Ruggieri, too, was a great scholar!"

"What a shame he's no longer around in order to help us bewitch Chantecoq!"

"Again, do not mock these things!"

"Let me laugh!"

"You know nothing of these matters, you…"

"And you?"

"There are certain secrets handed down from generation to generation."

"Those of Locusta?"

"And those of Circe," the Belle Imperia said with emphasis.

"The fact is," Gabriele acknowledged, "you're gifted with powers of enchantment which I'd defy anyone to resist."

Then brusquely, he said, on hearing the chimes of a clock, "Ten o'clock! Princess, if we had made a wager, you would already have lost. Météor has not yet arrived."

At the same moment as he spoke those words, the door opened to reveal Marco, the butler, who brought a business card on a platter, which he presented to the Princess.

Hardly had she set eyes on it than she let out an exclamation of surprise. "Chantecoq!"

"Chantecoq!" the masked man repeated with no less astonishment.

Gemma passed him the detective's card.

"Ah," he growled, "what does this mean?"

"We shall soon see!" the Belle Imperia said.

"You're receiving him?" asked Monsieur d'Orvieto.

"Why shouldn't I receive him?"

And Princess Rascolini, who had entirely regained her composure, added, "I've already done business with him. He's a very gallant man. Marco, show Monsieur Chantecoq into the Louis XVI salon."

"Right on time!" Gabriele exclaimed. "I love seeing you like this, full of guts, life, and energy!"

And, lowering his voice, he whispered in his accomplice's ear. "I'll leave you alone with this policeman. But don't worry, however long his visit lasts, I'll be keeping my eyes peeled, and I'll be ready to intervene if need be."

The Italian replied. "Thank you, my dear, but I hope the panther won't need the tiger to help her overcome the fox."

She left in her guise as a proud and magnificent goddess.

Alone, Monsieur Orvieto took a moment to grumble. "I'd be curious to know what the king of detectives is doing coming here."

***

Obeying the Princess's orders, Marco, who had also wondered as to the motives behind the great bloodhound's visit, had shown Chantecoq to the Louis XVI salon.

It was a room of modest dimensions, located on the first floor.

Its furnishing was rigorously of the period, the Beauvais tapestries, which could have rivalled those of the Château de Compiègne, the wonderful *objets d'art* spread over the tables, the console tables and corner furniture were worthy of much better than a foreign princess, that is to say they were fit for a queen, and in particular for the one to whom we owe the delightful little rooms at Versailles.

When the Belle Imperia, who had quickly changed her night attire for a day dress, a masterpiece by Madeleine Vionnet, the undisputed queen of haute couture, presented herself on the threshold, Chantecoq appeared to be absorbed in the contemplation of a collection of ancient watches, locked in a glass cabinet.

It goes without saying that he was well aware of the Italian's presence.

But manoeuvring as always with a remarkable prudence, he preferred to take his time and to begin the conversation only at the precise instant chosen by him.

Duped by his game, Princess Rascolini wore a slight smile that, from the corner of his eye, the great bloodhound picked up in passing, thanks to a mirror which showed him the reflection of his beautiful and dangerous adversary.

For a few seconds then, the Florentine watched Chantecoq, who was well aware of her, and Chantecoq was watching the Florentine without her knowledge.

The French detective had therefore just scored over the great Italian lady a first advantage which, however slight, was no less of a good omen.

"Hello, Monsieur Chantecoq!" Gemma began amiably.

Sharply, the detective spun round, as though he had been torn brusquely from an examination that had entirely grabbed his attention.

Then, bowing respectfully before the lady, he said, with all the hallmarks of a perfect gentleman, "I beg your pardon, Princess, I was just admiring all these splendours."

"You're welcome!" The Princess declared with her most amiable smile.

And, while pointing out a chair, she continued. "Please reveal to me the purpose of your visit…"

Chantecoq, whose natural distinction and sober elegance made him resemble a diplomat much more than a detective, replied.

"Allow me, Princess, to offer you all my apologies for the early hour at which I am visiting you, as well as all my thanks for the good grace and promptness that you have shown in receiving me."

The Florentine inclined her head. Never had her nickname of Belle Imperia been more fitting.

In her voice which had a naturally metallic timbre but which, when she wanted, she knew how to make sound as harmonious and captivating as a love song played on a viola, she spoke.

"I supposed that, for a man as busy as you to announce himself in this way at the home of a woman as distant as I, there would have needed to be a pressing reason."

"Indeed, Princess," Chantecoq confirmed with a smile full of deference. And he added, "I don't believe it would be useful to reveal it to you, because you already know it as well as I do."

This simple sentence was enough for the Princess to understand that battle had been joined.

But she remained defensive. "Monsieur Detective," she said to herself, "we'll prove to you that Italian fencing is still capable of keeping French fencing at bay."

Out loud, she replied, "Monsieur Chantecoq, I can't tell you how satisfied I am that you're not trying to use cunning with me."

"What use is that?" the detective said. "Your time is precious, as is mine. It's much better to get straight to the point."

"I'm listening."

With complete calm, the king of detectives continued.

"Yesterday, Princess, no offence, you made a serious mistake."

"Really?"

"I won't hide from you that it surprised me greatly, on your behalf. Why, instead of sending your chambermaid to intercept my secretary, didn't you ask me to come and see you?"

"Because you would have refused!" the Florentine responded assuredly.

"Disabuse yourself of that notion, Princess. I would have come running, much as I did as soon as I knew that you were desirous to acquire certain little papers that I was holding, and with which you fear that I might cause you some difficulties."

The Princess defended herself. "Monsieur Chantecoq, you are making a serious mistake, if you imagine that the fact of your having succeeded, by means that I prefer not to qualify, in extorting a few lines of my handwriting from me, has provoked the least disquiet in me."

The bloodhound riposted with flair. "I'm sure of it, Princess, as you're telling me." And completely innocently, he added, "I was guilty of swearing a reckless oath, and I'm sorry for it. But condescend to admit, Princess, that I have the right to do so, in extenuating circumstances.

"Was I not right to suppose that you attached a considerable importance to this letter written and signed by your hand, as well as a certain other document which, for all that it is not initialled with your name, nevertheless bears your authentic mark, since you have offered my secretary, via your chambermaid, a sum of one hundred thousand francs if he managed to rob me of these two items and return them to you."

This right hook, splendidly delivered, appeared to make no impression on the Florentine.

"Monsieur Chantecoq," she said, "your secretary hails from the Midi, isn't he?"

"No, Princess, he's a pureblood Parisian, born in Montmartre, of parents who also first saw day on that hillock."

"That surprises me, because your collaborator seemed to me gifted with a meridional imagination. He seemed to me called to play Tartarin rather than Chantecoq. Doubtless he was trying to impress you, by attaching such considerable importance to my chambermaid's approach?

"That's not at all how things happened. I'll straighten this out. I won't hide from you that I was extremely chilled by the method you used to get hold of a sample of my handwriting. I don't recognise your method there, Monsieur Chantecoq. Generally, you show more skill, more delicacy, more tact, more dexterity…

"Let's see! How is that a detective such as you didn't foresee that while I confess that I fell into the trap that you set for me, I wouldn't quickly learn that you were toying with me?

"That's what happened. Quarter of an hour after your employee's visit, I was fully apprised of the facts.

"Instead of lodging a complaint with the 'official' police, I preferred to act myself, and so I sent my chambermaid after your secretary.

"She didn't offer him, as he pretends, a hundred thousand francs in order for him to return I don't know what unsigned document written by me, to which you just alluded, but five thousand francs, no more or less, if he retrieved my letter to the Marquis de Sorrento."

And while training her sorcerous gaze on the great bloodhound, who was listening to her, silent, unmoving, his face impenetrable, the Italian continued.

"At this moment, I grasp the depths of your thoughts all too clearly. You're telling yourself: 'For Princess Rascolini to be so determined to recover this letter, this can only mean that she fears seeing it become a dangerous weapon in the hands of those with malicious intentions…'

"There's some truth in that, Monsieur Chantecoq, but it's not the whole story.

"I've no idea what shady designs you're concocting against me. I sense just one thing: it's that, to have acted in this way, it can only mean that you have some intentions towards me which aren't exactly friendly. Perhaps you're acting on behalf of Mussolini, the Prince's enemy, or on behalf of people who want to pick a fight with me? Perhaps, in all good faith, you accepted a mission that you believe to be just and which rests only on fantasy and lies?

"It remains the case that the act of hostility that you committed towards me demanded a response. It could have been more severe. I didn't want that. I detest fuss, and I loathe scandal still more. I aspire to nothing more than retirement, to the most absolute retirement, to forgetting a life which will have been for me nothing but a smile for a few days, and years of mental torture that you could not suspect.

"Believe me, Monsieur Chantecoq, when God calls the Prince back to him, the new life that awaits me is not in this world; it's in a Spanish convent, at Carmel, that I'll go to bury myself, and I have only one desire, to hear the monastery's heavy door close behind me.

"But I am still Princess Rascolini, daughter of the Duke of Grambaldi, a living hyphen between two of Italy's most illustrious families; I didn't want a private detective to hoard a letter signed by me, obtained from me through secrecy, and the use to which he wished to put it couldn't be in good faith and appeared suspicious to me.

"There you are, Monsieur Chantecoq, the whole truth. If you don't believe me, would you like me to summon my chambermaid?"

Still with the same calm, Chantecoq replied. "I believe, Princess, that there's no point dragging a servant into this business. I'll ask only your permission to correct certain little errors, quite involuntary, I'm sure, that have slipped into your account."

"Speak, monsieur, I promise to listen to you with the same attention as you granted me."

"First, Princess, you neglected to mention that your charming maid – because she is charming – had received from you the order to reclaim from my secretary not only the original of your letter, but also the carbon copy and any photos I might have taken of it."

"That's correct," Gemma acknowledged, "anyway, I believe that's natural enough."

"Perfectly," conceded the bloodhound. "I'm not insisting, as we're absolutely in agreement on this point. But there are one or two of your allegations in particular against which I will protest, when you declared that I might be an agent for Mussolini or for people who, to use your expression, would pick a fight with you. No, Princess!"

And, meeting the Princess's stare with his own deep, penetrating, sharp, searching gaze, the king of detectives intoned, "I am accomplishing, according to your own words, a mission that I believe to be just and which, contrary to your claims, rests on neither fantasy nor falsehoods, but on justice and truth."

The Florentine, this time, did not buckle under this attack. But, standing, shivering with a rage which, great actress as she was, she knew how to give the appearance of barely contained indignation, she cried out.

"So, monsieur, it's in the name of justice and truth that you have attacked me?"

"Yes, Princess," the detective confirmed, with formidable aplomb.

"Then what are you accusing me of?" asked the Italian who, through an effort of extraordinary willpower, had immediately regained all her sang-froid.

"Careful!" Chantecoq said to himself, "I think I've found a worthy adversary here."

And he replied, with the calm tone from which he had not strayed since the start of the encounter.

"Princess, I'm sorry that you're forcing me to dot the i's… but I'm not the sort of man to duck such a direct question. I'm therefore going to respond to you in a fashion as plain as that with which you have interrogated me.

"I've been charged with locating a missing person, Raymond Kérénot. A letter from yourself, unsigned, but whose handwriting I was able to identify thanks to that which, to use your words, I had successfully extorted from you, taught me that you had been that young man's very intimate friend.

"Pardon me for mentioning these details of your private life, but you demanded a complete and decisive explanation from me. I'm not the kind of man to mince my words. I give you that explanation. However, if I'm offending you, tell me. I'll be silent immediately."

"You offend me greatly indeed, Monsieur Chantecoq," declared the Belle Imperia, adopting the attitude of an outraged queen. "But I'm also not the kind of woman to mince my words. So go on, to the very end, but be assured that I'm capable of answering you."

"I already noticed that," drawled the detective, with a smile of absolute serenity.

And he continued. "As soon as I discovered the mysterious links that bound you to this boy, I thought that it was by coming to visit you that I had the most chance of being informed accurately.

"It goes without saying, Princess, that if you deign to

answer me, all this will remain between ourselves, forever. I know of nothing more respectable than a lady's intimate secrets. In other words, I'm incapable of revealing your own, so long as you don't force me to do so."

Although Gemma had detected all the threats hidden beneath these last words, she appeared untroubled by them. And it was with complete assurance, and even aggression, that she replied.

"Monsieur Chantecoq, I have nothing to fear from you, and the best proof is that I refuse to continue an interview that has already lasted all too long."

She stood, to show that she was taking her leave of the detective who, also abandoning his chair, said in the most natural tone possible, "Princess, I am far sorrier for you, than for myself. I came here with the most conciliatory intentions; I wasn't looking to declare war against you. The proof is that I've not hidden from you any of the weapons that I have at my disposal and that I immediately unveiled my infantry to you. I shan't insist further, I am retiring."

And with a rather disquieting courtesy, the great bloodhound added, "Just know, Princess, that having been charged by a mother to seek and locate her lost son, I'll neglect nothing in order to achieve this end. If there's some scandal, too bad! Thank you for listening, and farewell!"

The detective made a move to leave, but the Italian held him back. "Monsieur Chantecoq?"

"Princess?"

Haughty, insolent, the Belle Imperia continued. "It's my turn to ask you an indiscreet question."

She stared fixedly at the bloodhound as she spoke. "How much did Madame Kérénot promise you, should you find her son?"

"Madame Kérénot promised me nothing," replied Chantecoq, who didn't seem shaken by this insidious question.

He continued without hesitation. "And I asked nothing from her!"

"I was unaware, Monsieur Chantecoq, that you were working only for glory."

"In certain cases, Princess, it's more agreeable for me to oblige for free my friends and even sometimes persons who are simply pleasant to me."

"You make it back on the others."

"I practice my profession, Princess, but I do so honourably, and I trust that you won't commit the error and injustice of confusing me with the bosses or agents of certain shady outfits who make blackmail the basis of the majority of their operations."

These words, pronounced carefully, but with energy, must have warned the Florentine that she was venturing into dangerous territory because, beating an instant retreat, she replied.

"If I had, Monsieur Chantecoq, such a disagreeable opinion of you, I would certainly not have asked you, some time ago to look into that jewellery theft of which I was the victim.

"If I felt able to ask you about the sum of entirely legitimate expenses that you must be incurring as a result of the mission Madame Kérénot entrusted to you, it's because I was keen to protect your interests."

"How so?"

"I'll tell you. If, for example, it had been agreed to pay you a sum of ten thousand francs in order to recover Raymond Kérénot, I intended to offer you five times as much in order to abandon your search."

With an ironic smile, Chantecoq shook his head. "I can see, Princess, that quite contrary to what you told me this very instant, you have misjudged me very badly."

"No, no."

"Oh, yes, Princess, as you believe me capable of dishonouring myself for fifty thousand francs."

"Dishonouring yourself?"

"Could one debase oneself any further, than by betraying an unfortunate woman, a mother who weeps for her son and who would give her life to hear news of him alive?"

In a dry, hostile voice, Princess Rascolini declared, "This Raymond Kérénot was not a very interesting person."

Chantecoq riposted, reinjecting the steel into his voice. "You must have noticed that better than anyone."

The Italian gave a small shiver… but this jab, instead of intimidating her, to the contrary stimulated her nerves, stretched to their limits. And as a ferocious expression hardened her beautiful face, she said, "Better for him, and for everyone, that his name be forgotten."

"Then go and try making a mother understand that!" the detective cried.

"You are persuasive enough, Monsieur Chantecoq, to manage even that."

"I shan't even try." And, raising his voice a little, he added, "Princess, the moment has come to cease these games, and to put our cards on the table. Is Raymond Kérénot dead or alive?"

Nothing seemed to disconcert the Florentine, who replied. "Ah! Monsieur Chantecoq, do you never read the newspapers, then?"

The bloodhound riposted. "Make no mistake, Princess, I

read twelve every day and sometimes more."

"Then you read poorly."

"Why?"

"What! So you haven't seen, in one of these numerous sheets in which you delve, that a judicial enquiry was opened into the subject of Raymond Kérénot's disappearance, and that the enquiry concluded that he had been the victim of a villainous crime?"

"The word was 'suggested'…" the bloodhound corrected her.

"Let's not play games with words."

"Words, Princess, in these circumstances, have enormous importance. The proof is that I don't share the official police opinion at all. Raymond Kérénot wasn't lured into an ambush, nor was he robbed. If he has been silenced, it was not by professional thieves, but by someone with an interest in being rid of him."

"Me, I take it!" said the Belle Imperia who, despite all her cunning, was a hundred leagues from suspecting that Chantecoq was in the process of manoeuvring her with formidable skill, and that he was playing with her as a cat toys with a mouse.

Chantecoq's smile widened. Now, he was sure of it, he had his adversary. The fox had beaten the panther.

"Princess," he said, "I'm too loyal not to reveal to you that, when I discovered that the day after Raymond Kérénot had disappeared, his apartment had been searched from top to bottom and that his correspondence as well as all his papers had been pinched, and that then I had in my possession a certain letter that, by mistake, he had left at his mother's, I had the unworthy, the awful thought that you wanted to rid yourself of this person who had become too encumbering, sending him or having him sent to a world from which there is no return.

"Don't leap up, Princess, as I recognise my faults. Isn't a sin confessed, a sin already half-forgiven?

"I quickly realised that I was on the wrong track. A lady such as you being capable of such a crime? Come off it!"

And, playing his game with an artfulness by which Princess Rascolini, as strong as she was, could only be duped, the king of detectives continued.

"It's enough for me to reread this letter in order to be sure of it. Raymond Kérénot is alive, isn't he… alive and indeed well, at that?"

And watching the Princess, whose face had relaxed instantly, he stressed, "The proof: is that he's here."

"Here?"

"Yes, Princess, here, where he hides himself under an injured man's mask and under the name of Gabriele d'Orvieto."

"This time," the Florentine cried, with a flourish of undeniable sincerity, "this time, your instinct is wrong."

"Not possible!"

"My secretary really does have a mutilated face and his true name is Gabriele d'Orvieto."

"I shan't be so insolent as to contradict you."

"I appreciate that, Monsieur Chantecoq."

"However, I must tell you that I have every reason to believe that your secretary is in no way who you claim him to be."

"I'm certain of quite the contrary."

"And I, I can prove to you that Count Gabriele d'Orvieto was killed at Goritzia on August 9th, 1916."

"An error, Monsieur Chantecoq," Gemma protested,

"That wasn't Count Gabriele d'Orvieto, but his younger brother Guiseppe, who died on that date on the field of honour. Gabriele was wounded in 1918, as demonstrated by his military record, which I'm quite prepared to show you."

Chantecoq, growing serious, cut her off. "It's not his military record I need to see… it's him, right away, and without his mask."

For the first time since the start of the duel between her and the detective, Princess Rascolini understood that he had not failed, without her suspecting, to score advantage after advantage over her.

Incapable of controlling her rage, she cried out. "Count d'Orvieto swore never to reveal his face to anyone. I won't ask him to break the oath that he made himself, just because a private detective has got it in his head that he was Raymond Kérénot."

"It would be better for him if he *was* Raymond Kérénot," murmured Chantecoq slowly, with an enigmatic smile.

"What do you mean?" asked the Princess who, feeling more and more hunted, had become incapable of hiding the anxiety that now bloomed within her.

"I'm speaking for myself," the bloodhound said. "And, as sung in Carmen, or more or less at any rate, 'I believe that it's not forbidden to… speak…'"

"Monsieur Chantecoq," replied the Italian, her heart pounding, her throat dry, "just now you said to me, 'let's cease our games… let's put our cards on the table…'"

"Indeed I did."

"Very well, where is all this leading?"

"To the Roscanvel case!"

The Belle Imperia pretended to be astonished. "The Roscanvel case?"

"What's the Roscanvel case?" she asked in a strangled voice.

"Don't you read the newspapers then?" the bloodhound asked, with an ironic shrug.

Gemma bit her lip and leaned against the wall. She felt as though the floor was sliding from under her feet. Chantecoq was going to complete his rout.

"You're not going to tell me that you're unaware of the drama for which an innocent man is in prison in Marseille?

"The Roscanvel case, oh, but you know all about it, Princess… You wrote to me in order to forbid me from looking into it, first a typed letter, and then a second written in a hand that was admirably disguised, but still not enough for an expert, with however little warning, to fail to attribute to you its… maternity.

"Come on, Princess, admit it. Admit that you arranged Raymond Kérénot's disappearance and…"

"Enough!"

"… That you murdered Robert de Roscanvel."

"It's not true."

"And that this impostor Gabriele d'Orvieto is your accomplice."

"It's not true, I tell you, it's not true!"

Brusquely pulling a Browning from his pocket, the king of detectives trained it on Princess Rascolini.

"While we're waiting," he ordered, "you're going to come with me to the police station."

He didn't manage it. A dry noise, a little like the crack of a whip, rang out, and Chantecoq dropped like a stone on to the rug.

At the same moment, a curtain was lifted and Gabriele d'Orvieto hurried into the room, holding in his hand the automatic pistol with which he had fired a bullet into Chantecoq's chest.

"What have you done?" the Belle Imperia cried, dashing towards him.

"This man had us," the mutilated man spat through clenched teeth. "He was going to ruin us, I took him out. But leave me alone."

"What do you want to do now?" the Florentine asked.

"To see if he's really dead." And then the wretch added with a voice full of dreadful cruelty, "And if he is still breathing, to stick a second bullet in his head."

Gemma clung to him. "You can see he's not moving. He must have been killed at once. Better to busy ourselves straight away with making his body disappear."

"That's no problem," sneered the masked man.

"And yet…"

Monsieur d'Orvieto insisted. "Let me do this, I tell you, leave me."

And, pushing Gemma away, he approached Chantecoq's body and, leaning over him, was going to put the barrel of his pistol against the detective's temple… but a cry escaped him.

With one prodigious movement, Chantecoq was kneeling upright. Then, he disarmed Gabriele with one hand and, with the other, he tore off his mask.

It was the turn of the king of detectives to cry out in surprise. A second black mask, of the same dimensions as the first, was still covering his adversary's face.

That adversary, who had recovered himself, threw himself on the policeman to take back his pistol, but a jab to the stomach sent him reeling on to an armchair.

He stood again, looking for something to throw at

Chantecoq's head while, panicked, the Belle Imperia hurried towards the door which opened abruptly, revealing Marco the butler.

Then, while covering the trio with his Browning, the king of detectives backed towards a french window which opened on to the garden, opened it, and shouted out in a bright voice.

"I could kill all three of you, but I'd much rather take you alive."

Before his adversaries recovered from their stupor, Chantecoq had disappeared.

"That man is the devil himself!" the Florentine cried.

Monsieur d'Orvieto, trembling with rage, turned on Marco and, grabbing him by the arm, demanded, "What did you come here for?"

The butler answered. "I bring important news to monsieur and madame."

"Speak!"

"His Excellency Prince Rascolini just gave up his soul to the Lord."

"Finally!" rasped the tiger that was Monsieur d'Orvieto, while the Florentine became flushed.

And the sinister flunkey added, in a tone full of hypocritical unctuousness, "This time, I strengthened the dose a little!"

8 REVELATION UPON REVELATION

The same evening, around ten o'clock, Chantecoq found himself in his studio in the company of Jacques Bellegarde.

"My dear friend," the detective said to his son-in-law, "I'm very grateful to you for coming running quite so fast at my call. As I just recounted to you, the Roscanvel case has taken an extraordinary turn and you see that I was right when I predicted that I'd be obliged to appeal to you.

"On no account, for the moment at least, do I want to involve the regular police in this matter. I'll do that only when I have the guilty parties' confessions, and that shouldn't take long.

"I'm not hiding from myself the fact that, in order to obtain them, I'll have to fight a gruelling battle; Princess Rascolini, and especially her secretary, are adversaries of undeniable stature, decisive, and ready for any crime.

"If I hadn't had the foresight to put on this special chainmail which makes me, at least in part, immune to bullets and knife wounds, I'd be a dead man.

"This mysterious mutilated man shot me full in the chest.

I'm lucky he didn't have the idea of shooting me in the head and found that, positioned as he was, my chest presented a much more certain target than my forehead.

"In brief, I willingly acknowledge I was extremely lucky to emerge unscathed.

"Now I have the impression that even when, during the war, I was hunting spies, or when two years ago, I was launched on the trail of Belphégor, the famous Phantom of the Louvre, never have I faced such great danger.

"But this sinister couple would indeed be wrong to rejoice at the victory that they think they've won over me, it's a Pyrrhic victory which will swiftly be followed by their swift defeat, because they've succeeded only in fortifying my conviction in their guilt.

"Now that I have them, I won't release them again, until the moment when, after having put handcuffs on both of them, I'll have, not the honour, but the pleasure of putting them in the hands of justice."

And, his eyes shining, the king of detectives concluded. "All the same, I'm curious to know which bandit is hiding under that mask. There, you see, my dear Jacques, is the key to the whole business."

"You don't think it's Raymond Kérénot," observed Bellegarde.

"No, though I declared as much to the Princess, for whom I wanted to set a trap, into which she was eager to fall. As soon as the vanished man's mother brought me up to date with everything, I was immediately convinced that Kérénot had been murdered.

"A moment of reflection was sufficient to convince myself of this. The Princess who, beneath her appearance of being a noble and honest lady, shows every sign of being a reincarnation of her famous compatriot, Lucretia Borgia, whose crimes and debauchery have made her forever immortal, may have a very sharp penchant for a lad gifted with every physical advantage and all the moral flaws that please that kind of woman.

"In practice, no sooner did she realise that he was going to cost her dearly, than another man appeared, the masked man, who took care of matters thoroughly.

"Oh, that one, he's top of his class, and they both decided to rid themselves of the nuisance that was Raymond Kérénot. That's as clear as a mountain spring."

"Indeed!" Bellegarde agreed, "But what I can't grasp, is the motive for which the Princess and her enigmatic associate murdered the Count de Roscanvel."

"I don't know either," sighed the great bloodhound, "and yet, I've rarely succeeded in accumulating so much evidence against suspects. If they weren't guilty, why would the Princess have written that threatening letter to me?"

"Are you completely sure it was her?"

"Not content with my own analysis, I took the different samples of her handwriting which were in my possession to my friend Delphane, Paris's greatest expert in this field. He assured me that I was not mistaken, and that the writing in the three messages I submitted to him was that of the same woman.

And, growing animated, the king of detectives continued. "And this Marco? And that Suzanne? Yes, this butler… and this chambermaid who, after having been in the Rascolinis' service, went, as if by accident, to the Roscanvels and, still as if by accident, resumed their place with their old masters, as soon as they'd furnished the necessary information to frame an innocent man for a crime committed by another."

"This is all very troubling," said Bellegarde, "and even displays a shocking clumsiness."

"It would be, for professionals," agreed Chantecoq. "But the Princess and her accomplice aren't professionals. They obviously have crime in their skin, they sweat it from every pore. They don't hesitate to accumulate corpses around them… because I'd bet a million that they hastened the Prince's death, in order to secure their liberty more quickly.

"And then, the supreme argument, the killer argument, if they had nothing to fear from me in the first place, and nothing to fear from justice after that, why would the masked man have fired on me, just at the moment when, under the threat of my Browning, Princess Rascolini, disarmed, vanquished, ready to confess, was prepared to follow me to the police station."

"Your reasoning is absolutely logical," declared Bellegarde.

Chantecoq pressed on. "Therefore, the only unclear point where the Roscanvel case is concerned, is the crime's motive. At one point, I said to myself, 'Though his wife insists to the contrary, could Count Robert have been the Princess's lover, and did the masked man want to be rid of him, as well as Kérénot?'

"But that doesn't stand up. It's much too complicated, or much too simple. And then, my instinct tells me: there's something else. But what… what? Never yet have I bashed my head against the wall of such an enigma. It's enough to make you sell your soul to the devil."

Calming suddenly, Chantecoq continued. "It's no use getting angry, that would not help things, quite the reverse. Especially since everything's going well."

"Indeed, the Princess and the other one can't presently

leave Paris, without arousing suspicions beside your own. Before taking flight, which must hugely figure in their plans, they'll be forced to wait until after the Prince's funeral, at least," Bellegarde observed, judiciously.

"Oh! Oh!" the king of detectives declared, "with birds of this kind, we must be ready for anything. They could well, to the contrary, spread their wings before that unfortunate Rascolini is laid to rest in his ancestors' tomb. As such, I took precautions and charged Météor and Gautrais to mount round the clock surveillance over them.

"That's also why, my dear Jacques, I asked you to come and give me a hand."

"Gladly."

"On this kind of expedition, I never use my ordinary agents, I appeal only to the intimate circle, that's to say to those of whom I'm certain, as certain as I am of myself."

"You can count on me completely."

"To whom are you speaking? Haven't I already seen you at work?"

"Oh! Yes, Belphégor! What memories…"

The bloodhound smiled. "Not to mention, that as in the case of the Phantom of the Louvre, I'm going to furnish you with the opportunity for a sensational report for your paper."

"I will be eternally obliged to you."

"Let's say rather that you are my collaborator, my friend, my son."

"Always! But boss – may I call you boss?"

"It's fine with me."

"Then, boss, give me your instructions. I won't hide the fact that I await them with impatience."

"They consist of going to relieve the brave Gautrais and the excellent Météor who, since this afternoon, have been keeping a discreet watch around the mansion on Chaussée de la Muette.

"Both are camouflaged as policemen. We're going to do the same and put on in our turn the uniform of keepers of the peace.

"It's not perhaps completely proper, but as we are currently carrying out the police's auxiliary duties, they wouldn't judge us if, in order to give them a serious helping hand and in order to repair the error committed by one of their representatives, we borrow some of their accessories from them, all in good faith."

Both of them went into the laboratory. Half an hour later, they emerged from it completely transformed, in every important respect.

The keenest eye would have been incapable of discerning in one of them the greatest bloodhound of his generation, and in the other the foremost reporter of his age.

On Avenue des Ternes, they hailed a taxi.

They got out at the junction with Chaussée de la Muette, and went to meet, on foot, Gautrais and Météor, who - no less 'natural' than themselves, were keeping an imperturbable watch, patrolling the hundred yards in front of the Rascolinis' home, on the opposite pavement, in such a way that they appeared to be watching, not the Princess's mansion, but another private property, inhabited by a considerable politician, who was currently the target of violent attacks from the Communists.

Chantecoq and Bellegarde on one side, Météor and Gautrais on the other, exchanged a cordial and professional military salute. Then, as though they were passing the time of day, they exchanged a few words in a low voice.

"Anything new?" Chantecoq asked.

"No, boss," Météor replied.

"The birds are still there?"

"I'll answer that!" Gautrais said. "From here they can be seen very clearly, on the first floor, where there's a light in the window."

The bloodhound raised his eyes in that direction.

Behind some net curtains, he could indeed see the silhouettes of the Belle Imperia and her secretary.

"Perfect!" he said, approvingly.

Then, he asked: "You've noticed nothing out of the ordinary?"

"Lots of comings and goings," Météor answered, "Undertakers, caterers, some very chic people who came to leave their card or to sign a register… but nothing in particular."

"Thank you, my friends. Go and rest, both of you. It's midnight. Come back around six in the morning."

"Goodnight, boss. Goodnight, Monsieur Jacques."

"Goodnight, gentlemen."

"I suspect this will be rather calm," the journalist said.

"Haha! You never know!" the detective insisted.

Gautrais and Météor were moving to leave, but Chantecoq called them back.

"You're quite sure," he said, "that the Rascolinis' mansion has no exit other than on Chaussée de la Muette?"

"Yes, boss!" Météor affirmed. "We, that is, Monsieur Gautrais and I, have made all the necessary checks."

"Thanks and see you tomorrow, at six o'clock."

"Earlier if you want, boss."

"No, it's fine."

Chantecoq's two collaborators left.

The king of detectives took another look at the lit

windows. The silhouettes of the Princess and the masked man had disappeared.

"They too have gone to bed," Bellegarde observed.

"I doubt it!" Chantecoq continued. "I even have a feeling that the night will not pass without incident."

And, spying an automobile with a race car chassis which was parked three doors down from there, he murmured:

"There's a carriage which tells me nothing useful. I'm going to cast an eye over it. Stay there, and intervene only if I call you."

With a slightly nonchalant gait, his arms hidden under his cape, Chantecoq approached the car.

It was a car with a powerful motor and bearing the insignia of a firm which had recently triumphed in an international race.

The detective noted that the four tyres, as well as the so-called 'emergency' tyre, were brand new.

As he couldn't see, from the exterior at least, any sign of luggage, he tried to lean inside, in order to better inspect it and, in particular, to discover the owner's name.

But, jumping on the seat, a German Shepherd dog, which was lurking at the bottom of the car, began to growl in a tone so clearly threatening, that Chantecoq considered it unwise to prolong his investigation.

And returning to Bellegarde, he told him. "I was not mistaken. There's a car that we would do well to watch attentively, because I wouldn't be surprised if it wasn't intended to spirit away the Princess and her secretary tonight."

And with a mysterious tone to his voice, he added, "But, this time, they won't escape me, because they're going to hit a bit of a stumbling block; to be precise, I speak of a block that they're hardly expecting."

Chantecoq was not mistaken. A drama was on the point of taking place, but a drama that he hadn't foreseen, and which singularly resembled a tile that their adversaries would have thrown over their heads at the moment when they were not expecting it.

Indeed, it had only been five minutes since Chantecoq had rejoined Bellegarde than they saw advancing towards them a man of about thirty years of age who was closely following two uniformed officers.

"Hmm," groaned Chantecoq, "this doesn't smell good."

The man, a strapping tall bloke, with the decided air of someone with whom one does not mess, headed directly towards the private detective and his son-in-law and, without the slightest sign of politeness, he ordered them in a tone which brooked no reply.

"Follow me, both of you. It's pointless to try and run or to resist us. I'm Monsieur Méjasson, the secretary of the district's police commissioner. I've got you, I won't let you go."

Chantecoq had no thought of running, but even if he had that intention, it would have been essentially impossible to realise it.

Two officers on bicycles, who had just dismounted, were arriving as reinforcements. And, while cursing internally, he fell in behind the secretary, imitated by Bellegarde who, in the presence of this unexpected avatar, had resolved to base his attitude entirely on that of his father-in-law.

During the journey, not a single word was exchanged.

Chantecoq thought.

"We have been reported and denounced… By whom? Egad! By those whom I'm pursuing, and who will have noticed our presence. It's therefore tonight that they intend to leave, in that car which must do one hundred and twenty kilometres an hour… and perhaps even more than that.

"It's lucky that I took down its number: 57-48-19. There's still that… though I know that they're capable of changing it on the road.

"All the same it's enraging to admit to myself that this miscreant and this knave are going to burn our politeness at the exact moment when I was about to play such a jolly trick on them of my own, as well as on their guard dog, which had every appearance to me of defending its owners' interests with a zeal as blind as it was formidable.

"Ah! Bandits, I didn't believe that they would give me so much trouble. It's a bit much, all the same."

In his fear that the Princess and the masked man were going to escape him, he was on the point of telling the secretary everything.

But he reflected.

"That won't change things at all. By the act of putting on these officers' uniforms, Bellegarde and I, we've committed an offence which justifies our arrest, and even if I revealed to this worthy representative of the law that I am Chantecoq the detective and that my companion is none other than Jacques Bellegarde, the well-known reporter for the *Petit Parisien*, this civil servant who doesn't give me the impression of being the sort to dally with his duty, and of being highly conscious of his responsibilities, would certainly not take it upon himself to make the decision to immediately restore our liberty, even provisionally. He would want to refer it to his superior in the hierarchy who, himself… etc, etc. This trip to the station is therefore absolutely inevitable.

"But it's still vexing to think that this Italian and her

masked man will profit from it by having it away on their toes, to use the English expression."

On arriving at the station, the secretary led the two delinquents to his office, as well as the two gendarmes who were accompanying him.

The two gendarmes on bicycles, who had contented themselves with forming an escort, remained at the station which was situated on the ground floor.

The secretary, sitting at his desk, cleared his throat and began.

"Your names, your addresses, your papers?"

"Before all that, secretary," Chantecoq replied with a tone of false humility, "we would be very grateful if you could let us know of what crime my colleague and I are accused."

"You know perfectly well," sighed Monsieur Méjasson with a shrug of his shoulders.

"I trust, monsieur, that you don't take us to be criminals."

"That's my business."

"In that case, you would be mistaken," the king of detectives said calmly, "because if, as you seem to believe, we were bandits, instead of following you peacefully, docilely, as we did, we would have sought by any means to evade your pursuit, and who knows if we might not have managed to do so?"

"In the meantime," Monsieur Méjasson ordered, "give me the two revolvers which are in those holsters."

"These holsters are empty," declared Chantecoq.

He opened his. Bellegarde imitated him. The bloodhound had been telling the truth.

Chantecoq, who appeared to have taken his part in the misadventure, continued, smiling.

"Which isn't to say that we're not unarmed, even armed

to the teeth."

Hardly had he spoken these words, than the two gendarmes, in one bound, rushed, one towards Chantecoq, and the other towards Bellegarde.

But, with a cordial gesture, the king of detectives reassured them.

"Don't trouble yourself with searching us," he said, "we have no intention of availing ourselves of the various offensive and defensive toys that we're carrying on our persons."

"In the meantime, if you'd be so kind as to take off your cloaks, both of you." Monsieur Méjasson, convinced that the fake gendarme was making fun of him, commanded in a gruff voice.

"Gladly," agreed Chantecoq. "I was even going to ask you permission to do so, monsieur, because it's very warm in your office."

Simultaneously, the great bloodhound and the journalist removed their cloaks.

Noticing a rectangular box of the size and shape of a jam jar, which Chantecoq was holding under his arm, Méjasson cried out.

"What's that?"

The officer standing nearest the great detective didn't wait for an answer, and brusquely he tried to tear the object from him, which seemed at least as suspicious to him as it did to his superior.

Chantecoq grabbed him by the wrist and, without the slightest brutality, but with a strength that defied any resistance, immobilised him immediately.

"Don't touch that, my friend, because there's a devil inside that would jump at your face," he said, in tones that were benevolent but which were however nuanced with a dash of irony.

"Enough of that!" cut in the secretary, striking his desk with his fist. "There's no point in playing this drama out any longer. This box contains a time bomb, and you are two communists, who were attempting to blow up Senator Micoulot's house.

Convinced that thanks to this virulent outburst, he had succeeded in intimidating two presumed conspirators, he continued.

"Now, are you ready to give your confessions?"

"Yes, monsieur," declared Chantecoq, "but on one condition."

"What! You're asking for conditions?"

"Yes, monsieur."

"You have some nerve!"

"Allow me…"

"I allow nothing!"

"One word," Chantecoq insisted, in a tone of deferential conciliation, "I simply wanted to tell you that we are ready, my friend and I, to tell you the whole truth. But beforehand, and simply out of curiosity, we would be keen to know how you learned that we were to be found on Chaussée de la Muette, near the residence of this worthy representative of the people that you are protecting so effectively."

"I have nothing to say to you," Méjasson snapped with ill humour.

"Then, monsieur, I regret to declare that our lips will remain sealed and that we will consent to break our silence only in the presence of monsieur the police prefect, in person."

Méjasson scratched his ear.

He was, indeed, very embarrassed! Certainly the arrest of two pseudo-communists was a success to his credit, but if he didn't succeed in making them talk, this success would become significantly compromised. Their confessions were vital, at all costs.

Judging that his strong manner would be useless and perhaps even dangerous, he said to himself, "Let's try persuasion instead. It's still the best way to lead them by the nose."

And, while keeping a gruff and threatening tone to his voice, he replied.

"What astonishes me is that after you were led here, with such docility, that you should adopt such a different attitude, now that you're here in my office.

"After all, as you insist on it, I don't see why I shouldn't satisfy your curiosity. It was by a telephone call - anonymous, naturally - that I was warned that two individuals, disguised as gendarmes, despite wearing the precinct number, were entirely unknown to them.

"It was then that I decided to visit the scene myself. Are you happy?"

"Delighted, monsieur, delighted!" the king of detectives cried, while Bellegarde inclined his head in a signal of appreciation.

"Then," Méjasson continued, "I suppose that you'll no longer refuse to answer my questions."

"We have only one thing to say, monsieur. We are very honest men."

"Your name?"

"Chantecoq."

"Eh?"

"Yes. Chantecoq."

"The king of detectives?"

"In the flesh, as they say in the movies."

"What is this nonsense?" Méjasson thundered.

"I'm speaking very seriously," declared the bloodhound, "and here's the proof."

Tearing off the moustache that he had glued under his nose, then, taking off his kepi, he looked at the secretary, who was contemplating him with fright.

"Do you doubt it now?"

And, pointing to his son-in-law, who was engaged in the same operation, he continued. "And here is Monsieur Jacques Bellegarde, reporter for the *Petit Parisien*.

Méjasson and his two agents were literally petrified.

Chantecoq's physiognomy indeed, was much too well known by all, for them not to be completely certain that they found themselves in the presence of he who was hailed as the world champion of detectives.

It was definitely him, with his regular features, his gaze that was at once deep and penetrating, his smile that was loyal, affable, but just a little ironic.

Disconcerted, Méjasson stammered. "Ah! I see! I would never have expected…"

Chantecoq's prestige was such, as much in police circles as among the general public, that the secretary no longer knew what to say or even what to think.

Then, he ended up stammering again.

"Monsieur Chantecoq, why didn't you make yourself known as soon as I arrested you?"

"First, because you wouldn't have believed me, and however much it cost me to abandon a surveillance operation which held great interest for me, I preferred that this explanation, which had become inevitable, should take place not outdoors, but in your office.

The secretary, visibly perplexed, was silent.

Guessing what he was thinking, Chantecoq continued.

"Now, it remains for me to offer all my apologies for having put you - oh, much against my will - in a rather delicate position. You are, at the moment, torn between the desire to be helpful by releasing me, as well as Monsieur Bellegarde, and the very legitimate fear, of your responsibilities.

Méjasson admitted: "The fact is that I am very embarrassed. I was just nominated, a few days ago, to this station. My commissioner, Monsieur Pétirat - perhaps you know him, Monsieur Chantecoq?"

"I know him very well! I know that he's not always the easiest fellow…"

"That's what I was going to say, Monsieur Chantecoq… I will even add that he has me in his sights a bit."

"Hold on, why? You seem like a brave lad."

"I am indeed, Monsieur Chantecoq; only, I'm from the Auvergne."

"So what?"

"For Monsieur Pétirat, that's a crippling vice, an indelible blemish."

"I don't understand."

"Monsieur Pétirat is a Parisian, and only likes other Parisians. Beyond them, nothing exists for him. And he has such contempt for provincials that, in order to avoid seeing them, he is never absent, and spends all his holidays and days off with his brother, who is a wine merchant in Bercy.

"It's like his officers. Here are two of them, who are excellent colleagues, very energetic and full of bravado for every challenge that comes there way. Nevertheless,

Monsieur Pétirat can't stand them, because one, Rinardi, is Corsican, and the other, Madurec, is a Breton."

"Oh, hell!" Chantecoq joked. "This is going to go very badly for us, as I'm originally from Loiret, and my son-in-law was born in Le Havre. Never mind! As I hope, my dear Monsieur Méjasson, to cause you the least possible inconvenience and, on the other hand, I would of course like to regain my liberty as soon as possible, I would be greatly obliged if you were to try and ask for instructions from your boss."

"The trouble is that this evening he's attending the banquet for the Paris for Parisians Society, of which he's the vice-president."

"It's nearly midnight; the banquet must have finished."

"Yes, but after the banquet, there's a concert in which Monsieur Pétirat is taking part."

"He's a musician then?"

"A humorous singer."

"I had no idea."

"But I hope that he won't linger, because, before going home, he always pops in for a quick tour of the station."

A footstep echoed on the staircase that led to the first floor.

Méjasson was not mistaken. It was indeed Monsieur Pétirat who, dressed in black tie, white waistcoat, and wearing a flat cap, swept into his secretary's office like a gust of wind.

"Aha!" he cried. "What's this meeting all about? Can it be, Monsieur Méjasson, that you're organising a Soviet cell here?"

"So you don't recognise me, then?" Chantecoq cried, standing before the commissioner.

"But… wait."

Monsieur Pétirat stared at him, widening his already round eyes. Then, he spoke in a hesitant voice.

"It could almost be…"

"Chantecoq," cried the detective.

With mixed feelings, the commissioner took a good look at him. "I was unaware that you'd resumed service in the district."

"Well, my strapping lad," the great bloodhound said to himself, "if you're trying to be smart, you're going to find someone who's more than a match for you here."

"Oh! For one night only," he said out loud, "as well as my son-in-law to whom I must introduce you."

Monsieur Pétirat barely registered the deferential greeting that Bellegarde addressed to him, and scowling, with a clearly hostile attitude, he replied.

"What is the meaning of this joke?"

Chantecoq answered him. "My dear commissioner, you have perhaps learned that, quite contrary to the principles that govern the modern police, I have always kept the habit, when I had an important lead to follow and especially when hunting easily-startled game, of using the old system dear to Vidocq, our model in everything: that is to say, disguise.

"Well, this evening, before completing a very delicate mission, a very tricky one for which I had asked Monsieur Bellegarde to come to my aid, I decided that we should dress ourselves as police, only because, in the present case, it was in my opinion the most effective and surest of disguises that we had at our disposal.

"I was mistaken, I acknowledge, as we were very quickly detected and your secretary, alerted by a phone call, came to arrest us with a dexterity that I'm duty-bound to praise to you."

His brows furrowed, with a self-important attitude, Monsieur Pétirat, who had deposited his headgear on his secretary's desk, replied while smoothing his abundant curly hair.

"Monsieur Chantecoq, I don't need to observe to you that you've got yourself into a very bad business."

The bloodhound riposted. "In law, maybe, but in fact, I think not."

The commissioner, 'who was not a good boy', intoned with importance, "However sincere my admiration for your talent, Monsieur Chantecoq, I'm obliged to charge you, as well as Monsieur Bellegarde, with wearing a uniform illegally, and with impersonating an officer."

"And no doubt also to keep us under arrest," the detective insinuated.

"I ought to," declared Monsieur Pétirat, "but in light of your good character and that of Monsieur your son-in-law, I consent to sparing you this measure."

"You are truly too adorable!" Chantecoq cried, in a rather mocking tone.

"But on one condition," insisted the magistrate, "and that's that you immediately remove these uniforms."

"My dear commissioner," protested the bloodhound, "you're not going to force us to walk home in our pants?"

Monsieur Pétirat who was not sorry to bully Chantecoq, because he nourished a particular animosity against all those who worked 'on the margins of the police force', replied.

"You have only to telephone home and they will bring you a change of clothes."

"That's going to take some time, my dear commissioner," the great bloodhound objected, "and I assure you that I don't have any to spare, I've wasted quite enough already, and I truly fear that the two big league rogues that I was pursuing will have profited from it in order to take off."

"Two big league rogues," repeated Monsieur Pétirat with ill humour, "but that's my business… rather than yours, Monsieur Chantecoq."

"That's very possible, monsieur, and even certain, given that it was my intention, as soon as I had them in my power, to bring both of them to you.

"But now, that's going to become very difficult, especially if, as I foresee, they've taken flight."

"They're thieves?" the commissioner asked.

"No, murderers."

"Brr!" Monsieur Pétirat tried to joke, "you're giving me goosebumps."

"Commissioner, you would be wrong to take this story lightly."

"Why was I not made aware of this officially?"

"Ask monsieur the director of the judicial police."

"What will he tell me?"

"He'll tell you that, in line with Inspector Menardier's report, which followed another lead, it was impossible for him to suspect the true culprits of one and even several crimes which, I have the right to affirm to you, without my intervention, strongly risked never being uncovered.

"And you, you know who they are?"

"I know who they are."

"You're sure of that?"

"Absolutely sure."

"You have proof?"

"I have it."

"Their names?"

"Oh! Monsieur, wait until I've caught them."

"I have the right to demand…"

"No, commissioner."

"Sorry?"

"Please listen to me."

But Monsieur Pétirat, deeply irritated, cried out. "I understand your tactic. You want to reserve for yourself, alone, the glory of a sensational arrest."

Subtly, the king of detectives observed, "When one's pulled the chestnuts from the fire, it's only natural for one to eat them."

"You refuse to talk?"

"No, but before naming my birds to you, I would like to be sure that they have not flown."

"And if they have flown?"

"I don't want to be deprived of the pleasure of recapturing them."

"A financial interest?"

"My word, no."

"A matter of pride, then?"

"Something like that."

"Then, Monsieur Chantecoq, through pride, you're refusing to be an auxiliary for the police."

"Not at all!" the bloodhound protested. "Since I began working for myself, I haven't ceased being its collaborator for one single instant, its constant associate and if one has sometimes put sticks in the spokes of the other, it wasn't me, I assure you, and all the same you can't blame me for succeeding where Menardier failed."

"I blame you for involving yourself in affairs that are none of your business," said the commissioner, growing ever angrier.

Chantecoq, whose calm contrasted with that man's agitation, declared: "We're not going to reopen that old quarrel between the state police and private investigators. No one is more respectful than I of this great institution, of which I was a member for a long time, and which has the mission of safeguarding society itself.

"I know all the immense services that it has rendered for our country, that it renders still, and that it will render even better in the future, under the active and intelligent leadership of those who govern it.

"I pay homage to these acts of selfless heroism, of devotion, too often obscure, of skill, initiative, tenacity and intelligence which honour daily, from the greatest to the smallest, those who serve in its ranks.

"And you're going to see, commissioner, if I'm making you feel good, that I have an unspeakable contempt for all those shady operators of whom there are far too many among us and who, under misleading phrases: family security, confidential information, etc, etc, are sometimes nothing more than con artists, and sometimes worse. So comprised, the private police would be an odious thing, a public danger. May it be wiped out! I would be the first to cry 'bravo!' and I'd even ask myself why, in high places, it's taken so long to take a safety measure that seems to be just as important as sweeping our streets and collecting rubbish.

"But let all that wrath be reserved for those who, as well as your servant, have only one goal, to complement the work of the 'officials', to associate as required by them in the tasks for which they often lack the necessary time and resources; I consider that a lamentable error, a supreme injustice.

"Is it that the question of pride ought to exist, when the defence of society is at stake? Is it that we ought not, to the contrary, official police and private detectives alike, maintain between each other an undercurrent of sympathy, of professional courtesy, which could only forge between us a true bond, an official basis for collaboration, and produce excellent results. Oughtn't we to complement each other's work?

"Your task, to you, so crushing, so formidable, would be considerably lightened and we'd no longer have to fear, as alas! I have seen so many times, that the intrusion by certain of yours, erring through lack of clear sight, excess of zeal, and let's say it too, sometimes by professional jealousy, demolishes all our work at the decisive moment.

"Now, who is it that profits from these rivalries? From this dissension? It's the criminals.

"That's why, as much as I'm the declared enemy of those vile collusions which rest only on a meagre and contemptible interest, so much do I champion a loyal collaboration, every time that necessity demands.

"But I'm rambling and time is marching on. I notice, commissioner, that I am going to make you go to bed very late, and, as you've decided, allow me to telephone my valet to bring me the civilian clothes of which we have need, my son-in-law and I, in order to return home decently."

"Do it, Monsieur Chantecoq," authorised Monsieur Pétirat, who seemed to have been greatly impressed by this eloquent speech from the king of detectives.

And gripped by remorse, he immediately declared, "After all, it's too bad! Go home just as you are. It's still the best solution. Madurac, go quickly and find a taxi."

While the agent was hurrying outside, Chantecoq said to the Commissioner: "My dear commissioner, I thank you endlessly for your courtesy. And I will add only one word.

"If I've succeeded in winning you over to my way of thinking, it will greatly ease my regret at having lost my two birds this evening."

"So much so," repeated Monsieur Pétirat warmly, "that I'm convinced that, if you wanted to take the trouble, they won't get far. But, all the same, I wouldn't mind knowing their names."

"Your word of honour that what I shall confide in you will stay between us?"

"You have it."

Chantecoq leaned close to the Commissioner's ear and murmured a few words.

Monsieur Pétirat started, then he proffered, "What, you believe that this woman…"

"I'm sure of it!"

"Ah! Well!"

"As to the man, it's another case, but for an amateur bandit, he certainly has as much audacity as a professional."

"Monsieur Chantecoq," the magistrate affirmed, literally flabbergasted, "if it wasn't you, I'd say that you've embarked on a very perilous adventure. That said, you know what you're doing, and you know what you want."

"I believe, indeed," said Chantecoq with a smile, "that I'm old enough to go out without my maid."

Madurec returned, announcing, "The taxi is outside, commissioner."

"Then," declared Chantecoq, "I bid you *au revoir*."

"You don't begrudge me?" Monsieur Pétirat asked.

"You have done your duty," replied the bloodhound, "now it's my turn to do mine."

The commissioner shook his hand as well as Bellegarde's and led them both to his office's door.

Then, returning towards Méjasson, he cried. "You, as gaffes go, you can be proud of making a lovely one tonight!"

"How so, commissioner?" the poor devil exclaimed, who had been anticipating something close to congratulations.

"To cuff a man such as Chantecoq…"

"But…"

"Shut up! I don't need your explanations which couldn't fail to be as preposterous as you yourself. If this story gets out, it's not on you, but on me, that all the ridicule will fall. Ah! You're doing good work, Monsieur Méjasson, it's obvious you're from the Auvergne!"

And, while opening the door that led to his office, he hammered home his final point. "It's clear to me, you'll never be Parisian!"

***

Climbing into the taxi which was parked in front of the station's door, Chantecoq had given out loud his address to the driver, who, persuaded that he was 'carting around' two authentic officers, had immediately set off.

But, hardly had the car covered a hundred metres, than the king of detectives, leaning close to the window, said to the driver.

"Take us down Chaussée de la Muette, and stop when I knock on the floor."

The chauffeur nodded, and Chantecoq leaned back on the cushions.

His adventure didn't seem to have drained him, instead a good-humoured mischievous smile played over his lips, and, to Bellegarde's great astonishment, even though he knew his father-in-law's character all too well, he soon began to whistle the tune to *Marlborough's Left For The War*, which revealed an extreme satisfaction on his part.

The *Petit Parisien* reporter said to himself, "Clearly, this man is prodigious. Anyone other than he would have been furious at having been interrupted in action, just as his goal was within reach. I wonder what he could be thinking at this moment. I'd wager any amount with anyone that he's already taken some advantage from this incident, even if it was seemingly designed to exasperate him, and I wouldn't be overly astonished if this night, already so eventful, doesn't still provide some new and even more captivating adventures for us."

Desirous as Bellegarde was to find out what might happen next, on no account would he have allowed himself to interrogate Chantecoq, because he had already been his collaborator too often not to have noticed that when the great bloodhound was on the trail, it was useless to question him as he would never bother to respond.

Not that he meant the slightest ill will by it or that it was a question of pride. No, absorbed in his reflections, he simply didn't listen to you.

He lived exclusively in his own thoughts, or rather his thoughts concentrated on a single point, leading towards a goal, from which nothing could deter him, prevent him from distinguishing and from observing any external demonstration, which was not linked directly to it.

This faculty which was so powerful and yet possessed by so few human brains, was demonstrated for many by that extraordinary self-control whereby, by conserving his strength, he permitted that other individual gift which nature had granted him, that is to say an extraordinary instinct, to exercise without distraction and in the absolute plenitude of his reasoning and his willpower.

That's why Bellegarde respected his silences so scrupulously.

Chantecoq knocked on one of the windows at the front of the car. The driver slowed down and stopped on Chaussée de la Muette, near the place where the detective and his son-in-law, an hour before, had been intercepted by Méjasson.

"There's no point getting out," said the bloodhound. He looked outside. "The car's no longer there. I was expecting that. Perfect!"

Then, turning towards his son-in-law, he added, "Tell me, Jacques, placed as you are, you must be able to see the Rascolini mansion much better than I."

"Indeed."

"The window where we saw the Princess and the masked man profiled earlier, is it still lit?"

"Yes, still."

"Aha!"

"I can also see the same shadows."

"Those of our birds?"

"Indeed."

"Oh! You're sure of that?"

"Absolutely."

"That's getting serious. Wait a moment, we're going to swap places. The best thing would be for me to get out first, and then you. Let's go."

They carried out the manoeuvre. As soon as he found himself sitting in his son-in-law's seat, Chantecoq took a small pair of binoculars from one of his pockets, and pointed it through the gates in the direction of the lit window.

After a few seconds of observation, he replaced the binoculars in his pocket calmly, while murmuring to himself.

"Egad, I was not mistaken. Our couple of bandits have well and truly fled while we were at the precinct."

"Then, who are those people who are replacing them, in such an exact fashion, that I could have sworn it was them?"

"Haven't you guessed?" asked the king of detectives.

"Hold on then! Marco… the butler."

"And the chambermaid, Suzanne."

"I'd never have spotted them," the journalist declared spontaneously.

"The fact is," pressed Chantecoq, "that they have disguised themselves well. Only there it is, they must have had to do it quickly, and they made a mistake which has betrayed them."

"May I ask you what mistake?"

"The real masked man had his cheek and right eye uncovered, this one, it's the opposite. Which proves that after spotting us and succeeding in getting rid of us by phoning the station, the Belle Imperia and her mysterious accomplice, convinced with good reason that as soon as we were free, we would return to lurk under their windows, tried to pull a switch on us and lead us to believe that they were still there, when, at this very moment, they are fleeing at top speed on Route X… Y… or Z…

"We can do nothing more than return home quietly. Tomorrow morning, it will be daylight and everything will unfold as though on wheels."

And in a joyful voice, he called to the chauffeur. "Now, Avenue de Verzy."

And while the taxi was setting off he started, no longer whistling, but singing the tune of *Marlborough*, which revealed he was in the highest spirits.

Bellegarde said to himself, "He's amazed me so many

times… but never so much as tonight. All in all, he's just chalked up a failure, and yet never have I seen him so joyful, so triumphant, so full of confidence in everything as well as in himself."

Suddenly, he felt his arm being shaken.

"Well, my dear Jacques," cried Chantecoq, "you're saying nothing. You wouldn't have the hump, by any chance?"

"Not at all, my dear father-in-law," riposted the reporter. "I thought that you were 'working' and I wouldn't have wanted to interrupt you."

"I detect your customary discretion there, my good friend, and believe me when I say I appreciate it. But I feel that's enough for today and that our beds are calling us."

And with a glint of mischief in his eyes, he added, "I believe we've earned it, and that we'll be able to rest on our laurels in peace."

"On our laurels?" Bellegarde couldn't help murmuring.

"Exactly!" Chantecoq said. "My optimism is disconcerting you, isn't it?"

"Well, I mean…"

"Come on, admit it, I won't hold it against you."

Colette's husband cried out. "I'd answer yes, if, with a man such as you, you shouldn't expect everything and beyond."

"All in good time! You just, my dear Jacques, posed the question on its true terrain. And now, you want me to give you in five seconds a critique of our operations, or rather that I repeat to you those that you have already been delivering yourself?"

"My dear father-in-law, believe me when I say that…"

"Aha! You imagine that I'm going to formalise myself because you're telling yourself that I committed an imprudence by transforming us into police officers, an imprudence which got us arrested and also allowed our 'clients' to burn our disguises.

"Well, not at all! I'll respond only that we were not embarrassed with choice and that it was still more aleatory to disguise ourselves as barrel organ players, beggars, camels, etc, etc.

"It wasn't the first time that I'd put on a copper's uniform and never before had it presented the slightest problem. This evening, that was the hitch, wasn't it? Well, not at all!

"Did you imagine that I hadn't foreseen this eventuality? As well as its consequences. Result: the adversary is beaten, as they're fleeing. Pursue them? In this taxi? A match between a snail and a swallow!

"But that they're leaving, to the contrary, that's superb! Magnificent! Haven't they left behind two quality hostages? Marco and the chambermaid who, even if only to explain the disappearance of their mistress and her lover, are going to have to remain there, at least until after the Prince's funeral rites. Oh! Then, those two, I'll see to it that they'll be cooked in five seconds, and I'll obtain from them the address of their dear employer whom we'll pick up quietly and whom we'll gather no less discreetly not in Paris, but in Marseille, as well as her masked man.

"You can already imagine Judge Ribécourt's face. Ah! My friend, what a fine supper we'll enjoy that day, accompanied by a good bottle of that exquisite wine from Cavalaire that warms your heart and delights your brain."

"You're simply marvellous!" Bellegarde said, admiringly.

"Oh no!" Chantecoq affirmed with all modesty. "I know my job and I love it. There's my secret.

"And then, you see, you must always work from the

principle that obstacles and difficulties are the best guarantees of victory.

"Indeed, they force us to reflect, to take heart from everything, including some errors from which no one is exempt, to profit from the slightest circumstances and, above all, to never be discouraged, nor to let oneself be surprised."

The taxi stopped. They'd arrived on Avenue de Verzy.

Chantecoq paid the driver and entered the house with Bellegarde. Everything was calm and silent. They reached the laboratory, in order to get rid of their police costumes.

Bellegarde made for the bedroom that he stayed in, each time that, alone or with his wife, he spent the night at his father-in-law's house, when the silence was broken by the telephone ringing.

Both of them hurried to the room, Chantecoq grabbed the receiver and listened.

Immediately, he held out the second receiver to his son-in-law. "It's Colette calling."

The young woman's voice echoed through the machine. "Come quickly both of you. Something has just happened here that I can't explain by telephone, but it's serious enough to require your immediate presence. Don't worry about me, or for her. Everything's fine, but what news!"

"We'll be there in half an hour," replied Chantecoq.

"I'll go and get my car, which I left in the garage," decided Bellegarde.

"Splendid! In the meantime, I'll compose a note for Météor and Gautrais. The setting has changed, and there's no point in them going to Chaussée de la Muette at six o' clock tomorrow morning, since we won't be there."

"I'll wait for you on Avenue des Ternes," said Bellegarde.
"Very well."

"I'll be there in ten minutes."

"Me too."

The reporter left. Sitting at his desk and taking up his pen, Chantecoq murmured. "For Colette to telephone me like this, there must have been some serious mayhem over there. There's no point in racking my brain about it, as I'll be there soon.

"But I wouldn't be overly surprised if Rascolini and her mysterious lover have left their calling card there."

9 WHERE CHANTECOQ REALISES THE ENIGMA HE HAS TO UNTANGLE IS MORE COMPLEX AND TRAGIC THAN HE EVER IMAGINED

Since their marriage, two years previously, Monsieur and Madame Bellegarde had lived in a very pretty house, situated between Saint-Germain and Carrière, on the hill which overlooks the Seine, almost on the edge of the forest.

It was in this delicious and discreet shelter that Chantecoq had chosen to hide away Madame de Roscanvel, where the best welcome had been reserved for her by the young homemaker who, straight away, was struck with sympathy for the charming young lady, whose painful misfortune the detective had narrated to her.

It had been agreed that, as far as the servants were concerned, Madame de Roscanvel would pass as a friend of Madame Bellegarde, who had come to spend a few days with her following her husband's death.

Chantecoq had strongly recommended that the Countess

should not go out, or show herself to anyone, and to avoid the slightest encounter which might provoke a denunciation and so attract the police's attention in her direction.

The young lady had formally engaged herself to obey the detective's proscriptions, and he was so much more reassured, because he knew he could entirely count on his daughter who, before her marriage, had been his secretary and collaborator for three years and was, as a result, well versed in his methods and his principles.

That's why, while making his way at top speed on the road from Paris, in the six cylinder car that Bellegarde was driving, with thoroughly professional skill, the great bloodhound was saying to himself, "There's no error, there's been a Waterloo moment over there, and Colette must have the full account, but as she tells me all is well, there's no need to worry."

As always, Chantecoq was not mistaken.

On arrival at the Bel Air house, he was going to see his predictions confirmed beyond even the slightly vague limits that he had been thinking of.

Colette, who had been watching out impatiently for her father and her husband, was running towards them as soon as she heard the car come to a halt before the wooden gate, covered with a little thatch roof, that gave access to the property.

Chantecoq and Bellegarde quickly jumped from the car, each kissing Colette, who seemed visibly emotional.

While Bellegarde was opening the gate, returning towards his six cylinder car and prepared to drive it into a garage situated at the bottom of the garden, behind the house, the king of detectives asked his daughter, "What's happened, then?"

"Madame de Roscanvel will tell you herself," replied Madame Bellegarde in a low voice, looking around her instinctively, as if she feared being spotted by an invisible watcher.

"And the servants?" the detective asked.

"They're not awake."

"So much the better."

"Indeed, but you can judge that for yourself."

While speaking, they had followed a path which led to a cottage of pleasing architecture and quite huge dimensions.

They entered a hallway and from there a small living room with very subdued lighting, but enough however to reveal Countess de Roscanvel on the divan who, on seeing the detective, stood up saying:

"Ah! Monsieur Chantecoq, how good you are to have come so soon after your daughter's call."

And pale, shivering, she cried out. "I'm going to reveal a fact to you, that you will judge to be impossible, unbelievable, absurd… and yet it is the truth."

"My husband is alive!" she declared in a feverish voice.

Despite his formidable self-control, the great bloodhound started.

"What did you say, madame?" he said in an incredulous tone.

With a tone of conviction and sincerity, which made her claim even more overwhelming, Madame Roscanvel repeated herself.

"*I'M SAYING THAT MY HUSBAND IS ALIVE!*"

And she continued, oppressed and still under the influence of the shock whose traces she still bore on her face. "Don't think that I'm lying to you."

"Oh! Madame, the thought never crossed my mind."

"Nor that I've been the victim of an error, of a hallucination or the plaything of a dream, or a nightmare. No, I was wide awake, and completely conscious of reality."

And forcing herself to remain calm, Madame de Roscanvel explained.

"In line with your instructions, Monsieur Chantecoq, I spent the whole day in my bedroom, where Madame Bellegarde very kindly wanted to keep me company. I came down only for dinner, and as it was a very lovely evening, at nightfall, as you had authorised me to do, I went, still with your daughter, to take a little walk in the garden.

"The weather was magnificent. We sat on a bench at the edge of the terrace that looks over the road leading to the forest. We lingered there until eleven o'clock at night. It was so lovely. Around us, everything was silent. This pure air, imbued with the lovely scent from the neighbouring leaves was so sweet to breathe, that I felt a great physical relaxation, soon followed by a boost in my spirits, which did me no end of good.

"And then, my charming companion's conversation being so agreeable, it all made time fly for me so that, when midnight's dozen peals chimed from the clock of a nearby church, I had been convinced that it was no later than eight o'clock.

"We returned to the house. I went up to my room.

"For the first time in so many long and sad days, I had high hopes of getting a good night's sleep. I felt less desperate. A kind of interior voice predicted that, thanks to you, Monsieur Chantecoq, my anguish was going to come to an end and that the abominable accusation that was weighing on Monsieur Guèret and also on myself, was going to founder lamentably, when, upon undressing, I noticed that a jewelled brooch that I had been wearing on my bodice had disappeared.

"I valued it all the more, since it was the last gift that my husband gave me.

"I remembered that a few moments beforehand, when I was on the terrace bench near Madame Bellegarde, standing up, I had made a sudden movement after which I had heard quite clearly the sound of a light object striking a piece of wood, and to which I had not paid any attention.

"I told myself that this was perhaps my brooch which had become detached and had hit the bench as it fell. I resolved to go and look for it straight away."

While Madame de Roscanvel gave her account, Bellegarde, after having parked his car, had returned into the little room on tiptoes and was now also listening to the narrator who was continuing.

"I went down quietly, so as not to wake anyone. I reached the garden and as I was approaching the bench, I thought I saw a shadow which was crawling in the shelter of the privet hedge which ran along the length of the terrace.

"I stayed rooted to the spot. From the place where I was standing, it was impossible for the person who had entered the garden to notice me. I was therefore not risking anything.

"The strange but irresistible curiosity which incited me to see, to discover, had completely dissipated the fright that this sudden apparition had caused me at first.

"At that moment, I heard the little sounds of cracking branches. The shadow, which had been hidden behind the hedge for a moment, reappeared much closer to me, becoming more defined thanks to the light from the stars, and I then distinguished clearly, from a distance of around twenty metres, the silhouette of a man of tall stature who was crouching low and trying to approach the house, slipping across the glade, which was opposite the front door, above the main path.

"You will observe, Monsieur Chantecoq, that although very emotional, I was not at that moment unduly troubled, as I could note all these details and they have stayed engraved clearly in my memory."

Chantecoq gave an approving nod, and Madame de Roscanvel continued.

"Now, I clearly heard in the direction of the clearing, behind which the nocturnal visitor was hiding, some very light, very measured footsteps, which crunched in the gravel on the path.

"I made a movement to turn towards the house.

"As I was no more than a few metres away, I suddenly saw the man launch himself from the clearing, charge towards me, his hands stretched out before him… as though he was trying to strangle me.

"I had no more time to call for help. Believing myself lost, I pretended to faint and let myself fall to the ground.

"The man leaned over me… I then noticed that he was wearing a black mask that hid three quarters of his face.

"He stared at me for a moment. I held my breath…

"I asked myself 'is this a burglar, or a policeman?' And I cursed that curiosity, or rather that mysterious force which had forced me to linger there, and had prevented me from raising the alarm, when a strident whistle rang out in the direction of the forest.

"The masked man straightened up. I breathed a little more freely. He was going to leave, but suddenly a bright light surrounded us. The electric lamp at the front of the house had just illuminated, filling the area around us with its powerful rays.

"The man let out a cry. I shuddered. I felt as though I knew the sound of that voice.

"Galvanised, I stood and pushed by a sudden and furious instinct, I launched myself towards the man who was escaping the circle of light from which he had suddenly been surrounded, and was hiding in the undergrowth.

"I caught up with him just as he was about to reach the terrace.

"Then, turning back towards me, he pointed the barrel of a revolver at my chest. I had the terrible feeling that I was doomed, that any attempt to escape was impossible…

"But instead of pulling his gun's trigger, my attacker dropped to the ground, and Madame Bellegarde, rushing from the shadows, seized my arms, saying, 'Not a word, I just stunned him with a blow to the neck. Let's attempt, both of us, to drag him into the house, while avoiding waking up the servants.'"

"Bravo! Colette!" exclaimed Chantecoq, "I see that you've not forgotten my lessons or my advice."

And he added, addressing the Countess, "Forgive me, madame, for interrupting your tale at such a palpitating moment, but I couldn't resist the impulse to compliment my daughter and my pupil."

"And as for me," declared Bellegarde, "I can't resist the impulse to kiss you."

"I only did my duty," said the young woman defensively.

And after having given her husband a long and tender kiss, she nodded to Madame Roscanvel. "Please continue, madame."

Marie-Thérèse continued. "Not without difficulty, we managed to transport the masked man's inanimate body as far as the utility room. Madame Bellegarde switched on the lights. I stayed standing, immobile, as though petrified, in front of this man who was showing no signs of life.

"Madame Bellegarde, who had regained her marvellous sang-froid, said to me, 'Now, let's take off his mask.' She crouched down, lifted up the stranger's head, still unmoving, and pressed it against the wall.

"Very carefully, she lifted the thick veil of black silk that covered the man's face.

"There was a second one underneath. In case of surprise, the… I no longer know how to refer to… he, I suppose, had taken every precaution.

"The second mask suffered the fate of the first. A cry of stupor and shock burst from me, I recognised my husband."

A sob tore from the chest of the unfortunate lady who, though broken, at her wits' end, continued.

"I hurried towards him, I wanted to see him up close, to be sure indeed that I was not mistaken. It was he. I couldn't doubt it. I called to him, 'Robert, Robert…' He didn't answer me, and yet he was breathing. His eyelids even began to crack open. He had to see me, to recognise me…

"I didn't stop calling out 'Robert! Robert!' Then his eyes opened wide and I'll never forget their terrible expression, full of hatred and atrocious fury. His hands, fingers spread wide, reached towards me, as though he was still trying to strangle me, then he fell back on one side, unconscious again."

Exhausted, Countess Marie-Thérèse could now only murmur.

"Madame Bellegarde, I can't go on. Please, tell your father what happened next."

Colette took up the tale straight away.

"I believed that Madame de Roscanvel was about to faint and I hurried over to her. At that moment, our prisoner suddenly rose to his feet and, leaping through the door which had remained open, he darted into the garden and vanished even before I could make a move to follow him.

"The only clue that I was able to gather was the noise of a fast car which sped off in the direction of the forest. Then I rejoined Madame de Roscanvel, I helped her to this room and I telephoned you immediately."

"Good!" said Chantecoq simply, having restored all his apparent impassivity. Then he went on.

"I had foreseen that our quarry from Chaussée de la Muette might come to leave their calling card here, but I never would have believed…"

He stopped, as though he feared reviving again the pain that was tormenting Countess Marie-Thérèse.

But that lady, valiantly, forced herself to react, replying, "Speak, Monsieur Chantecoq, I implore you. However frightful this encounter was for me, I can't forget that we have an innocent man to save, and that now we possess proof that Julien Guèret couldn't have murdered my husband, as he is still alive.

"Madame," Chantecoq replied gravely, "first, permit me to admire your courage. Despite the dreadful blow that has just struck you, you have not ceased for a single moment to think of he who is being forced to atone for a crime that he didn't commit."

Gaining strength against the depression that had struck her, Madame de Roscanvel declared, "Whatever may happen and even if I must die from grief and shame, I want justice to be done… and thanks to you, Monsieur Chantecoq, it will be."

"In any case, madame," affirmed the detective, "I'm going to do my very best. Before that, I would need to be certain that you haven't been duped by a hallucination, or by some phenomenon of auto-suggestion."

"I'm certain!" the young woman exclaimed.

"Encouraged by the example that your daughter gave me, I had at that moment regained my composure, and it's impossible that I might have committed any error."

Chantecoq smiled. "It is, however, very easy to be sure."

And taking from his wallet the photo of Count Robert that he had taken on the evening where he had searched the house in Rue Henri-Heine, he placed it in front of Colette, saying, "Is this him?"

"Yes, father!" Madame Bellegarde replied, without hesitation.

"Now," concluded the detective, "all that's left is to catch him, just as soon as I discover his address, which won't take long."

"Monsieur Chantecoq," intervened Madame de Roscanvel, "in order to be so decisive, you must certainly know many things already."

"Quite a few, indeed."

"And perhaps you may already be able to explain to me how a man who gave me so many proofs of his love and who, a few seconds before disappearing, spoke to me with a tenderness that I still hear ringing in my ears, could have betrayed me in this way, passing himself off as dead, allowing Julien Guèret to be accused of murdering him and me of having been the accomplice and even the instigator of this crime?"

"I could, indeed, answer you," replied the great bloodhound frankly, "but that would push us too far. You need, Madame, to recover from the tragic emotional turmoil that you have just experienced, and I need to take the few hours of sleep I need in order to be fighting fit tomorrow.

"I'll content myself with telling you, Madame, that it's one of two things: either Count Robert de Roscanvel is the most blatant and shameless scoundrel, or he's been struck by some kind of dementia which dragged him down the slippery slope, at the bottom of which you have just found him.

"The facts that I already possess rather make me lean towards this second hypothesis."

"The poor man!"

"I can't, at this time, tell you anything more. Follow my advice. Force yourself to remain calm, very calm. Go back to your bedroom. Colette will go with you and tell you that you are surrounded by friends here who will do anything in order to defend you, and also to console you."

"You are right, Monsieur Chantecoq, I shall retire. I shall see you tomorrow, shan't I?"

"I fear that might force you to get up very early… because I intend to return to Paris first thing in the morning."

"I shall be up! Goodnight, Monsieur Chantecoq. Goodnight, Monsieur Bellegarde. If you only knew how touched I am by everything that you've done for me!"

She held out her hands to the detective and the reporter, both of whom clasped them with effusion.

"I daren't wish you a good night. I'll just say: brave heart!" Chantecoq said simply.

Colette left with Madame de Roscanvel who was now shedding quiet, very quiet, tears.

Alone with his son-in-law, the great bloodhound cried out, suddenly beaming: "Ah well, now I grasp the whole affair. It can be summarised thus: Rascolini bewitched the Count de Roscanvel and made a bandit of him. That's the lot!"

"There is a corpse, however," objected Bellegarde.

"By Jove! And this corpse is that of the Kérénot boy."

"How did they manage to pass it off as that of Count Robert?"

"First, because it was hugely disfigured, and then because his murderers had taken the precaution of slipping some objects and documents belonging to Roscanvel in his pockets."

"That's all highly plausible… but how do you explain the matching clothes?"

"Nothing simpler. Kérénot and Roscanvel were, as their photos indicate, of the same size and of the same build. Nothing would have been easier than for Rascolini, who must have prepared her trick a long time ago, in agreement with Roscanvel, to send him a sports jacket exactly the same as that which Kérénot was wearing when he left Paris in a car in order to fall into the trap that the Belle Imperia had set for him."

"Yes, that must be it!" gasped the reporter.

"This couple of bandits planned this business with a masterful hand. For an authentic Princess and a no less noble Count, it was good work. One thing's for sure, when people from high society decide to be crooks, they don't do it by halves!"

"And yet," objected Bellegarde, "they had other options available to achieve their goals. Why all these complications? Why this crime, which seems pointless? While admitting that led by an irresistible shared passion, they had the willpower to regain their liberty, didn't they have divorce as an option to free them?"

"Indeed," conceded Chantecoq, "the mystery of the Blue Train is not yet elucidated. There remain certain matters to resolve, such as that which you pointed out to me. But have patience, my dear Jacques, everything will become clear. Nothing will remain in the shadows, and when you recount this story to your readers, none of them will be able to reproach you for having neglected or forgotten the smallest detail, I give you my word. Now. Upstairs, let's get some sleep."

"I'll tell Colette to prepare your room."

"No need. I'll be perfectly happy on this divan. What time is it? Two o'clock… magnificent, that gives me five hours of sleep. That's more than I need in order to have no need of sleep the following night."

The detective and his son-in-law shook hands with affection.

A few minutes later, Chantecoq who, among other unique gifts, possessed the power of being able to fall asleep and wake up at will, was in a deep slumber.

At seven o'clock in the morning, he was up, as fresh and rested as always.

A few minutes later, Bellegarde, just as full of vigour as he, met him in the dining room, where they were served an excellent hot chocolate.

"My dear Jacques," said the detective, "I'm going to ask you to drive me back to Paris and, if you can, to stay with me today, because this day must be decisive, and I'll certainly have need of your services."

"I'm only too happy to be useful," the reporter affirmed. "I phoned the paper this morning to tell them that I was working on a sensational story, which is the absolute truth.

I'm therefore completely free."

"All in good time!" Chantecoq declared. "I wouldn't be put out for you to be there in the final battle, which is going to take place, and without doubt I'll need more than one witness, that is to say assistant."

"I'd be delighted!"

"You already gave me enough evidence of your courage and knowhow during the case of the Phantom of the Louvre, so I knew I can count on you completely."

And Chantecoq added, with a thin smile, "Anyway, I don't think we're going to be bored."

"I'm sure of it," Bellegarde replied. "And I'd be very happy and proud if I could help you to cuff two sinful bandits and to proclaim the innocence of Julien Guèret and Madame de Roscanvel."

"Good morning, father," called a voice full of harmony and youth.

It was Colette who, delightful in a dressing gown, was walking towards the detective.

"Good morning, my dear," he said, giving her a paternal kiss. "Not too tired?"

"Tired, me?"

"After last night's events?"

"I see the king of detectives has forgotten that I'm his daughter."

And with a charming frown, the young lady continued. "In fact, I'm furious."

"With whom?"

"Myself."

"Why?"

"What, father? Can't you guess?"

"Indeed not!"

"Didn't I let the masked man escape?"

"It was already very impressive that you succeeded in disarming him and preventing him from murdering his wife."

"The fact is that it all started very well, but it could have ended a lot better."

"Console yourself, my dear Colette," replied the great bloodhound.

"It's a good thing that Monsieur de Roscanvel succeeded in running away," he said with a slightly mysterious tone.

Colette gave a small start at that, but she fell silent.

Chantecoq continued. "You would like to know why, my incorrigibly curious one?"

"Father, if I am curious, I'm no less discreet."

"I gladly admit that, and to reward you for your discretion, I'm going to satisfy your curiosity."

"How you spoil me!"

"You richly deserve it, doesn't she, Jacques?"

"She always deserves it," emphasised the reporter with a voice full of tender and joyous conviction.

Chantecoq explained. "First. Roscanvel's flight has spared us a cruel scene between him and his wife, which is not to be overlooked. Second. Knowing Princess Rascolini to be at liberty, he would certainly have refused to talk, which wouldn't particularly help in solving the Mystery of the Blue Train. Now, when I take on a case, I don't content myself with half a solution, I want to push on to the end and not for the whole world would I put a full stop on some hypotheses.

"Third. Finally, I mustn't forget that I've been charged with another case, a mission which was entrusted to me by a mother: Madame Kérénot.

"Of however little interest her son may be, I promised that poor woman that I would bring it all out in the open.

Now that I'm certain he was murdered by the Princess, probably in cahoots with Roscanvel, the murderer or murderers must be punished. They will be. So, my little Colette, are you happy?"

"Yes, father. As always I discover that you are, first and foremost, better than a soldier, a champion of justice."

"Now, let's move on to this poor Madame de Roscanvel."

"Last night, exhausted with fatigue, she dropped into a heavy slumber. She needs more rest."

"There's no point in waking her."

"That was my thought too."

"The poor woman!" Bellegarde said. "It could be said that she's living through a true Calvary."

"A Calvary which is only just beginning," observed the detective's daughter, "To tell yourself that a man you cherished, adored more than anything, in whom you had unlimited faith and by whom you believed yourself to be loved jealously, not only has he betrayed you abominably, but he has become the most odious of criminals! Isn't that enough to break a heart forever? To plunge you into mourning for the rest of your life?"

"That's true!" the reporter admitted.

His eyes lit with a glint of luminous goodwill, Chantecoq declared, "Certainly, Madame de Roscanvel must have suffered atrociously and no doubt she is still suffering. Such a wound will take time to form a scar. And while admitting, which is possible, that the horror which can't help but be inspired in her by her husband's dreadful conduct won't be sufficient to wipe from her the haunting of the atrocious drama that she has just lived, won't she have the consolation of telling herself that there exists a man who loved her heroically enough, immensely enough, to confess to a crime that he hadn't committed in order that she herself was not tainted by odious suspicion.

"To this supreme proof of love she will be able to respond only with a fervent recognition. And time will do the rest."

"I know that you're a good prophet," replied Colette, "and I hope that as always, your prediction will come true."

"And me too!" Chantecoq exclaimed. "And now, time to leave for Paris."

Bellegarde stirred. "I'll go and get my car out."

He was moving towards the door, when it swung open…

Pale, her face still overwhelmed by the emotions of the previous night, but with a moving beauty even in her mourning clothes, Madame de Roscanvel entered the dining room.

"Monsieur Chantecoq," she said, "as I said to you last night, I didn't want to let you leave without taking leave of you. And furthermore, I wanted to say a few things to you."

Bellegarde and his wife made a movement as if to retire, but Countess Marie-Thérèse shook her head. "Stay, do please stay."

And in a serious voice, she continued. "Last night I had a terrible nightmare. I don't believe in warnings, in omens. Although I'm a Breton, I'm not superstitious.

"In brief, this was my dream. I saw Julien Guèret in his prison. He was calling to me. He held out his arms to me, I tried to go to him, but an invisible barrier separated me from him. Suddenly, in an act of desperation, I saw him throw himself headlong into the wall of his cell, and fall down with a shattered skull. I could then approach him. He was dead. I woke up prey to a terrible anguish and, from that moment, I can't stop repeating to myself: 'As long as he doesn't kill himself! As long as the truth isn't known too late!'

"So, I'm asking you, Monsieur Chantecoq, in order to ease my conscience, if, after what happened here last night, I don't have the duty to warn the authorities immediately that my husband is alive, and that the crime of which Julien Guèret is accused therefore never took place?"

The king of detectives replied. "I may only, madame, bow respectfully before the sentiment which inspired your desire to make such a gesture.

"I doubt, indeed, that Prosecutor Ribécourt would accord to your declaration all the credence that it deserves. His position is fixed. He believes Julien Guèret to be guilty, you too, as he has signed a warrant for your arrest. He would not listen to you. You'll object to me that there's Madame Bellegarde's testimony, but Madame Bellegarde is my daughter. I had been charged by you to make enquiries whose aim is exonerating you, as well as Julien Guèret, of the accusation of which you have been the subject. Monsieur Ribécourt will therefore take no notice of Colette's statement.

"I'm asking you not to risk compromising, through an action that is generous but premature, our final and decisive success which can't be far away. I beg your patience for a delay of only forty-eight hours. Is that too much to ask?"

"Certainly not, Monsieur Chantecoq."

"As to Julien Guèret, you can rest easy. Yesterday I telegraphed his lawyer to say that everything was going well, and that he could, without fear of raising false hopes, affirm to his client on my behalf that I was within touching distance of the prize. Everything's therefore also going well on that side."

"Monsieur Chantecoq, you think of everything."

"I'm thinking of you, madame, and of he whose admirable attitude, whose magnificent devotion to your cause, has rendered sacred to me!

"Be at peace, your heart will soon know the solace that your conscience must already taste."

Madame de Roscanvel held out her hand to the detective, when Bellegarde who, a moment ago, had reached the window, approached his father-in-law and whispered a few words in his ear.

Chantecoq went over, in turn, to glance outside.

"Ah! The rogue," he murmured through gritted teeth. "He has denounced her. But he who laughs last, laughs best."

The doorbell rang.

"My dear Jacques," said Chantecoq, "go and let them in."

And rejoining Madame de Roscanvel who, seized by sudden anxiety, had approached Colette, he said: "Madame, I beg you to save all your composure right away. Your bolthole is discovered. They have come to arrest you... but promise me, swear to me that you will keep yourself from saying to anybody that Count Roscanvel is still alive."

"I promise you."

"Brave heart! This is the final test. It will be brief, I guarantee it. Monsieur Ribécourt doesn't suspect the show that I'm preparing for him."

10 THE FINAL BATTLE

That same day, around ten o'clock in the morning, two men knocked at the door of the house on Chaussée de la Muette.

One, dressed in a redingote and black trousers, topped with an impeccable top hat, carefully gloved, wore the officer's rosette of the Légion d'honneur. His hair was greying, as was his fan-shaped beard, and he gave every impression of being an important legal figure.

The other, younger, respectably dressed in a dark blue suit, his black moustache and beard well-groomed, his blinking gaze behind a pair of pince-nez glasses which seemed immovable, was already demonstrating the gravitas befitting a Minister in waiting.

The house's shutters were closed as a sign of mourning.

The cast iron gates opened a crack to reveal the silhouette of a porter who had already put on mourning livery and who, in an unctuous tone, asked the visitors: "Have these gentlemen come to sign?"

And without waiting for their response he pointed them towards the register in which several pages had already been covered with numerous important and even illustrious signatures.

"No," replied the older of the two men, "I'm Monsieur Donon, notary, and this is my senior clerk. I have a very urgent communication to deliver to Her Highness Princess Rascolini."

Still with the same unction that suggested on his part an inflexible loyalty to the duty that had been assigned to him, the porter replied.

"I truly regret to inform you, monsieur, but it will not be possible even to let the Princess know that you are here. Doctor Angelotti, who cares for the Princess, has formally forbidden access to her apartments to anyone other than the senior chambermaid."

"Couldn't we see this woman?" the notary asked.

"No, monsieur. Mademoiselle Suzanne is not leaving the Princess's bedroom."

"Is there a steward here?"

"No, monsieur."

"Someone in authority… a butler, perhaps?"

"Yes… Monsieur Marco."

"Could I speak to him?"

"I don't know… maybe."

"Could you do me the service of finding out?"

"I shall see, monsieur."

The porter turned on his heels and headed towards the master staircase which led to the first floor.

When he had disappeared, Monsieur Donon leaned towards his clerk and spoke to him in a low voice.

New people were entering, well aware that the following day international newspapers would publish their names. There was no small advertisement.

Soon, the concierge returned.

"Monsieur Marco is coming down," he announced, "If you gentlemen would care to follow me."

Immediately the notary and his colleague followed him in.

The servant showed them into the office whose door opened under the master staircase and where we have already observed the Belle Imperia holding a rather… singular meeting with her butler.

Very politely, he invited them to be seated. Then he said, "Monsieur Marco will be with you in two minutes."

He withdrew, closing the door behind him quietly.

The clerk, who had approached his boss, opened his mouth, but with a brief and very clear sign, that employer motioned him into silence. And both of them took a seat, each on a chair.

It wasn't a long wait. Almost immediately, Marco, dressed in black, with a sombre and even saddened air, came into the room. Monsieur Donon and his clerk got to their feet.

With an affected dignity which showed that he was deeply convinced of his own importance, the butler gave them a curt nod, and said, "Monsieur Donon… notary?"

"Indeed," replied the ministerial officer in a tone which clearly indicated that he was resolved to maintain his distance.

"Please be seated, monsieur," invited the stooge, who had the tact to remain on his feet.

"No point," declined the scrivener. "I have only one thing to say to you: I must see Princess Rascolini as soon as possible."

"The Princess is suffering," Marco affirmed.

"So I've been told already! But was she on her deathbed I would still insist on being admitted to her presence."

However strong his self-control, the butler could not repress an imperceptible shiver. Then he replied.

"Despite my desire to be of service to you, I am forbidden to satisfy your demand on this matter. The Princess has been so overwhelmed by the Prince's passing, which was so sudden, that any new emotional disturbance is forbidden her.

"That is why I have an absolute duty to bar the door against anyone attempting to cross its threshold."

"I can only congratulate you on your devotion," stressed Monsieur Donon, "but perhaps you would be less intransigent if you knew the purpose of my visit."

"Whatever it may be, my dear sir, I will maintain the same attitude."

"Very well…" growled the notary. Then he continued. "In fact, doesn't Princess Rascolini have a secretary?"

"Indeed," declared Marco, "Count d'Orvieto."

"Could I speak to him?"

"Not at the moment."

"He's ill too, is he?"

"Monsieur the Count has gone out."

"Do you know when he'll return?"

"I've no idea."

"This grows tedious," sighed Monsieur Donon. "I would so much have preferred this formality to have been accomplished with the Princess's permission…"

"The fact is," said the clerk, "that it would have been better not to involve the police in this matter."

"The police!" the butler repeated, in spite of himself.

Monsieur Donon repeated to himself, as though he hadn't heard. "Her intervention will not fail to provoke in certain papers, always avid for sensational gossip, some speculation which strongly risks unleashing a scandal and of compromising certain persons belonging to the entourage of *de cujus*."

"I don't understand what you're trying to say," declared Marco, whose nostrils were beginning to clench.

"*De cujus*," explained the notary kindly, "is the term that we use in order to designate the deceased whose final wishes are deposited at our chambers."

"Ah! Good! Very good!" said the butler, more and more troubled.

With the same bonhomie, Monsieur Donon continued. "After all, as I can't be received by the principal interested party, nor by her secretary, I don't see why, to you who must be her trusted confidant, I should keep the reasons that bring me here a mystery any longer."

And calmly, as though it was the most natural thing in the world, the notary made his revelation.

"Around three months ago, Prince Rascolini sent me a document which was entirely written, signed, and initialled by his own hand in the presence of two honourable witnesses, and in which he declares the demand that after his death, his corpse should undergo an autopsy by two surgeons that he expressly requested: Professors Desmottes and… and…"

"Sardonce," supplied the clerk.

"That's right, Sardonce," repeated Monsieur Donon. "What is more serious is that Prince Rascolini orders that if this clause has not been respected within forty-eight hours following his demise, he cancels all his other arrangements, which made his spouse his sole heir, and instead leaves his entire fortune in order to support Italian refugees in France."

And, looking Marco straight in the eye, the lawyer concluded. "You see, Monsieur Marco, that I was not misleading you when I told you that I had a serious reason to see the Princess straight away."

Marco could no longer manage to hide the state of embarrassment and fear into which the notary's words had plunged him. "Indeed," he stammered. "It's very regrettable."

"So much more so," Monsieur Donon expounded, with his peculiar air of talking about nothing in particular, "if there were to be discovered in Prince Rascolini's body any traces of toxins or if the medical examination demonstrated simply that the dose of painkillers that were administered to him daily had been increased, it could land in hot water, not only those who gave such an order, but also and especially those who would have carried it out."

Growing livid, Marco shouted. "Are you implying, monsieur, that the Prince was poisoned?"

In a voice which had suddenly become metallic, even strident, Monsieur Donon intoned, "Indeed I am, and you know that better than anyone."

"Me, monsieur?"

"Yes, you… as it was you who administered the dose."

"But…"

"Yes, you. It's futile to deny it, your pallor and your anxiety have betrayed you. Now, monsieur butler, to lunch! It's your turn to be served."

"Monsieur notary," protested the Italian who, feeling trapped by a superior force, had completely lost his head.

"There's no use trying to persuade me, no more than trying to butter me up," replied Monsieur Donon. "I know your pedigree. You're not called Marco, but Marcolini. You're the pawn, and never has that qualification been more accurate, of Princess Rascolini.

"You made yourself, as well as your mistress, the chambermaid Suzanne, an accomplice who was richly rewarded through all her infamies.

"It was you who helped her to kill one of her lovers, Raymond Kérénot, in an ambush where he met his death. It was you who, infiltrated like a spy in her pay into the service of the Count and Countess de Roscanvel, falsely declared to the Marseilles prosecutor that you had caught Julien Guèret in the very act of kissing Countess Marie-Thérèse on the lips, the day after her husband had been crushed by the Blue Train.

"It was you who allowed the accusation against that man of letters and that unfortunate wife, of having murdered Monsieur de Roscanvel, while you knew full well that he was alive, and that he was hiding away in this house beneath the mask of a fake war invalid under the borrowed name of Gabriele d'Orvieto. Deny it then, wretch, I defy you. I've got you now, and I'll not let you go."

Pallid, teeth chattering, sweating with fear, the rogue stuttered.

"How… you… you… a notary… how could you know all that?"

"I'm no notary, but a decent detective."

"De...tect…ive?"

"My name is perhaps not unknown to you, because this is not the first time that I've come to this house."

"Chantecoq!"

"Yes. Chantecoq."

"I'm lost!"

"Not necessarily!" declared the great bloodhound. "Listen to me, Marcolini. You're a blackguard, and even a scoundrel. That Suzanne whom you want to make your wife barely deserves better than you. You're therefore destined to make a very well-matched couple. I'd like to separate you, and it's up to you to realise your dream, which is to go far, far away from here, with her to profit from the nest-egg that you already possess, which your multiple infamies have earned you.

"Perhaps you would become honest when you have the means to be so. That's the grace that I wish for you. It's certain that justice would be better satisfied and morality better served if I had you arrested, but when it's a question of saving two innocents and to tear them off, one to the guillotine, and the other to prison, it's permissible to strain that morality and justice of which I remain a zealous defender.

"This principle outlined, this is what I propose: you'll tell me immediately where Princess Rascolini and the Count de Roscanvel are hiding, if not, I denounce you, and you face the music."

Collapsing, Marcolini groaned. "Monsieur Chantecoq, I can tell you nothing… I don't know."

"Don't be an imbecile, man."

"Monsieur Chantecoq, I swear to you that I have no idea, and Suzanne too, where they've gone. You really think they would have told us anything, us, mere servants…"

"Come off it! They chose you as accomplices for their crimes; you can't expect me to believe that they didn't also take you into their confidence with their getaway plans."

"On my father and my mother's soul, I swear to you that I'm telling the truth."

"And on your own, do you swear that too?"

"Yes, Monsieur Chantecoq, even on my own."

"Take care, Marcolini, your head's already not sitting so

very steady on your shoulders."

"Monsieur Chantecoq," moaned the cowardly wretch, "if I knew, I'd already have told you."

"My dear Jacques," said the king of detectives to his son-in-law, pointing out to him a telephone, "would you be so kind as to get the prosecutor on the line, please?"

The reporter reached out towards the receiver when one of the panels of the huge bookshelves that filled one of the walls entirely pivoted on itself.

A woman appeared, her face convulsed, prey to an unspeakable dread; it was Suzanne who rushed towards Chantecoq, saying, "Mercy! Pity! I was there… hidden behind the secret door, I heard everything. He wasn't lying to you, Monsieur. He knew nothing. But me, I know…

"Yesterday evening, I overheard a conversation between them. The Count said, 'I fancy that we're being trailed by Chantecoq, and that he won't wait for the Prince's obsequies before striking a decisive blow.'

"'So, what should we do?' asked the Princess.

"Monsieur d'Orvieto replied, 'Go into hiding.'

"'Where?'

"'In Paris, that's still the best when you want to disappear.'

"'And afterward?'

"Monsieur d'Orvieto replied. 'Afterward? First, we'll have to eliminate Chantecoq, because as long as he doesn't find us himself, he won't denounce us to the police, and once he's dead, we'll have nothing more to fear from him.'"

"Not possible!" the king of detectives underlined, in passing.

Suzanne concluded her account. "There you are, Monsieur Chantecoq, all I can tell you, and what I've told you is the pure truth."

"I really want to believe you," conceded the bloodhound, "but there's one thing that you've completely forgotten to reveal to me."

"What's that, then?"

"The address of the place where the fugitives are hiding."

"That's right, sorry, I was and I am still so anxious."

"Come on, out with it."

"57, Rue Henri-Heine."

"Eh! Roscanvel's own house!" Chantecoq exclaimed. "That's… that's gutsy! And after all, it's not so daft a place."

Then he added. "That's easy to check, in any case. If you haven't been messing me about, I'll keep the promise that I made you, and you'll have time to shelter yourselves before the police come to bother you.

"If not, this evening, you'll both be sleeping in a cell.

"I warn you that there's no point in trying to flee, I have taken every precaution. And be very sure that I never bluff.

"Above all, don't get it into your heads to give your boss a quiet warning that I'm preparing to pay them a little visit, because I warn you that in that case, I would be like the gendarmes, that is to say pitiless."

The telephone rang. Chantecoq grabbed the device and listened.

"Hello!" came a man's voice on the other end of the line. "Is that you, Marco?"

"Yes, Count," replied the detective, borrowing the butler's Italian accent.

"Any news?" Roscanvel asked.

"No, Count."

"Do you know if the man in question has returned to Paris?"

"Yes, Count."

"Doubtless he'll turn up there under some mediocre disguise or other."

Chantecoq replied without frowning. "He already has, Count. He came disguised as a notary, under the pretext of communicating to the Princess a will from the Prince, in which he demanded that an autopsy be carried out within forty-eight hours of his death.

"But I spotted him straight away, and I got rid of him. Not without difficulty."

"Well done, Marco, stay watchful," the Count's voice commanded. "But I believe that soon the coq will end up being the one making us cockadoodle-doo."

"If I could help you," the detective insinuated.

"Would you?"

"With pleasure and I believe I've proved it, but these are things that can't be said over the telephone."

"I understand. Come and find me under some mundane disguise."

"Where's that?"

"57, Rue Henri-Heine."

"I'll be with you in an hour."

"I'm waiting. While you're about it, bring us some provisions."

"Understood, Count."

Chantecoq hung up the device. Concealing under an impassive mask the great satisfaction that he felt, he said: "You have not lied to me, mademoiselle, and I congratulate you for that, that gives me confidence for what comes next. But one more time, I warn you, you are under surveillance. So, watch out!

"But if everything happens as I hope, from this evening

you'll be able to take your turn to make a run for it. In that case, good luck, and may the devil take you."

Chantecoq and Bellegarde retired, leaving the butler and the chambermaid literally consternated, desperate, stunned.

"What a man!" Marcolini murmured, "I really thought I was lost."

"Lucky that I was able to give him the address," declared Suzanne.

"Without that we would have been done for," the stooge said, still trembling.

"Nevertheless," observed the maid, "we've lost big time."

"Nevertheless also," concluded Marco philosophically, "we couldn't have got away with it any easier. As soon as I can get out of here, I'm going to light a candle to the Blessed Virgin."

***

About an hour after the scene that we have just described, a plumber who was wearing a leather bag as a bandolier, which contained the tools of his trade, stopped in front of the house on Rue Henri-Heine. He must have been watched for impatiently, because hardly had he raised his head towards the first floor windows, than the little tradesmen's entrance was opened quietly, without revealing anyone.

The plumber headed towards the door immediately, and disappeared inside.

"Is that you, Marco?" asked Roscanvel, who was standing in the dark corridor.

"Yes, Count," replied Chantecoq, imitating Marcolini's voice and his intonations marvellously.

Count Robert, a hundred miles from suspecting that it

was the king of detectives who was trailing after him, climbed the servants' staircase which led straight to the second floor, where, sheltered from all indiscretion, the Belle Imperia and her lover had established their headquarters.

In order to avoid any light being visible from outside, not only did the shutters of all the rooms remain closed, but some thick curtains prevented the slightest rays of light from filtering through to the exterior.

Princess Rascolini was half-lying on a divan. The subdued beams from a skylight illuminated her beautiful face softly.

Roscanvel closed the door. The bloodhound bowed respectfully before the Princess then, putting down his bag on a table, he withdrew from it in succession a bottle of champagne, a terrine of foie gras and a rectangular tin which from its shape and dimensions strongly resembled that which he was always carrying with him on his expeditions, and with which, he had inspired true jitters in Monsieur Méjasson the night before.

Around the tin ran a white stripe glued to the sides and on which could be read these words printed in red ink:

Baltic Herrings
From Captain Brown's Recipe

While the fake plumber made these preparations, the Princess murmured in Roscanvel's ear.

"He's really transformed himself very well."

Count Robert outdid her. "You could almost say it was impossible to recognise him."

Out loud, the Belle Imperia said, "So it appears, Marco, that you have found a way to rid us of Chantecoq."

"Yes, yes..." affirmed the detective, while attacking the tin with a special key that he had taken from his pocket.

Roscanvel stepped forward. "I would be curious to know

how you're going to do that."

While beginning to open the tin which contained or rather was supposed to contain some Baltic Herrings, the detective replied, still imitating Marco's voice and accent.

"I'll tell you: it's really very easy. This evening…"

But he stopped, his ears pricked. Then, he said, "I think I heard a noise."

The Princess and the Count exchanged worried glances. With a wave of his hand, the fake plumber reassured them and went towards the door.

"Whatever happens," he said, lowering his voice, "don't move from this room, I'll take care of everything."

He darted outside and closed the door behind him.

"Provided he's not been spotted and followed by Chantecoq," said the beautiful Florentine fearfully.

Count Robert cried out, drawing a Browning from his pocket. "If ever that accursed detective shows his face here… next time I won't hesitate to blow his brains out."

"Be quiet!" the Princess cried. "That sounded like a lock, nearby, in the bedroom."

Roscanvel strained his ears. Absolute silence reigned in the house.

"No," he said, "it's nothing."

"I assure you that I heard it."

"You're mistaken."

"Not at all."

"If you insist, I'll go and see."

Count Robert headed towards the bedroom door. He tried to open it, it resisted him.

"Locked," he observed, stupefied.

"That's impossible," said Gemma, "it was open not ten minutes ago."

"You can see it's not!" Roscanvel observed.

Seized with a sudden suspicion, he went towards the door which led to the staircase, and through which the fake plumber had vanished.

It was also impossible to open.

"We're locked in!" he said in an irritated voice.

"By whom?" the Princess asked. Roscanvel did not respond.

The Belle Imperia put a hand to her brow. "Could Marco have betrayed us?"

Her lover shook his head.

"Then who?" demanded the Princess.

Count Robert remained silent.

Gemma rose to go towards him, when, with a sudden gesture, he put a hand to his forehead.

"What's the matter?" asked the Princess.

"A spot of vertigo."

"I just had a dizzy spell too."

"That's strange."

"I'm afraid, Robert."

"You!"

"Yes, I'm afraid!"

The Florentine staggered and fell back on the divan.

Slowly, Roscanvel said in a hoarse voice, "We've fallen into a trap that Chantecoq set for us. That man just now, he wasn't Marco! It was him!"

Reeling like a drunkard, he approached the table on which the detective had earlier deposited the bottle of champagne, the terrine of foie gras, the bread and the Baltic Herrings. With a groping hand, he seized the bottle.

"Empty!" he said, "It's empty! By Jove, I understand… it must have contained some sleep-inducing gasses that have filled the room, and that's why I…"

He stopped, contemplating with haggard eyes Princess Rascolini who, stretched out on the divan, was showing no signs of life. He approached her.

"Asleep," he said.

He tried to shake her, but in vain. For this was no sleep, but a lethargy that had paralysed her completely.

"Fly! Fly!" yelled Roscanvel, who seemed increasingly overcome by an irresistible torpor. "But this room has no exit other than these doors."

He advanced towards a curtain, drew it, and reached out his hand to a window latch.

"What good is that!" he said to himself, "he must be waiting for us down there. Surely he has alerted the police. I'd rather die than let them take me alive."

He drew his Browning.

"Her first," he snarled, "then me."

He trained the barrel of his gun at the Italian's chest. But just as he was about to pull the trigger, a cry escaped his lips, and twirling around, he collapsed on the carpet, at the feet of she whom he had tried to murder before dying.

***

That morning, Judge Ribécourt, on entering his office, gave a sharp start of surprise on noticing the presence of a huge wooden crate which certainly must have contained a grand piano, such as are seen in Cologne, Pasdeloup and at the Conservatoire.

"What!" he asked his clerk who, already there, was contemplating this mysterious parcel in a stupor, "What can this box contain?"

"That's exactly, what I was just wondering, your honour."

Monsieur Ribécourt who had approached it, read these words written on a large label nailed to the crate: *To Monsieur Judge Ribécourt, Palais de Justice, Marseille.*

"This is no error, it's indeed for me," declared the magistrate. "But what can be in there? Tell me, Cadière, do you know who brought this here?"

"Monsieur, I already made enquiries, and no one could furnish me with any information at all."

"One moment then," replied Monsieur Ribécourt, who had continued his inspection of the label, "there's something written here, yes, indeed: *Sent by Monsieur Chantecoq, private detective.*

"Chantecoq, private detective, isn't that the old Security agent who set up on his own after the War, and whose nickname is the king of detectives?"

"Indeed, Monsieur."

"I wonder what he could have sent me in this true Pandora's Box, on which he's taken the trouble to write, in large letters, *THIS WAY UP*, and *VERY FRAGILE*. And also, why all these little holes here and there?

"In the twenty years that I've been a judge, nothing like this has ever happened to me."

"Why don't we open it and find out?" the clerk suggested.

"No, it's not pressing," declared Monsieur Ribécourt. "It'll turn out to be some sort of practical joke, or worse. It would be much better to proceed with that operation when I'm not there.

"In any case, this morning I need to interrogate Princess Roscanvel who was sent to me from Paris yesterday. She must have arrived."

"I'll go and see, monsieur."

There was a knock at the door.

"Come in," said the judge.

It was a policeman who was bringing him a card.

No sooner had the magistrate glanced at it than he exclaimed, "Chantecoq! It's him… we're going to have the key to this mystery. Gendarme, show in Monsieur Chantecoq straight away."

The great bloodhound appeared, smiling with a deferential amiability under which a clear eye would not have failed to detect a light irony. He bowed to the judge who immediately addressed him, while pointing at the enormous crate.

"Monsieur Chantecoq, I've indeed received your parcel, as you can see. I've not yet had time to open it. But as you're here, you'll certainly tell me immediately what it contains."

With an assurance capable of disconcerting Saint George himself, the king of detectives riposted.

"Proof of the innocence of both Julien Guèret, and Madame de Roscanvel."

"Eh! What! What are you saying?" Monsieur Ribécourt exclaimed, raising his arms to the ceiling. "Monsieur Chantecoq, is it your intention to make a mockery of justice?"

"I have only one intention, monsieur, and that is to serve justice."

"It seems to me that you have a funny way of going about it."

"Let's say 'original', monsieur. Knowing to what extent, all in good faith which I must acknowledge, you have been obstinate in seeing guilt in two innocent people, I wanted to convince you through facts which are material, brutal, and undeniable, that you are mistaken."

"No!"

"Yes, monsieur, as Monsieur de Roscanvel is still alive!"

"The Count de Roscanvel alive! What is this sick joke? Come along, this farce has gone on long enough. Monsieur Chantecoq, I must ask you to leave."

"Not before having demonstrated to you, monsieur, that the Count de Roscanvel is indeed alive!"

And approaching the crate, he pressed on a secret switch that made its front panel crack open along its full height and width.

Dumbfounded, half-crazed, Monsieur Ribécourt and his clerk saw, strapped solidly to two stools, the top and the bottom of their bodies supported by some belts whose extremities were fixed to the crate's supports, immobile, still anaesthetised, and sitting face to face, a man dressed in a very chic sports jacket and a woman wearing an elegant day dress.

Triumphantly, Chantecoq made the introduction. "The Count de Roscanvel and his mistress, Princess Rascolini."

"I'm dreaming!"

This was all that the unfortunate Ribécourt could say, falling heavily in his armchair, while Cadière, wiping away the sweat that was beading at his temples with his sleeve, cried out, "Indeed, such things could only happen in Marseille!"

Not wanting to compromise his dignity any further, Monsieur Ribécourt strove to recover himself. Still half choked, he continued. "Monsieur Chantecoq, will you explain yourself to me…"

"It's these two who are going to explain everything to you themselves."

"But they're dead."

"In a simple lethargic state, monsieur. I can, in a matter of seconds, bring them out of it, as soon as you please."

"But how!"

Chantecoq approached the crate and took from his pocket a case containing a flask that he uncorked and which he held in turn under the noses of the Count and the Italian.

Two minutes later, they had both awoken, bruised, aching, numbed, stunned, baffled, not yet understanding much and looking around them with eyes that were heavy with sleep, frightened, under their heavy eyelids.

In a jiffy, Chantecoq released their bonds, and said to them in his mordant voice: "Monsieur Count de Roscanvel, and Madame Princess Rascolini, please allow me to introduce you to Judge Ribécourt, who is now going to take very special care of you."

The Italian gave a cry of rage. Roscanvel contented himself with grinding his teeth. The clerk approached the seats. Both were incapable of standing upright. They fell heavily back on their chairs.

The implacable face of justice, Chantecoq continued. "When you're feeling a little better, Princess, no doubt you'll explain to the judge how you arranged the disappearance of a certain Raymond Kérénot and the manner by which you took it on yourself to make that unfortunate's corpse pass for that of Monsieur de Roscanvel.

"I'll say nothing," snarled the Italian.

But recovering suddenly, as though he had just regained all his strength, Count Robert cried out.

"Very well, then! I'll talk. I was crazy about this woman. Blind to anything else, she had literally bewitched me. Both of us, we wanted to belong to the other without sharing. We were both married. We couldn't divorce, she, because, as you know, divorce is forbidden under Italian law, myself, because I wanted to spare the very Christian family to which I belong the shame of seeing one of their own disobeying the Church's commandments.

"Gemma swore to me that she would rid herself of her husband as soon as I had taken out my wife.

"Though I was capable of anything in order to keep for ever the love of she who had inspired in me such senseless passion, I refused to sacrifice a woman that I had once married, believing I loved her, and who loved me still with all her soul.

"I would do anything for love, but I wouldn't do that.

"So we decided, Gemma and I, to stage my death. Gemma had confessed to me that before meeting me, she had a lover, an individual from whom she had separated, and who was trying to blackmail her. We resolved to draw him into an ambush, to kill him, and to put his corpse on the tracks so that his head would be crushed by the Blue Train.

"The plan worked. It was she who shot him through the heart with a revolver a few minutes before the Express passed through. Me, I put some papers belonging to me in his trouser pockets. You know the rest, Monsieur Judge. Do your duty, I've nothing more to add. My lawyer will doubtless plead insanity. Perhaps he'll be right, because it's a true insanity that took hold of me from the day I met this woman.

"Previously, I was an honest man, a gentleman, Monsieur Ribécourt, she turned me into a bandit, a murderer…

"Here's my head, take it."

Monsieur Ribécourt turned to the Princess. "What do you have to say to that?"

"Nothing!" replied the Italian, whose eyes were glowing with the lights of hell, "or rather... yes. Monsieur de Roscanvel has forgotten a detail which will no doubt have some importance, in your eyes."

"What's that?" asked the magistrate.

"It's that, in accordance with the promise I made him, I didn't hesitate to take out my husband by ordering my butler to administer him with a dose of morphine strong enough to put a definitive end to his suffering."

Frightened by this cynicism, Monsieur Ribécourt cried out, "This woman is a monster."

"Let's rather say a hysterical criminal," Chantecoq suggested.

"What a business!" lamented the judge, who had completely lost the plot.

And directing a begging gaze at Chantecoq, he said, "How am I going to get out of this?"

"Monsieur Judge, nothing could be simpler," declared the detective. "First, you only have to lock up these two guilty parties."

"You're right. Cadière, draw up two arrest warrants."

"Then," continued the bloodhound, "you immediately sign an exoneration of Julien Guèret and Madame de Roscanvel."

"Of course."

While the judge, aided by his clerk, set about these formalities, Chantecoq approached the two prisoners, to speak to them.

"You tried to defy me. You see my response."

And he added, "It's good to see that from time to time vice is still punished and virtue rewarded!"

EPILOGUE

That same day, Julien Guèret and Madame de Roscanvel were released. Chantecoq was waiting for them outside the prison.

The detective was not a man for effusion. In spite of everything, he was greatly touched by the expressive manner in which the two expressed their gratitude to him.

He took them to the house where he was staying, and where they met Jacques Bellegarde, who had accompanied his father-in-law and who was ready to gather, the perfect reporter that he was, the first impressions of the two innocents.

"What a fine book you'll be able to write," the journalist told the novelist.

But he replied, "No, because the ending would be too painful."

"And yet, here you both are at liberty."

"Yes, but..." Julien Guèret stopped himself, letting out a deep sigh.

Chantecoq approached, took his hand, and said,

"Patience! Your admirable sacrifice will soon reap its own reward. For the moment, she who loves you is still too injured by her own suffering. But already she knows to what extent you adore her, and I can tell you that she would have preferred to die rather than to see you convicted.

"At the moment, in the face of her husband's infamy, who didn't hesitate to denounce her to the police and to have her arrested, she can only be a poor pained and distraught creature. And it's towards you that, tenderly and forever, her heart will go."

And with a smile full of exquisite generosity, the king of detectives added, "Trust me on this... I've always been a good prophet."

FIN

CHANTECOQ AND MÉTÉOR WILL RETURN IN...
CHANTECOQ AND THE HAUNTED HOUSE

ABOUT THE AUTHOR

Arthur Bernède (5 January 1871 – 20 March 1937) was a French writer, poet, opera librettist, and playwright.

Bernède was born in Redon, Ille-et-Vilaine department, in Brittany. In 1919, Bernède joined forces with actor René Navarre, who had played Fantômas in the Louis Feuillade serials, and writer Gaston Leroux, the creator of Rouletabille, to launch the Société des Cinéromans, a production company that would produce films and novels simultaneously. Bernède published almost 200 adventure, mystery, and historical novels. His best-known characters are Belphégor, Judex, Mandrin, Chantecoq, and Vidocq. Bernède also collaborated on plays, poems, and opera libretti with Paul de Choudens; including several operas by Félix Fourdrain.

Bernède also wrote the libretti for a number of operas, among them Jules Massenet's Sapho and Camille Erlanger's L'Aube rouge.

ABOUT THE TRANSLATOR

Andrew Lawston grew up in rural Hampshire, where he later worked for a short time as a French teacher. He moved to London to work in magazine publishing, alongside pursuing his interests in writing, translation, and acting.

In addition to translating the chronicles of Chantecoq for the English-speaking world, Andrew has written a number of science-fiction and urban fantasy books, full of his particular brand of humour. Andrew currently lives in West London with his lovely wife Mel, and a little black cat called Buscemi. There, he cooks curries, enjoys beer and quality cinema, and he dreams of a better world.

ALSO AVAILABLE

CHANTECOQ
Chantecoq and the Aubry Affair
Chantecoq and Wilhelm's Spy I: Made In Germany
Chantecoq and Wilhelm's Spy II: The Enemy Within
Chantecoq and Wilhelm's Spy III: The Day of Reckoning
Chantecoq and the Mystery of the Blue Train
Chantecoq and the Haunted House
Chantecoq and the Aviator's Crime
Chantecoq and Zapata
Chantecoq and the Amorous Ogre
Chantecoq and the Père-Lachaise Ghost
Chantecoq and the Condemned Woman
Chantecoq and the Ladykiller
Chantecoq and the Devil's Daughter

By Andrew Lawston
Detective Daintypaws: A Squirrel in Bohemia
Detective Daintypaws: Buscemi at Christmas
Detective Daintypaws: Murder on the Tesco Express
Zip! Zap! Boing!
Voyage of the Space Bastard
Rudy on Rails

Printed in Great Britain
by Amazon